A Billionaire for Lexi

The Barrington Billionaires

Book 3.5

A Holiday Novella

by
Ruth Cardello

Author Contact
website: RuthCardello.com
email: Minouri@aol.com
Facebook: Author Ruth Cardello
Twitter: RuthieCardello
Goodreads
Bookbub

Clay Landon has never taken himself or his life of privilege seriously. He has spent his life going where he wanted, when he wanted, and keeping his relationships as casual and open as his lifestyle. It's a pretty damn good life until he meets Lexi Chambers, an equally free spirit who is completely unimpressed by him or his wealth.

Having her becomes his obsession.

Lexi Chambers knows how to get into trouble and does so with a skill acquired by doing it a shit—Let's just say a lot. Her sister, Willa, recently married into the wealthy Barrington family and Lexi is trying to stay on her best behavior.

One too-sexy-for-his-own-good, Clay, will test her resolve.

He'll make her laugh and push her to, once again, believe in possibilities.

COPYRIGHT

Dedication

This book is dedicated to my six year old daughter, Serenity. Thank you for giving me a sentence to use in my book. "With no street lights it should have been dark, but the light of the moon glistened on the freshly fallen snow in an almost mystical way."

Always better together!

A memory from Ruth Cardello

Christmas, 1971
Ruth Cardello, Jeannette Winters

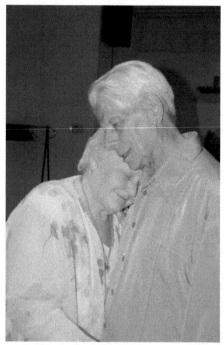

The parents of Ruth Cardello and Jeannette Winters, 2006
Memere and Pepere to Danielle Stewart.

Although they're both gone now, they are with us every day in the love
we show each other.

Dear Reader,

It's the holiday season and I'm feeling grateful. First, if you've chosen to read this novella anthology, chances are you've read the first half of my Barrington Billionaire series. You may already know why this particular project is important to me, but if you don't. . .come with me as I journey back in time.

Picture me in 2010, writing in the basement of my 850 square foot house while my youngest daughter played at my feet and the washing machine hummed behind me. I was a kindergarten teacher back then with three children and a dream of one day sharing my writing with others.

An economic slowdown hit my area, and my teaching career became less stable. I kept getting laid off. Twenty-two years of teaching ensured that I would be employed in the district in some capacity, but not as a kindergarten teacher. I took whatever position I could but I wasn't doing what I loved anymore. So, I took a leap of faith.

My brother, Gerry Labrecque, suggested I self-publish. In 2011, I sat down with my computer, read every blog I could about how to self-publish, and put Maid for the Billionaire up for FREE. The rest, as they say, is history.

I love that my brother was part of my publishing journey because, as the youngest of eleven children, family has always played a large role in my life. We grew up poor, but blissfully ignorant that life was different for others.

How poor was I back then? When I was in elementary school my clothing always came from donations people gave us in trash bags. My father worked three jobs to afford the house we lived in. My parents were God-fearing, hard working, second generation Americans who raised eleven children to be strong and independent. They did occasionally dress us in some funny clothing, though. I'm still a little scarred from the colorful pair of pants my mother had made out of a beach bag. But I digress.

I live in an economically depressed area. When I first started making money from my writing, my first priority was to make sure no one in my family lost their homes. People warned me in the beginning that if I gave money to my family then they would only expect more of it. They don't know my family.

We've survived and thrived because we take care of each other. A few years ago, my niece sent me a most incredible story she had written and asked if I would help her self-publish it. I gave her a list of about sixty things she would need to do first. She called me back the next day and said, "I'm done. What else should I do?" After that, Danielle Stewart had her auntie's full support. She has about 20 books and novellas up now, and I couldn't be prouder.

Just over a year ago, my sister, Jeannette Winters, who had a full-time job as an analyst, told me she dreamed of making enough money from her stories to pay for the new roof her home needed. I gave her the same list and told her to bring me a completed romance. If she did that, I promised to get her the best editors I could afford, help her choose covers that would fit her books, and take over the business side of self-publishing. She joined the same author group my brother and I did and finished not only one, but two billionaire romances. And they're good. They're so good I could cry.

Danielle, Jeannette and I plotted out three series that intertwine through key scenes and character cameos. Working with the two of them, developing these storylines and characters together, has given me some of the most treasured memories of my life. We truly are ALWAYS BETTER TOGETHER.

My parents have both passed away, but I like to think they are looking down at my generation with pride. We're holding to the ideals they raised us with. Family comes first and our legacy is how we live our lives. My books are bathtub reads. They're fun. They're sexy. But they won't change the world.

My children, my nephews and nieces, and their children . . . if I show them that real wealth is having family (FAMILY is a flexible term to me . . . some are by blood, others by love) you care about who cares about you . . . then we have changed the world. At least, our little corner of it.

Ruthie

P.S.
Love seeing your favorite characters show up in other books? The perfect solution is our **Synchronized Series!** One world. Three authors. Character cross-over. Binge reading at its best.

Each series can be enjoyed individually but reading them all together weaves an exciting and unique experience.

A great example of the fun you'll find is when all the characters collide at a charity event and experience the same place in very different ways.

Ruth Cardello's
Billionaire
World

Synchronized Series

Always Mine · Stolen Kisses · Trade It All · Let It Burn · A Billionaire for Lexi

One White Lie · Tangle For Two · You & Me Make Three · Virgin For The Fourth Time

Fierce Love · Wild Eyes · Crazy Nights · Loyal Hearts

Chapter One

CLAY LANDON LEANED against the mantel of a fireplace and frowned. He'd spent quite a lot of time with the Barringtons over the past year, and the idea of spending Thanksgiving with them had sounded mildly entertaining. He hadn't expected the dark mood that was slowly taking hold of him.

His best friend, Dax Marshall, stepped away from his new bride to join him. "You're in a mood. Are you hungover or hungry?"

Clay kept his expression serious. "I'm hoping if I don't smile, Asher won't try to hand me his son again. Do I look like someone who wants to hold a baby?"

Dax laughed. "Better you than me, but don't panic. Fatherhood isn't catching."

Clay glanced around and arched an eyebrow. "Are you certain? Lance and Willa are preparing for twins. You and Kenzi married sooner than you'd planned. Kenzi's probably already pregnant and waiting to tell you."

Looking across at his wife, Dax's expression softened. "I wouldn't mind."

With a shudder, Clay folded his arms across his chest. "Like I suspected, highly contagious and you're already infected."

"Don't be afraid of growing up, Clay, it's not as bad as you think."

"Growing up. Giving up. Call it what you want. I prefer my life the way it is."

"Do you?" Dax's question hung in the air.

Clay dropped his arms and pushed off the mantel. "Look at them, Dax. All smiles and hugs. I can see the lure of it for you, but don't buy into the fairy tale. They're not as perfect as they want you to believe."

Unbothered, Dax smiled. "They're completely screwed up, but I'm pretty messed up myself." He clapped a hand on Clay's shoulder. "And you, my friend, fit right in."

Clay shrugged his hand off. "Remind me why I'm here since it's not for the pleasure of your company."

"I have two working theories of equal merit."

"I'm sure I don't want to hear either."

"One is that you are a lonely son of a bitch who actually misses me now that I spend more time with Kenzi than I do with you."

In a tone thick with sarcasm, Clay said, "Nailed it."

"Or you heard Lexi will be here."

Clay didn't respond at first because Dax's second guess cut too close to the truth. Lexi Chambers was slowly but surely ruining his sex life. At first he'd dismissed his attraction to her as the "twin effect." What man hadn't indulged in the fantasy of being with twins? After getting to know her sister, though, his interest had settled solely on Lexi. Willa was not only too sweet for his taste, she was also now married to his best friend's brother-in-law, which made her almost family.

Lexi on the other hand was a spirited, irreverent rebel who spiced up his late night dreams on a regular basis. She was not only gorgeous, but she knew how to use her body to reduce the men around her to babbling pools of drool. Her outfits were daring; her comebacks were sassy. Careers couldn't contain her. Neither money nor fame seemed to impress her. She ran wild and free with an abandon that was hotter than hell. The only flaw he'd found in her so far was that she was unimpressed by him.

Normally Clay would have moved on to another woman. He had enough eager women on speed dial to fill his bed for a month, but the mere thought of Lexi was enough to kill his desire for any of them. "Will she be here? Kenzi and Willa will be happy," Clay said in a bored tone.

"So you're here to see me? That's your claim?" Dax asked in a droll tone.

Dale, the patriarch of the Barrington family, joined them. "May I get you a drink, Clay?"

Clay shook his head. There was something about the wholesome vibe Dale and his wife, Sophie, exuded that stole the enjoyment out of catching a buzz. Although Dale wasn't from the same generation as Clay's grandfather, he had the same dignified authority. Being around Dale brought back fond memories even while leaving Clay feeling a little sad. "As always, thank you for including me, Dale. Dax was just saying he hopes he's the next to give you a grandchild."

"Friends never miss a chance to throw you under the bus, do they, Dax?" Dale asked with a smile.

Dax nodded and returned the smile, looking a million times more comfortable with his father-in-law than Clay ever imagined he would be. "No, they don't. Is Lexi here yet? Clay was just asking about her."

Dale's eyes twinkled with humor. "She said she's on her way, but that could mean she'll arrive before or after dinner. She's a tough one to figure out."

"She sure is," Clay said, instantly regretting it when the other men smiled knowingly. It was definitely time to change the subject. "I was looking forward to meeting your son, Andrew."

Dale's expression sobered. "He wasn't able to get back for the holidays this year. When that has happened in the past, we've been able to Skype with him. This year he said he's not in a situation that allows it. He won't say where he's deployed to. He tells me not to, but I worry about him."

Dax frowned. "Have you looked into it? Asked around?"

Dale shook his head. "He'd be furious if I did and he found out about it. Don't know if you've noticed, but I've raised some headstrong sons."

Dax nodded and accepted Dale's answer with an ease that meant he would look into it. It was still strange to see how protective Dax had become of this family. Before meeting Kenzi, Dax had been known to slice through companies with the heartlessness of a pirate from the past. He'd charged forward, avoided personal investment, and made no apologies for his choices. This new version of Dax still took some getting used to.

A family man.

How the mighty have fallen.

Clay glanced around the room again. Dale's wife, Sophie, caught his eye and waved him over. Turning to gain support from Dax, Clay realized he was standing alone. He made his way over to her, feeling slightly uneasy as he did. His own mother and father had died when he was a young child. His grandmother had cared for him, but she'd been more generous with her money than with her time or attention. Sophie was the opposite. He could have found a reason to avoid her, but he not only liked her, he also liked the idea of her. She was sweet and devoted to her family, like an old-fashioned mother in the movies.

"I am so glad you agreed to join us today, Clay. It's good to see you and Dax laughing together." She reached up and gave his cheek a motherly pat.

He wanted to dislike the gesture, but he didn't. The genuine affection in her eyes warmed Clay's heart in a way that confused him. This was Dax's new family, not his. He spent time with them out of curiosity, not because he wanted or needed this type of people in his life. "Dax hasn't stopped smiling since he met your daughter."

"Love does that to a man," Sophie said. "I couldn't have chosen a more perfect husband for Kenzi. How about you? Do you have anyone special in your life?"

"They're all special," he said lightly. "And I prefer it that way."

She smiled indulgently. "Boys. You all sound the same until you meet the right one."

Clay felt Lexi's arrival before he saw her. His attention slid away from Sophie to the doorway of the living room where Lexi was greeting Kenzi and Willa with hugs.

"Clay?"

Lexi removed her jacket, handing it to Grant, the second to the oldest of the Barrington sons. Her tight, orange dress might have been too bold on another woman, but she wore it with the confidence of a model. It hugged every curve, accenting her beautiful ass and amazing breasts. Her blonde hair was pulled back on both sides, revealing enough neck that he grew hard imagining kissing his way up it. Grant said something to her that made her smile, and Clay's stomach clenched with a jealousy he tried and failed to conquer.

Sophie laid a hand on his forearm, pulling his attention back to her. "I know a lot of single women who would love to meet you."

Clay looked down at Sophie. "I appreciate the offer, but meeting women has never been my issue."

Sophie sighed. "I didn't think this house needed more men in it, but having you and Dax around feels like I added two more sons to the family. So, when I say this, I mean it in the kindest, most loving way. You and Lexi are very much alike."

He gave a long look. "Is that a compliment or an insult?"

She gave his forearm a squeeze. "It's a warning to be careful what you wish for. I wouldn't like to see either of you get hurt."

"She's a beautiful woman, Sophie, but that's it. Don't worry. In my world, women like Lexi are a dime a dozen."

"Charming as usual, Clay," Lexi said as she wrapped her arms around a shocked looking Sophie and planted a kiss on her cheek. "Sophie, happy Thanksgiving."

LEXI CHAMBERS TOOK a moment to enjoy the red flush that spread up Clay's neck. *He's embarrassed. Good. He should be.* If she'd ever allowed herself to be, Lexi might have been intimidated by the Barringtons and the man who had just insulted her. The Barringtons were one of the richest families on the East Coast, and Clay was a financial notch above them. He was also drop-dead gorgeous.

Money didn't equate to a person's value, though. It didn't fill them with integrity or make them better than anyone else. And gorgeous meant little at the end of the day.

Sophie turned and gave Lexi a warm smile. "You're on time to eat with us; good girl. Willa wasn't sure you'd even make it."

"Hard to pass up a free meal," Lexi said lightly. She and Sophie were in a better place than they'd ever been and, for Kenzi and Willa's sake, Lexi wanted to keep it that way. "Thank you for inviting me."

Sophie hugged her. "You know you're always welcome here. Don't make us wait until Christmas to see you again. Join us for game night before then. You might be surprised how much you enjoy it."

"I absolutely will," Lexi promised and was still smiling as Sophie walked away.

"Liar," Clay said.

Without looking at him, Lexi answered, "It's called being polite. You might want to try it sometime."

"What you overheard was a joke, Lexi."

"Bite me," she said between gritted teeth that were still flashing a smile.

"I would, but you keep saying no," he countered easily.

She met his eyes, reached over, and adjusted his tie. "That's because I only sleep with men I like." She trailed her hand down his tie and loved his quickly indrawn breath. Despite what he'd said to Sophie, Lexi knew Clay found her attractive. The turn off was that he found many women attractive. She looked him over slowly, blatantly. There was no denying he was a good-looking man, but the size of his ego overshadowed the temptation to find out how endowed the rest of him was.

His hand closed around hers and held it against his chest. "Try me. You might be surprised how much you like it."

Despite the warmth that flooded through her at his sultry suggestion, Lexi threw back her head and laughed. "Quoting Sophie as a come-on? Honey, you're off your game."

His eyes narrowed. "You can deny it, but I know how I make you feel."

"Tell yourself whatever you need to." She gave his hand a squeeze then pulled hers free. Her smile was real now. They'd gone there before and would go there again. It was a flirtatious, harmless sparring. Although she would never do anything about it, these exchanges with Clay always left her feeling young and beautiful, which was sometimes harder to do as she neared thirty.

She looked across the room at her best friend, Kenzi, standing with her husband, Dax. "Is it strange for you to see Dax happily married?"

"Very."

Her attention slid to her twin sister, Willa, and her husband, Lance. "I can't believe my sister is married as well."

"Thanks to me."

Lexi arched a perfectly sculpted eyebrow. "You're still trying to take credit?"

"A bet is a bet, and I won."

"Too many shots of tequila were ingested before that bet was made—making it null and void."

"I beg to differ."

"I didn't take you for the type to beg," Lexi said cheekily.

He placed his hand on her lower back, bent near her ear, and growled, "I won't have to; I won."

Lexi ignored her racing heart and the way her skin warmed beneath his touch. The details of that inebriated bet hadn't survived her hangover the next day, but she wasn't about to admit it. "Double or nothing?"

"Normally, I wouldn't refuse such an offer, but I'd rather collect my winnings and go home. Or, more accurately, take you home and collect my winnings." His breath was a warm caress on her ear.

"Can't tonight, I have a date after this."

His hand tightened on her back. "On Thanksgiving? With who?"

"His name doesn't matter." It didn't. She wouldn't sleep with him. She'd been on one date with the man she was meeting after dinner, and it hadn't been an amazing one. He had, however, asked her to join him for drinks that night, and Lexi was certain she'd need a few later. She was happy Kenzi had found love, happy her sister had found the same, but things felt different now. Kenzi and Willa walked around with stupid grins on their faces, talking about babies and furniture like either topic was worthy of prolonged discussion.

Even though there had been times when Willa and Lexi had pulled away from each other, needing space, they'd always returned to each other. At the end of the day, they'd always been all the family each other had. It wasn't that way for Willa anymore. She had Lance now. She was blissfully pregnant and had attached herself to Lance's parents as if she'd sprung from Sophie's vagina.

And they love her right back.

Which is good.

Only it didn't feel that way for Lexi. Even if she wanted to, she would never fit in with the Barringtons the way Willa did. Willa was soft spoken, sweet. Lexi didn't know of one single person who hadn't automatically loved Willa. Lexi was honest enough with herself to acknowledge that not everyone had the same reaction to her. She was too much for some people. She always had been.

"You don't have a date," Clay said.

Lexi met his eyes. "You almost sound like you care. You'll get over it, though. Women like me, we're a dime a dozen."

Chapter Two

I T WAS A sweet torture to be seated next to Lexi during the multicourse Thanksgiving meal. He enjoyed their earlier banter about the bet because he suspected she didn't remember what she'd agreed to. The actual bet had been for a dinner out, but he was enjoying seeing how far she'd let him go with it before she called bullshit. That topic was temporarily on hold, though. They were close enough for an occasional accidental touch to be expected, but they were under enough scrutiny from the others that their usual sexually charged discourse was curtailed.

He lowered his voice and asked, "How is the job search going after Poly-Shyn?"

She studied his expression for a moment before answering seriously. "I always land on my feet. I'm doing some short gigs while looking for something more permanent."

"I heard you left suddenly."

There was a flash of annoyance in her eyes. "I really can't stomach another lecture on being more responsible."

His eyebrows rose in surprise as he realized he'd touched upon a sensitive subject. "I could hardly lecture anyone about anything."

Her expression relaxed. "Sorry. Didn't mean to snap at you. It has just been a frequent topic of discussion lately."

"Because you left without giving your notice?"

The look she gave him hinted that she had another snappy comeback that she held back. "Yes."

"Why did you?"

"Because I'm completely irresponsible, unable to understand how my actions affect others, and at the end of the day chronically ungrateful."

"Ouch."

"I could go on, but I'd rather not."

"I'd heard you were enjoying the job."

She pushed the food around her plate for a moment then laid her fork down and leaned in. "I slept with one of the project managers there and his wife threatened to make a public stink if I didn't leave."

"Lucky bastard if it were true, but it's not," Clay said softly. He didn't believe her. There was too much defiance in her tone. "Why lie to me? I don't care either way."

She sighed and pursed her lush lips briefly. "That old greasy pig made a pass at me, and I turned him down, maybe more harshly than I should have but he's married. Then, out of nowhere, his wife confronted me. She told me she knows Sophie and would tell everyone that I slept with her husband if I didn't quit." She looked across at her sister then back to Clay. "I don't want to mess things up for Willa. She's happy here."

Clay's hands clenched on the table. Poly-Shyn would be

down a project manager by Monday night. The family who owned the company, the Hendersons, could take care of him, or Clay would handle it himself.

She seemed to sense his thoughts because she reached out and touched his hand. "Please don't say anything to anyone. It's done, and I want to forget it. Willa doesn't need to know."

He turned his hand so it closed over hers. "This isn't about her, it's about you. No one should treat you that way."

Her smile was thin. "It's okay. I was ready to move on anyway."

"The bastard needs to learn a lesson."

"What he'll learn is that people like to think the worst of me. Please don't get involved."

"So, you'd rather leave him there to do it to another woman?"

She pulled her hand away from his. "Don't judge my choices. Before you tell me what I should or shouldn't do, why don't you share a list of how you've made the world a better place recently?"

Clay sat back and glared at her. He wanted to help her. Hell, all she had to do was ask and, with his connections, she could have her pick of jobs at any number of companies in any location on the globe. He had certainly never seen himself as a knight in shining armor, but her low opinion of him stung.

Because she's right. When was the last time I risked something for someone else's benefit? He lowered his voice again. "If you need money—"

"I don't want to work for you."

"You wouldn't have to." Her sister's short stint as his assistant had been enough to prove he didn't require one.

"And I'm not for sale."

That made him smile. "I do like how your mind goes there when you talk to me, but I was referring to a gift, free and clear, no strings attached."

She shook her head and picked up her fork. "Thank you for the offer, but taking money from you would be right up there with sleeping with that pig at Poly-Shyn. Neither would leave me feeling good, and I'd never hear the end of it from Willa if she found out about it."

He was torn between laughing and being offended. Lexi was one hell of a woman. She cared about not only her sister but was willing to put her own feelings aside for her happiness. A slow smile spread across his face as a thought occurred to him. He leaned over and whispered in her ear, "The reason you won't sleep with me is because you're worried it will affect your sister somehow."

Her cheeks turned a delicious shade of pink. "That's one of the reasons, yes."

"One?" He turned fully in his chair to face her. "There are others?"

Dale asked firmly, "Clay, could you pass the stuffing?"

Clay pulled his attention from Lexi long enough to do just that but grew confused when he saw the dish of stuffing was on the other side of the table. It was only then that he noticed all eyes were on him.

Asher, the eldest Barrington son, leaned forward from

across the table and said, "That's code for sit up straight and behave."

Low chuckles escaped a few tablemates but were stifled. Dax met his look and let out a hearty laugh. The others joined in, some with looks of amused sympathy.

Never in Clay's life had he been chastised for his behavior, and there was no reason for him to tolerate being the butt of this family's joke. However, when he looked down at Lexi he was surprised to see real concern in her eyes, and how he felt was no longer important. Did she think he was about to make a scene? Say something to embarrass her?

He turned and faced his plate again, deciding to laugh along with them—for Lexi. He sat straight and picked up his fork and knife. "Yes, sir."

There was a second wave of laughter then the moment passed. Everyone returned to their side conversations.

Lexi nudged his arm. He leaned down to hear her whisper, "Thank you."

Those two simple words warmed his heart, and he fell a little bit in love with her right there, right in the middle of all those damn Barringtons. He wanted to be the person she trusted to be on her side. Thanksgiving dinner, beneath a table of watchful eyes, was not the time nor the place to show her how much else he wanted to be for her.

She had a list of reasons she wouldn't sleep with him. A list. Chipping away at it would be his mission. *And she thinks I don't know how to make the world a better place.* He met her eyes and knew he had a big, smitten smile on his face. He laughed aloud even though it brought all attention back to him, then stabbed a piece of turkey and said, "When is the next game night? Lexi just said she could beat me at Scrabble, and I need to prove myself."

OKAY, WHO IS the man beside me and what did he do with the real Clay?

He was not only engaging in idle conversation with everyone at the table, he was also on his best behavior. When Dale had corrected him, she'd expected him to respond with something sarcastic, but he hadn't. He was acting like he cared what the Barringtons thought of him, and that didn't fit with her impression of him. Normally, he did what he wanted, when and how he wanted.

He turned then, caught her watching him, and smiled. The pleasure that rushed through her confused her all over again. She knew how to deal with the outrageously flirtatious Clay. She could easily dismiss the self-absorbed, easily bored billionaire he'd portrayed himself to be in the past. This Clay? The one who seemed to care how she was doing both that night and in general—*I could like him.*

No, he's still Mr. Turn-everything-into-an-innuendo Clay.

Tonight is an act and I'll prove it. Watch his pretense fall away when he hears this.

She tapped his arm and motioned for him to lower his head toward her. "So, I'm trying a new kind of cleansing program. I'm going cold turkey, completely celibate until the new year."

"Do you have a date for New Year's Eve? It's a day early, but a better choice for such an anticipated indulgence," he said without missing a beat.

His expression was so serious Lexi laughed louder than she meant to. *There's the Clay I know.*

Sophie piped in, "Lexi, dear, did I hear you mention New Year's? Does that mean you've decided to join us in Vermont?"

"I—I—" *Shit.* Kenzi had told her about the charity event her mother was planning, and Lexi had been deliberately vague about committing. An evening with the Barringtons was one thing, but a long weekend? Those were best avoided. Somehow, no matter how Lexi tried, she'd find a way to offend one of them.

Lexi acknowledged it was her own fault. Sophie hadn't met her at the best time in her life. Still reeling from the loss of both parents, Lexi and Willa had been sent to live with an aunt and uncle in Canada. Willa had withdrawn, practically non-verbal despite being in her teens. Scared, Lexi had tried all sorts of stunts to make her sister smile. She'd felt as if she were losing her sister as well and had been desperate to help her. Perhaps that was why the conversation she'd overheard between her aunt and uncle still stung each time she remembered it.

She'd been sitting on the bed beside with Willa when her aunt's voice had carried through the wall. "It'll be for the best. Boarding schools know how to raise children, we don't. If it were just one, just Willa, maybe we could do it. But Lexi's already difficult. Can you imagine her in a few years? I don't know if I have it in me to raise her."

Willa's eyes had filled with tears and she'd shaken her

head as if Lexi had let her down. The rebel in Lexi had taken root that day. A few months later, when Sophie had come out to their school to meet her daughter's new best friends, Lexi had enjoyed shocking her. Over the years, Sophie had invited Lexi and Willa on family vacations, but had always seemed genuinely afraid that Lexi would date one of her sons. It had made flirting with them childishly entertaining.

At twenty-nine, Lexi knew her pride was one of her greatest faults. She didn't blame Sophie for thinking the worst of her at times, especially considering the grief she'd given the woman for over a decade. In moments of weakness she still caught herself saying things to get a rise out of her, but it was a pattern Lexi was determined to break.

"Lexi and I have plans for that night," Clay said smoothly, "but we'll see if we can change them."

Kenzi hugged her husband's arm. "Did you know they were hanging out now?"

"I did not," Dax said blandly.

"It's been too recent to mention," Clay said.

"We're just friends," Lexi stressed at the same time. They both stopped and looked at each other.

Grant chimed in with a clarifying question. "So it's not a date?"

Clay turned toward him and asked, "And if it were?"

Grant's eyes narrowed. "I'd rather you called it off. Lexi has been part of this family for a very long time."

Asher spoke to his wife loudly enough for all to hear. "It's kind of cute to see Grant riled up."

Ian, the third son from the top and a career politician

like his father had once been, interjected. "I had no idea he had it in him."

Lance asked, "You don't think he—?"

"I don't. No offense, Lexi," Grant said gruffly.

"None taken," Lexi said with relief. Of all the Barrington boys, Grant was the most like a big brother to her. She didn't want him to like her in any way but that.

Grant continued, "Clay and I run in many of the same circles. I know how he operates. Don't bring that shit here. Be careful. That's all I'm going to say."

Dax leaned forward. "Grant—"

"Please pass the salt, Grant," Dale said firmly.

No one moved at first, held still in a tense silence. Clay opened his mouth then closed it. He looked from Grant to Dax and back.

Lexi doubted anyone knew what Clay would say, not even Clay.

Sophie took her husband's hand in hers and said, "Do you know what I am most grateful for this Thanksgiving?"

All eyes turned to her.

She smiled at Grant and then Clay. "All of you." In a perfectly proper voice, she added, "What Grant is trying to say, Clay, is that we love Lexi. Hurt her and my sons will line up to kick your ass." There was a shocked collective gasp, but Sophie continued on as if she hadn't said anything the least bit out of character, "Now, who would like coffee?"

Never one to hold back, Lexi stood, walked over to Sophie, and gave her a long, tight hug. Dale nodded at Lexi in approval.

Dax put his arm around Kenzi and announced, "I love this family."

Lexi returned to her seat and used her napkin to dab away the tears from her eyes. "Me, too."

"I'm still on the fence," Clay said with dry humor. When everyone looked at him, he smiled and added, "I *was* the only one threatened at the table tonight. Now, someone, please, pass the gravy."

Someone chuckled and the others joined in until everyone was laughing. It was the perfect release to lighten the mood. When the group broke into smaller conversations again, Lexi turned to Clay and said, "I can't figure you out."

"Sounds like a problem that can only be solved by spending more time with me."

"See, I still don't know if you're serious."

He took her hand and discretely brought it to his lap beneath the table and laid it across the hard bulge in his trousers. His eyes half closed with pleasure at her touch, then he returned her hand chastely to the table.

"Oh," she said and couldn't think of another thing to say besides, "I see."

The smile he shot her was sexy and private, his tone low enough for no one else to hear. "You could if you wanted to. Just say the word."

His eyes were mesmerizing. "Not afraid you'll get your ass kicked?"

He wiggled his eyebrows suggestively. "Something tells me it'd be worth it."

She laughed softly, doing her best to not draw the

group's attention back to them. This side of Clay was a temptation she wanted to give in to, but she didn't want to chance losing the ground she'd made with Sophie. Lexi had never imagined Sophie would feel protective of her. It changed everything.

Clay wants me, but for a night.

Maybe two.

Once the challenge is gone, he'll move on.

We're better as we are—dancing around what was never meant to be.

With that, Lexi took out her phone, sent a text, then stood. "I'm sorry to eat and run, but I have a date tonight."

When Clay didn't rise to his feet, Asher said, "That hurt to watch."

Deliberately not meeting Clay's eyes, Lexi said her good-byes to everyone and bolted. Clay might be disappointed, but he'd probably soothe that pain away in the arms of some woman that night. *Me? I'll down a few shots until my date's stories are no longer boring.*

It's better this way.

Chapter Three

THE FOLLOWING MONDAY morning Clay stared up at the ceiling of his office. His feet were propped on his desk and his arms were crossed over his chest.

Kate, Dax's secretary, popped her head in the door. "Mr. Landon?"

"Yes."

"I didn't realize you were still using this office. Does that mean Ms. Chambers—I mean—Mrs. Barrington is returning?"

"No. I'm flying solo this time." He realized he'd answered sharply when Kate went from relaxed to nervous.

"Well, if you need anything, I'll be at my desk." She turned and retreated to her desk outside of Dax's office.

"Kate," Clay called out, rising to his feet. He made it to her desk just as she was sitting down. "Do you have a minute?"

Eyes round, Kate glanced at her boss's closed door then back. "Of course."

"You're a woman."

"That's what I'm told."

"If you had to come up with a list of why you wouldn't sleep with me what would be on it?"

Kate blinked a couple of times quickly. "Besides the fact that I'm engaged?"

"She's not, so yes, besides that."

Kate laughed. "Mr. Landon, are you asking me for relationship advice?"

The last thing he needed was her amusement. He gave her a cold look. "When Dax gets in tell him I'm here." He turned and started back to his office.

"Mr. Landon?"

Clay stopped.

"I didn't mean to laugh. You just took me by surprise."

"Because you can't imagine someone like me needing advice about women?" he asked.

The twinkle in her eye wasn't flattering. "Yes, that's it."

His eyes narrowed. "I could own this company if I wanted to. Why aren't you at all afraid of me?"

"Honestly?"

Clay threw his hands up in the air. "If I wanted to hear lies that made me feel better I wouldn't be here waiting for Dax, would I?"

Kate scanned his face slowly, then said, "Fair enough. This is just my opinion but . . . you don't seem to take anything seriously, so people tend not to take you seriously."

He thought about how Lexi had said she couldn't tell if he meant what he said or not. Kate might just be on to something. "Go on."

She swallowed visibly. "Were you born rich?"

"Insanely."

Kate made a face. "A certain type of woman might think that's attractive, but other women might say it means you've never had to fight for anything."

"And that's a bad thing?"

Kate tapped her fingers on her desk. "Mr. Landon, I like my job here. Mr. Marshall is a wonderful boss. I don't really want to insult one of his closest friends."

Clay pulled up a chair in front of her desk. "Your job is safe. You've piqued my curiosity. Give it to me straight."

"You're a very attractive man," Kate started.

"Why does that sound like you're putting it in the negative column?"

"Do you remember the names of all the women you've dated in the past five years?"

Clay started to list them aloud, came across a couple he'd forgotten, then frowned. "Why does this matter?"

Kate looked away as if choosing her words carefully. "It paints a picture of a man some women might think will not stick around."

With a frustrated sigh, Clay slumped back into the chair. "Women have always liked me exactly the way I am."

"Certain women, I'm sure, but it sounds like you've come across one who is different."

"She certainly is. I texted her this weekend, and she didn't respond. Nothing. Who does that?"

"What did you do when she didn't answer?"

Clay shrugged. "What the hell was I supposed to do? She obviously doesn't want to talk to me."

"So, you only want women who come to you easily."

"No, I want this one."

"But you're not willing to fight for her?"

"Fight? Who? What? You're not making any sense."

Kate rolled her eyes heavenward. "I bet the top of her list of why she won't sleep with you is because she thinks you don't actually care about her."

"Of course I care about her."

"What have you done to show her that you do?"

"Beyond the text?" *God, I'm lame. I have the resources to do anything, and I stopped at a text.* "You're a genius, Kate!"

"Are you bothering my secretary?" Dax asked as he walked up to Kate's desk.

Kate stood. "Good morning, Mr. Marshall."

"We might have to share her. She's amazing," Clay said with a huge smile.

"You don't even work here, Clay." Dax waved for Kate to sit.

"That's cold, Dax. I have an office. Why would you deny me the ability to staff it?"

Dax rubbed a hand across his eyes. "Kate, is there coffee brewing?"

"Of course."

"Could you bring two cups into my office? I'm not awake enough for this." He looked down at his watch. "It's not even nine, Clay. You normally sleep until noon. Is something wrong?"

"Something was, but thanks to Kate I have a plan. Clear your schedule for the next few hours, Dax. I need your help on something."

Instantly alert, Dax said, "Absolutely. Come in. Kate, call Taylor and MacMillan and postpone our ten o'clock video conference."

Clay followed Dax into his office then sat at his desk, an act that sent both of Dax's eyebrows to his hairline. Nonplussed, Clay searched through Dax's desk drawers until he found a notebook and pen. He wrote jewelry then crossed the word off. "Jewelry is way overdone. Anyone can buy that. What do women love that most men can't afford?"

Indulgently, Dax took a seat in front of his own desk. "What the hell are you babbling about?"

Clay held a pen poised over the notebook. "If Lexi thinks I don't actually care about her, I'm going to prove to her that I do. Come on. This will be fun. You know her. What would she want?"

"You want my help with Lexi?"

With an impatient sigh, Clay waved a hand. "Didn't I just say that? I tried to text her after Thanksgiving, and she didn't answer me."

"Have you considered that she might not be interested in you? I'm throwing that out there as a possibility."

Shaking his head in disgust, Clay said, "Kate is much better at this than you."

"She's simply too afraid to tell you the truth."

"No. No, that's where you're wrong. I apparently don't instill fear in anyone. People don't take me seriously according to Kate. Do you agree?"

Dax ran his hand through his hair. "You don't want to

hear what I think."

Considering that Dax was known for speaking the truth even when it was uncomfortable to do so, his hesitation gave Clay a moment of pause. They'd been friends a very long time. Dax's opinion was one of the few that actually did matter to Clay. "Yes, I do."

"I think you're looking for the next game to entertain yourself with. You've been hanging around the Barringtons like they were a new and shiny toy you wanted to play with, but now that you know them you're bored. Lexi shot you down publicly. She's a challenge. I get it. But this isn't a game to me, Clay. This is my fucking family. You hurt her, you hurt Kenzi. I'm not going to let that happen. You sent her a text. She didn't answer. That's it. Drop it."

Clay laid the pen down on the table. "Why the fuck are we friends, Dax? That's assuming we are. Your opinion of me couldn't be shittier."

Dax stood and ran his hand through his hair again. He paced back and forth as he spoke. "I won't sugarcoat the truth. What do you want me to say? If we weren't friends, you wouldn't be around Kenzi or her family at all. I've let you into a part of my life that is very important to me. That doesn't mean I won't step in if you look like you're about to fuck it up."

"What makes you so sure I don't care about Lexi?"

"Because you don't care about anything."

And there it was—a reiteration of what Kate had said, but this time coming out of the mouth of his closest friend.

Clay rose to his feet. "I've been there every time you've

needed me. I doubt you could list the number of deals I've helped you facilitate."

"When it was convenient for you. When the projects were interesting enough or you had nothing better to do. Listen, I'm not saying I don't appreciate what you've done for me over the years, but if this is about being honest with each other . . . you'd definitely stand by me in a fight as long as it happens after you've had your beauty sleep."

"Fuck you." Clay slammed his hand down on Dax's desk.

"You asked for the truth."

Shaking his head, Clay strode toward Dax. "Is there anything else you'd like to share while I'm here? You know, just in case this is the last time you see me."

Dax looked him in the eye. "Pick something to care about. A cause. A charity. Hell, help Zuckerberg cure diseases like he claims he and others will by the end of the century. You'll be a lot happier. I'm not telling you anything I didn't tell myself a short time ago. I was a miserable bastard and didn't realize it. Caring about anything sucks. It has the power to rip you up and leave you in shreds. But you know what's worse? Caring about nothing. It leaves you numb. You don't even know how much of life you're missing because you're used to feeling nothing. You want me to believe you care about Lexi? Prove it. Leave her alone. Respect that she made her choice."

Shit. He'd felt a whole lot better after talking to Kate, but Dax was right. If things didn't work out with Lexi, it would affect more than the two of them. "Zuckerburg approached me for a donation. It sounded like an unrealistic project."

Dax shrugged. "A hundred years ago no one would have believed medicine would be as far along as it is now. I'm not saying it's the project for you, but if you don't change something, I know I'll hear about you in the news someday, a victim of an overdose. You're too old to party the way you do, too smart to do nothing of importance with the fortune you've been left, and too big of a pain in the ass for me not to miss if you let a little honesty end our friendship."

Clay let his friend's words sink in before answering. He sat back down at Dax's desk. "I can't see myself in an office every day."

"Then pick something that doesn't require that."

"I don't do drugs . . . anymore, but I could cut back on the drinking. It's not as much fun as it used to be."

Dax nodded. "That's what happens as you get older."

"Depressing, isn't it?"

"Not at all. What replaces it is fucking incredible."

"Having a family who gathers for game night?"

"Having a real partner and building a life together. I'm not trying to sell that to you, either, but I don't miss a single thing about my life before Kenzi."

Clay drummed his fingers on the desk as he processed the entirety of their conversation. "You're wrong about something."

Dax raised an eyebrow in question.

"I actually like the Barringtons, and I do care about Lexi. You're right, though. Lexi made her choice clear, and I need to respect that."

Dax let out a long sigh. "Good."

Leaning back in his chair, Clay propped his feet on Dax's desk. "I'll forgive you for the beauty sleep comment. How could you help but be jealous when I'm obviously better looking than you?"

"Obviously," Dax said dryly, folding his arms across his chest again.

"We do have a problem, though."

"We do?"

"Poor Kate is probably scraping together money to pay for her wedding. You need to give her a raise."

"Why is it that every time you come here it costs me money?"

"We could share her. I could go back to using that office as my business base."

"I'd rather pay her more."

Clay laughed and Dax joined in. Just like that things were good between them again.

ONE EVENING A week later, Lexi sat on the couch in the living room with her laptop still unopened beside her. She'd spent the week avoiding the man she'd almost slept with on Thanksgiving night. One more shot of tequila and it might have happened.

I'm done drinking.

The final cherry on the sundae of shit had been the next day when she'd received a text from Clay. He'd asked if she wanted to see him. She hadn't wanted to see anyone.

She still didn't.

She laid her head back on the couch and embraced the fact that she hadn't showered in two days. *It's not like I have anywhere to go anyway.* The last gig had been a catalog shoot for a department store. It had paid as much as she normally made in a month. *Which means I earned this opportunity to wallow.*

Her phone beeped with a message from her sister. While scrolling to it she saw how many messages her drunken mistake had sent. They were woven between unanswered messages from Kenzi.

Another person who will be better off with less of me as a part of her life.

She hadn't felt that way the year before. Kenzi and Willa had been as lost as she was. They'd been the Three Musketeers of not knowing what they'd do with the rest of their lives. Not anymore.

They both deserve the happiness they've found.

What do I deserve? Am I living it?

There were many great things about having an identical twin, but the negative was it made it too easy to directly compare one's life to another. *Willa always knew what she wanted. Now she has it.*

Do I even know what I want?

She threw an arm over her eyes and groaned. *Yes, I want to fast forward through the holidays so I don't have to sit there and pretend I'm happy for everyone else when I feel like this on the inside.*

There was a light knock on her door followed by a louder

one. It was probably Mrs. Silvester asking if she could borrow detergent. She'd been by earlier for fabric softener. It was hard to say if the woman actually needed all the items she asked to borrow or if she was simply lonely and used the visits as a chance to talk. In her seventies, the woman lived alone with her cats. *A fate probably waiting for me.* Lexi trudged to the door and opened it. "Let me guess, you're out of detergent?"

"Lexi, dear, I hope you don't mind me dropping in without calling."

Sophie. Shit.

Lexi ran her hand over her tangle of hair. "Sophie, what a surprise."

"May I come in?"

Lexi coughed into her hand and opened her mouth to say she was sick, but her eyes met Sophie's and the lie died on her lips. "Sure. Don't look around. The maid moved out when she married your son."

Sophie looked around and her nose wrinkled a little, but she made her way into the living room. She lifted an old pizza box off the couch and placed it on the table before taking a seat. "Kenzi mentioned she hadn't heard from you since Thanksgiving."

Smoothing her shirt over her hips, Lexi sat on the other side of the couch near her laptop. "I've been busy."

"Willa hasn't heard from you either."

Lexi wiped at the area below her eyes, hoping the makeup she hadn't removed wasn't making her look like a raccoon. "I meant to call her. Time just got away from me."

"Lexi, dear, I raised too many children to not recognize a lie when I hear one. Did we embarrass you at Thanksgiving? It's really no one's business if you and Clay want to be friends, or more."

Tears sprang to Lexi's eyes. "Oh, Sophie, it's not you. You and your family have never been the problem. It was always me."

After a long pause, Sophie said, "Did I ever tell you I had a sister?"

"Kenzi has mentioned her."

"She died a couple of years ago. I wasn't there when she did. We hadn't spoken for years. I know all about how time can slip through your fingers. But, you and Willa are not me and my sister. You have something beautiful. Whatever happened, don't close her out. She loves you."

"I love her, too."

"I know you do. So why are you avoiding her?"

With a sniff, Lexi pulled her legs up and hugged them to her chest. "You wouldn't understand."

"Try me."

"Sophie, you were right to be afraid I'd be the one to marry into your family. I'm really messed up on the inside."

"I was never—" Lexi shot her a doubtful look and Sophie stopped before saying something they both knew wasn't true. Sophie took a deep breath before starting over. "You and I are more alike than you know."

"I sincerely doubt it, and I mean that as a compliment."

"See, no one has to beat you up, Lexi; you're willing to do the job yourself. I spent more years than I care to admit doing the same. It affected my family and my marriage. I thought I didn't deserve to be happy. Once a year I withdrew from everyone I loved because I couldn't forgive myself. I wasn't just hurting myself, though. I was hurting my whole family. That's where you are now. What are you holding in, Lexi? What are you beating yourself up for?"

A lone tear slid down Lexi's cheek. "Willa and Kenzi have never been happier than they are now. I'm happy for them, but it's hard, too."

"Oh, honey, of course it is. A lot has changed this past year. You're feeling left behind, aren't you?"

Lexi nodded and wiped her check with the back of her hand. "Something like that."

"Well, you've had a good wallow over it, but now you're going to go take a shower, get dressed, and come shopping with me."

"That's a nice offer, Sophie, but—"

"It wasn't an offer. Get up," Sophie said in a firm tone as she rose to her feet.

Lexi slowly stood. "I love you for coming, but I'm not in the mood to go shopping."

Taking Lexi by the arm, Sophie led her across the room. "Lexi Chambers, you are a beautiful and intelligent young woman, but you've got a lot to learn about family if you think I'm leaving here without you. Get your butt in that shower, cover up the shadows under your eyes with concealer, and let's go buy you a new dress. It'll make you feel better."

Fresh tears sprang to Lexi's eyes. "You don't have to do

this, Sophie. I know I drive you crazy most of the time."

Sophie cupped one side of Lexi's face. "Sweetie, I raised five boys—on your worst day you don't come close to what they put me through. I'll always be grateful that Kenzi had you and Willa with her in Canada. You were her rocks when we didn't even know she needed one. You don't have to marry one of my sons to be my family, in my heart you're already one of us and you always will be."

Lexi laughed as she wiped another tear away. "I couldn't believe it when you told Clay your sons would line up to kick his ass if he hurt me. I meant to thank you for that."

"You did, honey. Now, stop stalling and get cleaned up."

Nodding, Lexi turned to do just that then looked back. "Thank you, Sophie."

"Go on. Have you eaten? We'll stop somewhere, get something to eat, and you can tell me all about what's going on between you and Clay."

Lexi nodded and trotted off to the shower. Never in her wildest dreams had she imagined that she would turn to Sophie for advice on anything, but suddenly she wanted to.

Before hopping into the shower she sent a text to Willa and then Kenzi. She told both of them she'd call them later but she was too busy to talk because she was heading out for an evening with Sophie. They both wrote back about how great that was and said they definitely wanted to hear all about it later.

A short time later Lexi applied the last touches of makeup and looked at herself in the mirror. She'd never had a mother figure in her life, but she did now. The miracle of it was that Sophie was taking on that role after seeing the worst of Lexi. She'd stuck out the tough times and somehow still loved her. The piece of Lexi's heart that had shattered long ago found its way back together. The fix was fragile, but it felt good.

And for the first time in a very long time Lexi liked the woman she saw in the mirror. She certainly wasn't perfect, but maybe, just maybe, there was hope for her yet.

Chapter Four

THREE WEEKS HAD never felt so much like forever. Clay sipped on spiked eggnog while watching Asher laugh at a face his young son made. There was a time when Clay would have thought Asher looked ridiculous interacting with a baby who probably couldn't tell him apart from any of the other men in the room, but this time the scene moved Clay. He thought about how Dax had said what came next was a million times better than the life he'd left behind.

The whole idea of marriage was crazy. Two people decide to choose each other over not only everyone they've ever met, but also anyone who might come into their lives later. He watched Dale reach over and take Sophie's hand as they listened to their children swapping stories from childhood. After many years of marriage, could they actually be that happy with each other? His attention moved to where Dax was standing beside Kenzi, smiling down at her. Would his friend one day stand in a room of his own children, still madly in love with his wife?

Clay placed the cup of eggnog down, unfinished. Christmas Eve had always been a night where he and his friends jetted off to some exotic location and partied hard enough that Christmas Day had always been a foggy recovery.

When Dax had invited him and told him to bring presents, Clay had been too curious to turn the invitation down. *So this is what Dax considers living.* He might as well have stepped into a holiday postcard. The Barrington home was ornately trimmed, from the bushes outside the home to every shelf and corner inside. Presents overflowed from beneath a ten-foot lit tree, the ones he'd brought were set with the others, but were in a distinct pile of their own.

"If you keep frowning you won't get more than coal in your stocking."

A warmth shot through Clay at the sound of Lexi's voice. He turned, a huge grin spreading across his face. "And you think you'll get better?"

Laughter lit her eyes. "If Santa knows what's good for him I will."

Clay laughed and allowed himself the indulgence of taking in the full beauty of her. The red dress she wore was a wrapping that did little to hide the gift of what lay beneath. He counted to ten and told himself to behave. "Beautiful dress."

She spun before him then leaned against his arm as she asked, "You like it? Sophie bought it for me."

"Really?" It was impossible to remember what they were talking about. Her mouth was close enough to claim, the warmth of her breast against his arm sent his blood rushing southward.

She leaned in even closer and lowered her voice. "We almost chose something conservative, but then I reminded her you'd probably be here. So, *Merry Christmas.*"

"You—it's—" *Damn.* He gave in to the lusty smile he'd been fighting to hold back. "Thank you."

Her laughter was light and heaven to his ears. She laid a hand on his forearm and said, "Hey, I'm sorry I never answered your text. I was going through something."

"Something? Or someone?" He hated that he'd asked that aloud. He'd never been the jealous type. Ever. But the thought of her with another man was slowly driving him mad. "Are you still with him?"

"Him?"

"Mr. Thanksgiving night."

She searched his face for a long moment. "More like Mr. Thanksgiving drinks after dinner, and I haven't seen him since. I shouldn't have gone out with him that night, but I was in a funk."

Good. "I hear Mr. Christmas is more attractive and Mr. New Year's is amazing in bed."

She shook her head, but she was laughing. "All I know is Mr. Christmas Eve is full of himself."

He raised and dropped a shoulder. "Is it bragging if it's true?"

She laughed again and linked her arm with his. "Don't ever change, Clay. You're a hoot."

A hoot? He wanted to be much more than that to her. "We all change, Lexi, especially when we discover that having what we want necessitates it."

Her eyes flew to his and her mouth rounded in preparation of saying something, but Willa interrupted. "Lexi, when did you sneak in?"

Lexi stepped away to hug her sister and Clay lamented the absence of her touch. "I just arrived."

"You must have popped in while I was in the bathroom." She looked Lexi over and her eyes popped. "That's the dress Sophie bought you?"

Clay briefly took in Willa's conservative, short-sleeved dress and marveled at how two women could have so much in common and still be so different. "It's lovely, isn't it?" Clay prompted Willa.

She hesitated as if she'd been about to voice a different opinion. Then she smiled. "It's definitely Lexi."

The two sisters exchanged a look of understanding that ended with Lexi smiling. "Yes, it is. Your dress really brings out your eyes, Willa."

"Thanks." Willa turned her attention to Clay. "Dax said you brought presents for everyone. That's so nice of you. Lance and I didn't know you were coming so you don't have anything from us, but will you be here tomorrow?"

"Please don't feel that you have to get me anything. I'm not here for the presents." He glanced briefly at Lexi and loved the blush that brought color to her cheeks.

Willa looked back and forth between them then said, "I should get back to Lance." She wagged a finger at both of them. "Be good."

Clay waited until she was out of earshot before he leaned down and whispered in Lexi's ear, "I'd rather be phenomenal."

Lexi laughed and his reward was that she linked her arm with his again. "You realize that if we ever do get together you'll have quite a lot of hype to live up to."

"If? If?" He put a hand over his heart as if she'd wounded him. "We have a date for New Year's Eve."

LEXI'S RESPONSE WAS a flutter of her eyelashes and a quick look away. She honestly didn't know how to take Clay sometimes. Although she'd heard that he might make an appearance at the Barrington's that night, she hadn't expected him to stay. She also hadn't expected him to act like he'd come to see her.

Clay had been a topic of many conversations over the last few weeks. Willa thought the idea of Clay marrying her sister was romantic beyond description, until Lexi reminded her that most men—especially men like Clay—weren't looking for marriage. She encouraged Lexi to be brave enough to believe in possibilities. Kenzi had said that although Dax claimed that he wouldn't get involved, he had smiled when Kenzi had suggested that Clay was sweet on Lexi. She thought Lexi should play it cool because Clay was used to women fawning all over him. In the end, it was Sophie's advice that Lexi took to heart. After listening to Lexi describe her interactions with Clay as strings of light flirtation sprinkled with moments when he sounded like a concerned friend, Sophie had said, "You need to decide what you want, Lexi. If you're looking for a few dates, it doesn't matter how you act. In the end, you're both adults. However, if you think there's a chance you might marry Clay—be yourself. If he's the right one for you, he'll cherish you the way you are."

Lexi had joked, "Shouldn't we go on at least one date before I think about naming our children?"

"You're not getting any younger, sweetie," Sophie had said, then laughed with such mischief that Lexi had joined in. Then Sophie had held up the red dress Lexi was presently wearing and said, "Try this on. If it doesn't stop him in his tracks and get him to ask you out again then he's not man enough for you."

So far Sophie's choice of dress had definitely turned Clay's head. He was full-on flirting with her, but that wasn't anything new, and it left Lexi wondering if she hadn't read more into Thanksgiving than had been there. "Did you really buy me a present?" she asked.

"Yes, Dax told me to buy for everyone."

Not exactly a grand, romantic gesture. "I bet I can guess it."

One side of his mouth curled up at the challenge. "You think you know me that well?"

"We'll see, won't we?"

He inclined his head and waited.

"Is it a large box or a small one?"

"A small one."

"Square or rectangular?"

"Rectangular."

"It's a bracelet."

His eyes narrowed. "Why do you say that?"

She referenced the room full of people. "You wouldn't

embarrass me, so I'm guessing the gift is a tasteful gift. You're a bit flashy so it would be something expensive. Considering that you don't know me that well, jewelry would be a safe choice." He looked unhappy with her guess so she gave his hand a pat. "Don't worry, I'll pretend to be surprised when I open it."

"I appreciate that."

His arm was tense beneath her touch, and she started to regret saying anything about the gift. She could hear Willa's voice in her head reminding her that the best response to any gift is a simple, "Thank you." *Why do I always open my mouth and make problems where there were none?*

Dale clapped his hands to gain everyone's attention. "Adhering to Barrington tradition, you are all allowed to open one gift tonight. Choose carefully. The rest will be given out tomorrow morning after breakfast."

As the youngest, Kenzi chose her gift first, the one from her husband. It was a monogrammed bed for her dog, Taffy. "I love it, Dax. It's perfect." She kissed him then put it down and snuggled to his side.

One by one the others went until only Lexi and Clay remained. "Ladies first," he said.

Lexi walked over to the tree and wavered between opening his present in front of everyone or not. *I wish I'd told him that I would love anything from him. That's how I feel.* She closed her eyes briefly, considered all the ways it could go well or badly, then opened her eyes and sifted through the gifts until she found the one for her from him. It was rectangular, but smaller than she'd expected. Definitely not a bracelet. "Thank you, Clay. I'm sure I'll love whatever it is." She opened it and discovered one simple, black flash drive.

"It's probably filled with a thousand photos of him," Grant said dryly.

"Behave," Sophie chastised softly.

Lexi returned the cover to the small box and smiled. "Better than a copy of his porn collection."

Willa covered her face with her hand, Sophie shook her head, but she was smiling. Dale wasn't smiling, but he looked like he was on the verge of it.

"That would require several flash drives," Clay added without missing a beat. Asher barked out a laugh and the others followed suit.

"You're next, Clay," Dale said.

Clay hesitated. "Is there one there for me?"

Lexi rushed forward. She wasn't sure about anyone else, but she'd brought one. Now that she'd seen his gift to her, she didn't feel guilty that she hadn't had a lot of money to spend on his. He accepted the box from her, bounced it in his hand for a moment, then a huge smile spread across his face. "I have no idea what this is."

"Then open it," Lexi said gently. It hadn't been easy to choose a gift for a man who could afford anything he wanted.

He took a moment and looked around the room before gazing back down at the package. "My family never celebrated Christmas. At least, never like this. Thank you."

There was an emotional silence where the women dabbed at their eyes and Dale nodded in approval at Dax.

Ian broke the mood by saying, "Open it already."

Everyone laughed.

Clay tore the paper off the box and revealed a toaster box. Lexi waved at him. "That's just the box I used. Keep going."

He pulled off the tape that held that box closed and took out two smaller, wrapped ones. He tore those open looking as if he were really enjoying the process. A moment later he held up the small digital camera and frame she'd bought him.

Lexi said, "I figured you probably have everything, but you don't have a photo of this Christmas. Now you do."

He replaced the camera and frame back in the box and closed the distance between them. Without warning he bent and brushed his lips briefly over hers and growled, "I love it."

Lexi dropped her present to the floor.

Dale clapped his hands loudly. "So, we'll see you all tomorrow morning. Be here by nine."

Chapter Five

CLAY PACED THE Boston Harbor Hotel's presidential suite he called home while in Boston. He hadn't expected Lexi to fall into bed with him right after the party, but he also hadn't expected her to skirt away while he was saying goodbye to Sophie and Dale. He was tempted to text her. No, he was dying to text her, but he wouldn't. Not this time.

This time he'd wait for her to contact him. And she would—as soon as she saw what was on the flash drive he'd given her.

He glanced at his watch impatiently. She had to be back at her place by now. Unless she was out with someone. That thought twisted his gut painfully.

I should call her just to make sure she made it home.

He took out his phone but stopped before choosing her number.

No. She has my number. If she wants to talk to me, she'll text me.

His phone rang and he almost dropped it in his haste to answer it. "Hello," he said trying to sound nonchalant but coming across as irritated instead.

"Clay? It's me, Lexi."

I know. "Hi."

"Is it too late to call? I'm sorry. I'm just looking at your present, and I didn't want to ask about it in front of everyone tomorrow."

He told himself to play it cool. "Good choice." *That's it? The best I can do? It's safe to say I'll never bowl her over with my wit.*

"First, I want to say I'm sorry for being a complete jackass at the party. Sometimes I don't think. When I open my mouth I have no idea what wild shit will come out of it."

Since he wasn't sure what part of their exchange she was referring to, he replied with a vague, "You have nothing to apologize for. I hope kissing you didn't embarrass you."

Long awkward pause. "No, that was nice."

Nice. Hmm.

She continued, "I should have said that I would love anything you gave me. And that's what I meant to say. I was just trying to be funny, and if it came out sounding ungrateful, I'm sorry."

This was an interesting side of Lexi. He had no idea that she worried so much about how others felt. "I probably would have bought you a diamond bracelet, but Dax and I decided what I gave you was a better choice."

"What exactly did you give me? I opened it, but as far as I can see it's simply a spreadsheet of companies and emails. Did you accidentally upload the wrong file?"

Now we see if the time I put in was worth it. "No, that's

the right file. I spent the last couple weeks calling people and asking them if they have a job for you. I wasn't sure if you actually loved HR or if you would choose something else if you had the chance, so start by picking the company you'd like to work for, then contact them with a description of what you'd like to do. They'll either give you a job they have or create one for you."

Lexi gasped. "You called everyone on this list? There's over a hundred companies."

"Then you should definitely be able to find a job you like."

"I don't know what to say."

"Thank you?"

She sniffed. "This is beyond nice. This is . . ."

Don't let her say "too much."

". . . phenomenal," she finished softly. "I could cry."

A feeling spread through him that was a million times better than any chemical high he'd ever had. Was this what Dax had referred to? "Don't cry. Find something you want to do. I hear life is a lot more enjoyable when you have a project you're passionate about."

"Do you have one?" Her tone was hopeful, and he was glad his answer was now a yes.

"I've recently become involved in a couple of charities. It can be difficult to choose one when there so many in need. Sophie's New Year's fundraiser sounds like my next big investment. I'd like to surprise her with something for it, but I'm still working out the details. With only a week left, I could use your help to plan it."

There was a long pause during which he held his breath. Finally, she said, "I'd love to."

"Great. I'll pick you up in the morning, and we'll go to the Barrington's together."

"I'd rather meet you there."

Hmm.

"Okay, if that's what you want."

"Yes." There was another pause before she said, "Clay, thank you for calling around for me. No one has ever done anything like that for me, and I don't know what to say, except that I'm grateful."

Deciding to lighten the mood, he purred, "Grateful or *grateful?*"

She laughed, "Good night, Clay."

"Good night, Lexi."

Later that night, Clay lay back in bed with his hands tucked beneath his head and tried to go to sleep. *It'll never happen.* He was anxiously awaiting Christmas morning.

And he was smiling.

ACROSS TOWN, LEXI lay in her own bed staring up at the ceiling with the flash drive Clay had given her still clutched in her hand. Whether it was the holiday season or being close to so many couples who were gushing love for each other, Lexi was sliding dangerously close to wanting to believe in love again.

It wasn't that she didn't believe in any kind of love.

She and Willa had a sister bond that nothing could ever break.

Although not related by blood, she saw her relationship with Kenzi the same way.

The last few weeks had proven to Lexi that Sophie and Dale saw her as more than simply Kenzi's friend. They accepted her as she was and that was more than Lexi had ever hoped for.

But Clay—

He was a whole other level. The problem with letting herself believe that his feelings for her might be real was that then she had to ask herself how she felt about him. Not just how flirting with him made her feel, but what she thought of him as a man.

He certainly wasn't humble by nature, but he had little reason to be. Very few people were born into his level of wealth. If life was fair, it would have compensated that good fortune by making him hideously ugly. Instead he had the classic, handsome features of the English with a height that hinted at a splash of Norwegian genes. He always dressed in a casual, but professional, style that could easy grace the cover of a men's magazine.

It wasn't that Lexi didn't think she could attract such a man, that part had never been the issue. It was everything that came after the initial chase that was a disappointment. Men didn't make an effort to know her, they wanted her on a basal level that didn't require a working knowledge of her favorite books or childhood memories. Repeated similar experiences had jaded Lexi toward men. Definitely toward men like Clay.

She held the flash drive above her face and studied it.

The Clay I know wouldn't spend weeks compiling a list of places he'd contacted for me. So, either there is another side to him—or he really, really wants to sleep with me.

The latter was depressing but easier to believe.

Lexi rolled onto her side and tucked the flash drive beneath her pillow. The digital clock beside her bed displayed the switch to Christmas Day with the same lack of fanfare Lexi associated with the holiday. She thought back to the confusing mix of emotions that had filled her each year during her childhood. The years that her aunt and uncle had picked them up from the boarding school had been awkward and stilted. The years after had been better, but still had lacked the magic people associated with the holiday. As a child as well as an adult she'd always found Christmas to be a sham, all build up but just another day in the end.

She rolled onto her back and slammed a fist onto the bed beside her. If she was this wide awake during any other time of year she would have flipped on the television, but her mood wouldn't be improved by the onslaught of holiday specials. They didn't represent any version of Christmas she'd ever known.

Men like Clay weren't looking for more than sex and the only magic Christmas held was its ability to make everyone spend more money than they should. *And I'll prove it.*

She picked up her phone from the table beside her bed and dialed his number. *He won't even answer. He's probably with someone else.*

"Lexi, is everything okay?" he asked in a voice deep from sleep.

"I—I—" She considered making up a reason she'd called. She could claim to have rolled over and hit redial by accident. She remembered what Sophie had said, though, about being herself. "Is this a bad time?"

"For you to call me? Never."

She smiled at that. "I couldn't sleep and . . ." Shaking her head, she waited for him to offer to come over. That's what men did, at least all the men she'd ever known. They wouldn't care what was keeping her up, they'd see it as an opportunity to comfort her—*intimately.*

"I couldn't either," he said, fitting exactly into what she'd expected him to say. "Christmas has always been my least favorite holiday, and I'm not used to remaining sober enough to experience it."

"I've always hated it, too," she said in genuine surprise.

"What's the worst part for you?" he asked gently.

"It's all the times people say if it lacks magic, it's because you don't believe enough. Is it my fault that I recognize commercial exploitation of families? If the stores could partner with religion to make Christmas a monthly holiday, they would. That's the magic of the season, that no one has caught on to how they're being manipulated."

"God, you sound like me. It's why I usually throw an anti-Christmas bash somewhere warm. It's too depressing to watch my friends cart trees indoors, make perfectly beautiful homes gaudy with decorations, then gather with people they don't give a shit about the rest of the year."

Lexi hugged her comforter to her and smiled. *We really are alike.* "I can't understand why I enjoyed the Barringtons' party."

"Besides the fact that I was there?" he added with humor.

Lexi smiled again. "Besides that. Did you enjoy it? The party, I mean?"

He let out an audible breath. "I didn't expect to, but I did. It felt a bit like stepping into a Norman Rockwell version of Christmas. The only imperfection I found was the absence of one of their sons. They said he was unable to come home for the holiday."

"Andrew. He has always been a tough one to figure out."

"They say the same about you."

"Me? Hardly. What you see is what you get with me."

He was silent a moment then said, "That's what you want people to believe, anyway."

Lexi laughed nervously. He wasn't speaking in sexy innuendos. He sounded sincere, and it made her nervous. "You don't know me as well as you think you do, Clay."

"That's easy enough to change."

And here it comes—the booty call request. She remained silent and waited for it. Hearing it would come as a relief in some ways.

"I meant what I said about wanting to brainstorm with you on ways I could support Sophie's charity event. You know her better than I do, and I value your opinion. I realize we'll see each other at breakfast, but what are you doing after that? Spend the day with me."

Lexi chewed her bottom lip. "Tomorrow?"

"Of course tomorrow. Or, considering the hour, today to be more precise. How brave are you feeling?"

Excitement and disappointment filled her. She wouldn't say yes to him, but she wasn't ready to say no to him either. "Brave? I don't think we should—"

"Sorry, forget it. It was a ridiculous idea. Blame the time of night."

Even though Clay was proving to be just like every other man she'd known, it didn't make him a bad person. It simply meant he wasn't any more special than they'd been. "It's my fault. I shouldn't have called." Her voice was thick with emotion.

"It's just that she asks me to visit every year, and I've always found a reason not to. I thought that since she's only a few hours away this might be the year I drop in."

Lexi sat up in her bed. "Drop in where? Who are you talking about?"

"My cousin Jacqueline. She grew up here in the United States and reconnecting with her has been on my to-do list."

There was something in his voice that lent this topic importance. "But you haven't."

"No. She can be—intense."

"So you don't like her."

"I didn't say that. It's a long boring story."

"I wasn't sleeping anyway," Lexi said gently.

With that, Clay began a story of a boy raised by grandparents who gave him everything and demanded nothing except he keep a low profile in their lives. If he didn't ask questions, didn't cause trouble, everything and anything he wanted was at his disposal. He described his childhood as a happy one except for the times when Aunt Gina visited with her daughter. Although Clay and Jacqueline had been similar in age, Jacqueline had always been the top of her class. She had an opinion about almost every topic imaginable and the business savviness to achieve the goals she set for herself. Her fortune had risen, dipped, then risen again, and each time she came back stronger. "I know exactly how she'll set me up," Clay said. "She'll list the companies she is now president or chief executive officer of now, then she'll give me this tight little smile and ask 'And what have you been doing?'"

"I hate that question. You might as well ask someone how much they weigh."

"Exactly."

"I can understand why you haven't gone to see her."

"She can be a real pill, but . . . she's my only living relative. Look at the Barringtons, they have their issues, but they work it out. I feel like I should at least try."

Lexi dug out the flash drive and hugged it to her chest. "And you wanted me to go with you?"

Clay cleared his throat. "Ridiculous, right?"

No, beautiful—the most beautiful Christmas present she'd ever received. "Let's do it. Let's go see that cousin of yours."

"If it's awful, I'll make it up to you."

"It won't be," she promised, although she had no way of knowing if it would be or not.

"What about your family, Lexi? You never talk about them. Where do they live?"

She told Clay about how she'd lost her parents early in life. Despite how different her childhood had been from Clay's, in the ways that mattered, they'd been similar. Both were in search of something better. Taking turns, they compared the stupid mistakes they'd made over the years. She'd been rebellious, he'd been self-indulgent. Neither had been happy in their own way. They were both at a place where they were ready for a change, but not sure what that meant.

Most of what Lexi said she would never had shared with anyone because she knew the type of helpful, motivating lecture that would be showered upon her. She didn't want to completely overhaul who she was, but she did have areas she could work on.

Clay was the same. He was by far not apologizing for the privileged life he lived, but he wanted to be more—for his time on the planet to have mattered. As Lexi listened to him describe his vague, nagging discontent with how he was living his life, she had to stop herself from saying, "I know exactly how that feels," over and over again.

The sun came up and filled the room with light. Lexi looked at the clock beside her bed. "Oh, my God, it's morning. We've been talking for hours."

"So we have. What time do you want me to pick you up?"

A mild panic spread through Lexi. The last few hours had been good, so good, that she felt unexpectedly vulnerable. She wanted to believe.

In him.

In herself.

In possibilities.

Lexi had survived the loss of her parents and everything

else life had thrown at her by telling herself she didn't care. She had consistently chosen the thrill of the new over investing too much of herself in one person or even one career. Other than her sister and her best friend, Kenzi, she'd kept her attachments to a minimum. The less she cared about, the less life could rip away from her. It was a survivor's philosophy, and she'd felt comfortable with it until recently.

Unlike the men she'd dated in the past, Lexi didn't feel that Clay wanted to control her, or worse, change her. Her stomach did a nervous flip. Part of her wanted to spend the rest of the morning getting to know him. Part of her wanted to hang up and never speak to him again.

Something told her that if she wasn't careful, this man could do something no other man had. *He could break my heart.*

Only if I give him the power to. One good conversation doesn't need to change anything.

He wants to take me with him to see his family, but that means nothing more than he simply doesn't want to go alone.

"I'll meet you there."

He chuckled. "Afraid if you let me in your door we'll miss breakfast and spend the day in bed?"

"Yes," she said honestly. A rush of desire spread through Lexi at the image. With nothing more than his voice, he'd lit a need in her so raw she wanted to suggest he come over right then, but she didn't.

He groaned. "You're not making it easy for me to respect your decision."

"My decision?"

"To wait until New Year's Eve."

Oh, yeah. I forgot about that. She'd been testing him, sure he would back off as soon as he realized she wasn't going to drop into bed with him. She could tell him now that she'd been joking, but it might be better if he thought she'd been serious. "It wasn't meant as a countdown."

"So you're reneging on your bet? Even though I won fair and square."

"I wouldn't have bet sex." *Shit. I hope I didn't bet sex.*

He made a deep sound in his throat. "Don't tell me you can't remember what you promised if you lost."

"We were both drunk."

"I remember every moment of that night."

"Good for you. A gentleman would realize that whole conversation was a joke, and he'd drop it."

His laugh was sexy and tempting. "I have been accused of being many things, but being a gentleman was never one of them. And you can claim to want one, but we both know I'm more your taste."

"Keep telling yourself that," she answered lightly. The way he said *taste* had her licking her lip as she remembered the heavenly feel of his mouth on hers. Even as she told herself the wisest course of action was to keep things casual, she couldn't help but smile.

"That's it, I'm definitely collecting on the bet."

"Thankfully, I know when you're not serious." Lexi's breathing came quicker. This was the other side of what they had—the sizzle.

"Do you? I'm going to enjoy testing that confidence of yours."

No, don't. It's already unsteady. "I'll see you at breakfast, Clay."

"Say my name again."

"Clay," she said with a light laugh.

"Not like that. Softer, huskier, like it turns you on when you say it."

"Clay," she whispered in her best bedroom voice. Giving him what he wanted was its own pleasure. Not wanting him to see that she was equally affected she added, "Yes. Yes. Oh, yes, Clay."

He made a pleased sound. "I'll take that for now, although that last part will sound even better when I'm sinking into you again and again. On New Year's Eve. Just like you promised."

Lexi closed her eyes as a wave of hunger for him rocked through her. New Year's Eve was a week away. Would they even be talking by then? If so, wouldn't sleeping with him be a mistake? He wasn't some guy who would fade out of her life afterward. As Dax's best friend he would always be there, a potential long-term reminder of how she still wasn't strong enough to make better choices.

But, oh, what a good bad choice he'd be. "Bye, Clay." This time her voice was richer, full of the need he'd lit in her.

"Better. For now. See you at breakfast."

Chapter Six

THE NEXT EVENING, after a couple of hours of light conversation that took them most of the drive home, Lexi turned in the bucket seat of Clay's car and swiped through the photos on the camera she'd given him. Kenzi had taken it for a while, and there were at least twenty photos of Clay and Lexi.

Flirting.

Sharing a joke.

Lexi gazing at Clay across the room with a look of longing. *I need to end this before I get in too deep.*

She turned the camera off and said, "Don't forget that my car is still at the Barrington's."

He shot a quick smile at her. "I may forget on purpose. I'm enjoying you being dependent on me."

Deciding it was best to ignore that comment, she set the camera back in the case. They'd done the Christmas thing together, spent time with both the Barringtons and Clay's cousin's family. This was when they were supposed to return to normal and not see each other until the next holiday. "Jacqueline wasn't as bad as you described. You can probably go visit her now without a buffer."

He frowned at her. "Is that what you were tonight? A buffer?"

"I'm not judging. There's plenty of situations I'd rather not go into alone. She cares about you, though. I could tell."

His hands tightened on the steering wheel. "Her eyes nearly popped out when you mentioned being a background singer one summer for Stained Souls. Then you said you'd helped Senator Bidly write his acceptance speech. She had no idea what to think of you. I was surprised to see you share so much with her."

Lexi rubbed her cold hands together. She'd wanted to steer Jacqueline's attention away from prying into Clay's business, and it had worked, but Lexi was used to sometimes having a backlash from her methods.

He took one of her hands in his and brought it to rest beneath his on his warm thigh. "Why did you do that, Lexi?"

She shrugged. All she'd done was put herself in his position and asked herself what he wanted. If she was about to be lectured on oversharing, then so be it.

"I shouldn't have told you she interrogates me about my life. You put yourself in the line of fire, didn't you?"

Lexi glanced out the front window. The way he understood her was disconcerting. "If I said yes, will it dent your fragile male ego?"

He raised her hand to his lips and kissed it. "No, it would simply affirm why we're so good together, and it'll only get better."

Her eyes flew to his and her hand shook. "Don't say

that."

He frowned again. "Why the hell not?"

She pried her hand free. *No, we can't. Today proved it. Anything beyond this is dangerous.* "We're friends, we have fun together, but that's as far as it can go—as far as I want it to go."

"I thought you were braver than that."

What she had with Clay had earned the truth. "This has nothing to do with being brave. I don't know about you, but my track record with relationships sucks. If they make it a month I'm shocked. I don't want to ruin what we have by taking it there."

"Taking it where?"

"I don't know." Lexi was at a loss for how to describe what she felt toward him. Yes, she wanted to sleep with him, but she also simply enjoyed his company. He could make her laugh like no one else, but he also listened in a way that kept her honest with him. *What do you call that?* "We both know how quickly things can get ugly after people have sex. Suddenly it's all about how bad you can make each other feel."

"You've been with some serious assholes."

"Maybe." She tucked her cold hands between her knees. "But, tell me, how long was your longest relationship?"

Clay returned to clenching the steering wheel again. His silence confirmed what she already knew about him.

They drove along for a while with a heavy silence hanging over both of them. Eventually, Lexi cleared her throat and said, "I'm sorry. I know this is awkward, but we're going to see each other at every Barrington function and beyond. My best friend married your best friend. If you were anyone else, I'd sleep with you and be done with it, but this is complicated."

The corner of his mouth twitched. "Lexi Chambers, you're hard on the ego, but damn, you're sexy." He picked up her hand again and turned it in his. "So, no dinner tomorrow?"

"It's for the best."

He pulled up to the sidewalk outside the Barrington home and parked before turning toward her. "Are you going to Sophie's fundraiser in Vermont?"

"I told Kenzi this morning that I would."

"I'll be there, too. I'm flying up the day before."

Lexi swallowed hard. "I'll—"

He cupped her face and silenced her gently with his thumb over her lips. "Meet me there, I know. I didn't need your protection today, but thank you for going with me. You have every right to doubt me. I've never stayed with anyone. I've never dedicated myself to anything. If I were a better man I'd respect what you're saying and try like hell to be your friend. I can't do that, though." Without hesitation he took her face in his hands and kissed her deeply until they were both shaking and clinging to each other, then he dropped his hands and sat back. "I want you so damn much it's slowly driving me mad."

She slumped back, breathless in her own seat and nodded.

I know exactly how that feels, too.

CLAY SPENT A restless night tossing and turning. He wasn't the kind of man who tortured himself with the ethics of a decision, but this one had him confused. On one hand, he actually enjoyed being with Lexi, a hell of a lot more than he could ever remember with another woman. And it wasn't all about sex. He liked her, more and more with each side of her he got to know.

She was brazen in the face of authority, but the first to judge herself harshly. She preferred to appear irresponsible, but her loyalty to family and friends was proof she wasn't. Kenzi said she and Willa had moved to Boston because they thought she needed them, and now he believed Kenzi was right. Nothing came between Lexi and those she cared about. She'd do whatever she could to help them. *Like spending Christmas telling my family about all the times she jumped from job to job just so they wouldn't ask me questions about my own life.*

She went because she thought I needed her.

The realization that she was the first to do anything like that for him rocked through him. Women tended to see him in terms of his wealth, his looks, and what he brought to the bedroom. They didn't worry about him. The women he knew would have been more concerned about what his cousins thought of them than how he felt that day.

Lexi was not only a woman he was chomping at the bit to sleep with, she was also quickly becoming a friend. He didn't have friends in general, not real ones. Dax was the exception. His life was full of people who wanted to spend time with him, but few who would stay if he suddenly lost his fortune. He liked to think Dax would. He had a feeling Lexi would, too.

Which made her special.

Too special to sleep with?

He'd wanted to disagree with everything she'd said about what happened to people in the aftermath of being intimate, but he couldn't. Things would change. They might be civil. They might be tumultuous, but they wouldn't be the same.

He'd also been unable to deny his history with women. She thought putting two people together who had no idea how to sustain a relationship was a recipe for disaster. How could he argue that?

Dax had said that if Clay wanted to prove he cared about Lexi, he needed to respect her decision. He wasn't used to not getting what he wanted. There'd only been a handful of things in Clay's life that had been impossible, regardless of how much money he had. He couldn't bring his parents back. He couldn't stop people flocking to him simply because they saw him in terms of what he could do for them financially. Some things were non-negotiable in life.

That's not how he wanted to view Lexi.

He remembered what Kate had said about giving up too easily. *I've done a hell of a lot more than send her a text, though. I called everyone I know and told them to hire her. I took her to meet my family. What more does she want?*

Chapter Seven

"WHAT DO *YOU* want to do?" Kenzi asked from her spot at the end of the couch. She was still in her pajamas, and her hair was mussed from sleep. Not that she could be blamed since Lexi and Willa had shown up on her doorstep without warning that morning.

Dressed in stretch jeans and a loose blouse, Willa looked down at the laptop she had perched on her knees and sighed. "Clay must really like you to have gone to all this trouble."

Lexi leaned forward to take the computer back. "It's just a list. He gave *you* a job. I'm not here to talk about Clay, though."

Not taking the hint, Willa looked across at Kenzi. "Do you remember how jealous Lance was of Clay when I worked for him? It was the only reason Dax gave Clay an office in his building. He wanted to watch over us. They were both worried about nothing, though. Clay only has eyes for Lexi. I'm so glad he's finally doing something about it."

Kenzi chuckled. "He really is smitten, Lexi. You should have seen Dax's face when he heard that Clay took you to meet his family. Clay has never taken anyone there, not even

Dax."

Lexi closed the laptop and placed it on the table in front of her. Of course she wanted to believe what Kenzi was saying, but it didn't change her decision. She and Clay would remain friends. Just friends. "I didn't wake you both up to talk about Clay. This is serious. What do I do with this list? Is it okay to actually take a job from it?"

Willa looked confused. "Why wouldn't it be?"

With a sigh, Lexi smoothed the hem of her dress down over her leggings. "If I remember correctly, Willa, you were the one who asked me to try to keep work and this family separate after I left Poly-Shyn."

"Willa," Kenzi said in surprise, "the Hendersons were fine with her leaving abruptly. It actually worked out for the best."

Willa wrinkled her nose, a tell that she felt guilty for saying it. "I'm sorry, Lexi. I didn't mean to sound that judgmental, but the way you left was wrong. You didn't even give them notice. They took a chance by hiring you, and you acted like it meant nothing."

Lexi let out a long breath and counted to ten. She could explain herself to Willa, but she really wasn't in the mood to throw herself at her feet and beg for understanding. Sometimes it was easier to simply stare her down. "Just to be clear, you're both okay if I take one of these jobs. I don't want to get grief later if I choose one that doesn't work out."

With a shrug, Willa said, "That would be between you and Clay."

"There is no me and Clay." Lexi stood impatiently. "I

don't even know why I bother sometimes. You don't listen. I'm happy that you are now a Barrington, Willa, and I'm trying to navigate your rules, but if you're going to pretend you don't care about this, then I'll do what I want."

Kenzi waved a hand in the air. "Wait. Willa, Lexi's been part of this family just as long as you have. There's nothing she could do, short of become a nun, that would shock us. What are you worried about?"

Willa looked back and forth between them, then blurted, "Things are so perfect. Lance is amazing. Your whole family seems happier." She placed her hand on her stomach. "I never thought I could be this happy, and I'm afraid—"

Kenzi scooter closer to Willa, putting her arm around her in support. "What are you afraid of?"

Lexi crossed her arms in front of her and looked down at them. She'd spent most her life protecting Willa, but on this one subject, she wouldn't. "Say it, Willa, although I'd be shocked if you have the nerve to. Frame it just right, though, or you may sound like you're not a saint."

Willa looked down at her hands and blinked back tears. "I never said I was a saint."

"What are you talking about?" Kenzi looked up at Lexi. "What don't I know?"

With her chin held high, Lexi said, "Willa is afraid I'll somehow screw things up between her and your family. She blames me for the early issues she had with Lance, but there's more, isn't there, Willa? You blame me for something much bigger."

Willa shook her head. "I don't."

"You do," Lexi insisted. "Just say it."

Wiping a tear from her cheek, Willa said, "It was a long time ago. It shouldn't affect me at all now, but . . . when our parents died we went to live with our aunt and uncle for a short time. They sent us to boarding school because they couldn't handle us."

"Me," Lexi said. "They couldn't handle me."

Willa looked down at her hands again.

Kenzi stood. "You don't know that."

"Oh, we heard them say it, didn't we, Willa? They made their reason for sending us away very clear."

Willa rose to her feet and went to stand in front of Lexi. "All you had to do there was follow their rules, but you did whatever you wanted to do—just like you always have. It didn't matter that I wanted to stay. You ruined it for both of us."

"And you're afraid I'll do that again."

Kenzi stepped between her two best friends. She took Lexi's hand in one of hers and Willa's in the other. "The two of you were my family at a time when I thought I'd lost mine. Don't you dare treat each other with less love than you both deserve. Willa, you are the most kindhearted person I've ever met. Lexi, I believe you'd take a bullet for me or Willa without a thought of what would happen to you. The past holds some ugly memories for all of us, but we decide how much power to give them. Not one of us is perfect, but we're always better together."

Willa nodded. "I'm so sorry, Lexi. I didn't even realize I was holding on to that day."

Lexi sniffed. "I know. I came here today because I want you to stay just as happy as you are today." She looked at Kenzi. "Both of you. I don't want to do anything that jeopardizes your happiness."

Wiping her face with her free hand, Willa said, "It could be the hormones, but I could bawl my eyes out right now. I love you two so much."

Lexi hugged her sister. "I love you, too."

Kenzi wrapped her arms around both of them. "Now that I'm adding puffy red eyes to my glorious morning look, can we talk about something safe, like this weekend?" She dropped her arms and returned to the corner of the couch. "They're predicting a big snow storm for Vermont. Dax and I are going to try to fly up the day before. How are you two getting there? I'd say you could come with us, but I know you don't fly, Lexi."

Willa chewed her bottom lip. "Do you think you could do it this once, Lexi? Maybe take something for the trip? It's a long drive otherwise."

"I don't mind going up on my own," Lexi said. "You're pregnant, Willa; don't feel that you need to make the drive with me. And it doesn't make sense for you to come with me, Kenzi. You'll probably have your whole family on your plane."

"We could have a car take you," Kenzi said slowly as she mulled ideas.

Willa took Lexi's hand in hers again and gave it a squeeze. "Or you could drive up with Clay."

Lexi shook her head. "No way."

"Why? It's the perfect solution," Kenzi exclaimed.

"Because—because—" *Oh, what the hell?* "I'm trying not to sleep with him."

Willa wrinkled her nose. "It's okay if you do. You like him. He likes you. It's fine."

"It's not fine if it's going to cause issues between us, Willa," Lexi said quietly.

Willa pulled Lexi in for another tight hug. "It won't, Lexi. No matter what happens between the two of you. Don't let me ever make you feel bad about who you are or how you live your life. If the Barringtons ever decide we aren't good enough for them, it'll be their loss."

"Hey," Kenzi laughed. "Barrington over here."

"Not anymore; you're a Marshall now," Lexi and Willa said in unison.

Kenzi laughed again. "I love when you sync up like that and say the same things at the same time."

Willa and Lexi both turned and stuck their tongues out at Kenzi, then saw each other doing it and laughed. When they stopped laughing, Lexi said, "I'm not calling Clay and asking him to drive me to Vermont."

Kenzi took out her phone and started typing. "You won't have to. I'm telling Dax right now that you're driving up to Vermont all by yourself in a potential snow storm. If Clay likes you half as much as I think he does, he'll contact you."

About ten minutes later, Lexi's phone beeped with an incoming text. Lexi smiled. "It's Clay."

Willa and Kenzi came to huddle around her. "What did he say?"

"He wants to know how I'm getting to Vermont."

"So, tell him," Kenzi urged.

I'm driving, Lexi typed.

Alone?

Lexi hesitated before answering. "I don't know, guys. Are you sure you're both okay with this?"

With a straight face, Willa said, "Bring condoms."

"Okay, then." Lexi burst out laughing.

Kenzi chimed in. "Dax wouldn't have told Clay if he thought Clay wasn't serious about you. Give Clay a chance to prove Dax is right."

Yes, alone.

Not anymore.

Shouldn't you ask if I want the company?

Oh, I'm taking you. All the way.

Lexi laughed at the double entendre. "He's so bad."

"You love it," Willa said with a smile.

"I do." She texted: *Because halfway would be disappointing.*

Don't worry, it'll be a long drive. One that you'll like so much you'll want to do it again. And again.

Lately I've been driving myself everywhere so this will be nice.

Oh, yes. Much better. I promise. Lexi laughed again.

Kenzi leaned forward. "Should we ask what you two are saying?"

"No," Lexi said with a huge smile. "No, you shouldn't."

"So, you're going up with him?" Willa asked.

"I sure am." Lexi nodded. *Up. Down. Either. Both.* The miracle would be if they made it to the charity event at all.

CLAY TUCKED HIS phone back into the inside pocket of his jacket and strolled into Dax's office. "I'm driving her up," he announced as he plopped into the chair.

Dax raised his hand for Clay to hold off on saying more and ended his call. "Good. Now, can I get back to work?"

Rubbing a hand over his chin, Clay said, "So, I'm interviewing staff today. I was hoping I could get a few tips from you on how to weed out the riffraff."

"What do you mean you're interviewing? For what? And why are you doing it here?"

"My office is here," Clay said with mock outrage. "I don't have employees, and you won't share yours. How am I supposed to run a business with no staff?"

"Whoa. Stop right there. You're starting a business?"

"Don't sound so fucking shocked. I've made a ton of money for you over the years. My networking skills are unparalleled. Everything I touch turns to gold. Why shouldn't I run a business?"

"Here? In my building?"

"Are you suggesting I relocate? That can be devastating for a young company."

Dax leaned back in his chair and looked heavenward for strength. "Does this new business have a name?"

Clay held up the notebook and pen he'd used earlier with Dax when they'd brainstormed for places Lexi might want to work. "I thought we could choose one this morning."

Throwing up his hands, Dax used his intercom to ask Kate to hold his calls. "Is it for profit?"

"Why wouldn't it be?"

"I thought you were looking into partnering with charities."

"I am and I've already donated to several. This is different. I want to build something of my own. Prove that I can do it."

"Okay. You could start a foundation."

Clay spread his hands out in the air as if stretching the word. "The Landon Foundation. I like it. There's room on the front of this building for an iconic L."

"No. No there isn't."

"Let the idea sink in before you reject it." He tapped his pen on the still blank page. "What's the next step?"

"Most foundations are established as nonprofit corporations with the purpose of making grants to various organizations or groups. You should have one you focus on."

Nodding, Clay wrote: *Find interesting cause.* "This is good stuff."

"Sophie is active in many charities. She'd be better at helping you with this than I am."

Clay made a face. "I want to look like I know what I'm doing before I take this to the Barringtons."

With a shake of his head, Dax said, "Why?" Then he smiled. "This is about Lexi, isn't it? You want to impress her."

Clay shrugged. "She doesn't think I can commit to anything."

"Can you?"

"I think so. I hope so. If I thought anyone was listening

I'd send up a request for a little guidance, but no amount of Christmas lights will convince me we're not alone. I have what I need for now, though." Clay stood. "Oh, and one more thing. I'll need you to clear out five more offices for me."

"Really? Why?"

"I told you, I'm hiring staff today."

Dax groaned then pressed the intercom again. "Kate? Drop what you're doing. You're helping Clay this morning. It appears he's conducting interviews, and he'll need your expertise with organizing it. He may also need a few offices cleared out. Move Jamison's team up one floor."

Clay leaned forward. "I knew you'd share her with me. Congratulations Kate, you just got a huge raise, double your present salary."

"Really?" Kate exclaimed.

Dax lifted his finger off the intercom. "You're paying her."

"No problem."

"And she's the only employee of mine you get to talk to. That's it. Don't mess with anyone else."

"I promise."

Dax pressed the intercom button again. "Really. I'll send a memo down to HR. You can say no, Kate, even after today. My office is your priority, but if Clay needs it, then I guess you can help him out from time to time."

Clay propped his feet up on the corner of Dax's desk and laced his fingers behind his head. "The Landon Foundation."

Dax leaned forward and knocked Clay's feet off his desk.

"Housed, temporarily, in the Marshall building."

"Don't worry, Dax, you won't even notice I'm here."

Chapter Eight

WHATEVER ROMANTIC IDEAS Lexi had had about the drive to Vermont with Clay had taken a backseat about halfway into the trip, when the light snow that had been falling in Boston was replaced by heavier flakes as they drove northward. Lexi's phone beeped with an incoming message. She read it then said, "Willa is watching the news. She said the storm is intensifying. Ice and snow. They can't fly out today."

Clay kept his eyes on the road. "I didn't expect it to be this bad. How far out are we?"

Lexi looked at the GPS. "We're halfway there, but I don't think that means less than two hours. Not with the snow sticking to the road the way it is. I'm sorry. I should have checked the weather more carefully."

"Hey," Clay said, taking her hand in his. "Don't worry about it. The guy I bought this Hummer from said it could drive through anything."

"Have you had it long?" Lexi asked. It looked new.

"A couple of days."

Lexi looked down at their laced fingers. "Did you buy it

for this trip?"

"I did."

"You're crazy."

"My Jaguar wasn't built for snow, and I'm driving with precious cargo."

That made her smile. "Thank you, but you realize you can rent cars, right?"

"Renting is for people who don't know what they want. I do. I made my choice, and I have no problem committing to it."

The way he said committing sent Lexi's heart beating wildly. *Don't read anything into what he says. He's a flirt. Like me.* "I had no idea you were so serious about cars."

"I'm serious about a lot of things." The Hummer swerved a bit as it hit a small patch of ice. Clay returned his hands to the steering wheel. "Although, right now, I should focus on getting us there in one piece."

Lexi turned down the radio. "I hope you can see farther than I can."

"It's fine, Lexi," he said in a tone that made her realize she must have sounded nervous. "A lot safer than trying to fly in this weather."

Lexi turned to watch his profile. "Most people think I'm crazy for not flying."

"Most people didn't lose their parents in a plane crash."

He said it the same way she would have, a little bit angry with a dash of rebellion. *He gets it.* "Exactly. Every time I think it shouldn't bother me anymore, I try to board a plane and panic at the last minute. I've even bought plane tickets then driven anyway. Willa says I'll never see the world if I don't get over it. I'm not sure I can."

After a quick glance at her, Clay said, "There is something called a boat. Now, I don't know too much about it, but I hear it floats instead of flies. People have even been known to use them to get across large bodies of water."

Lexi smacked his arm, but she smiled as she did it. "Thanks. I'll look into them."

"I happen to own a rather large yacht. It's bigger than most. Not too big. Too big is almost as bad as too small." He shot her another look and winked.

Lexi was still laughing as she asked, "Is there anything you can't make into a sexual innuendo?"

With a completely straight face, he said, "Me? I was referring only to my boat. You are completely responsible for where your mind went."

"I'll remember that," she warned. She turned forward just in time to see a pair of headlights coming straight at them on their side of the road. "Clay?" She smacked his arm again. "Clay, do you see that?"

"Holy shit," Clay exclaimed and pulled into the other lane. The car flew past. He looked over his shoulder. "What the hell was that?"

Just then the Hummer hit a patch of ice that sent the vehicle into a spin. Clay fought to correct it, but there was too much ice and too much momentum. They started into a spin that took them back across the road and into a ditch.

As soon as the car stopped, Clay turned to her. "Lexi, are you okay?"

Lexi nodded, but took a moment before answering. "I think so. Are you?"

Releasing his seat belt Clay ran his hands over her face and then her arms. "Did you hit your head?"

"No, no . . . I'm okay."

He released her belt as well and pulled her into his arms, holding her tightly against his chest. "I thought—for a second there—"

"Me, too," Lexi mumbled into his chest, loving the feel of his strong arms around her.

He pulled back enough so he could see her face. "I can't lose you now; I just started believing in—"

He stopped and Lexi raised her hand to caress his cheek. *Me, too.* "What? What did you just start believing in?"

A look entered Clay's eyes that Lexi had never seen before. Desire laced with something else. "Me. You. Us. The whole thing. When I'm with you, I feel like I can do anything. When we're apart nothing matters more than being with you again. I've been in a sleepless, nauseated, and euphoric state since we met."

"Is that a good thing?" Lexi asked, her eyes brimming with laughter as well as tears.

"I don't want to be your friend, Lexi. I want so much more." His mouth closed over hers and Lexi welcomed the claiming.

It was more than a kiss. Clay used his lips, his tongue, to declare a hunger for her that would have scared her if she hadn't felt the same for him. She opened her mouth wider to him, wrapped her arms around his neck to hold him as they explored each other with abandon.

He lifted her easily so she was sitting across his lap and ran his hands up beneath her shirt to caress her bare skin. She inched her skirt higher so less material would be between his hardness and her eager sex. They ground against each other like teenagers giving in to wild urges. He undid the first button of her shirt and kissed the skin it exposed then reached for the second.

A loud knock on the window made them both jump. "Are you all right in there? Do you need an ambulance?"

Clay eased Lexi back onto her own seat and straightened the front of her shirt before rolling down the window. "We're okay."

A tall bearded man who looked like he was in his late fifties peered into the vehicle. "You shouldn't be out tonight. We're sanding the roads but the ice is pretty bad."

"I noticed," Clay said dryly. "Thanks for checking on us."

"Do you need a ride? Will it start?"

"It should," Clay said. The engine kicked on.

"You might want to see if you can pull out of that ditch. The roads are closed so you won't see many come by here after me."

Clay put it in reverse. The back wheels spun, but the front made a nasty, grinding noise.

"Looks like you broke an axle," the man said. "You're not driving anywhere in that thing tonight."

Clay slammed a hand on the wheel before turning back to the man and offering his hand for him to shake. "Clay

Landon. Could we offer to compensate you for a ride to anywhere but here?"

"Kenny Meade. I have to finish sanding this route, but you can come along. There's a motel a few miles from here. They should have open rooms."

Lexi expected Clay to demand a better option, but he didn't. He simply thanked him then turned to Lexi. "Are you comfortable going with him? We'll grab our smaller bags and come back for the rest tomorrow."

Lexi peered past Clay to the large sanding truck the man had driven. "He doesn't seem dangerous."

Clay checked his phone. "I have no service here. How about you?"

"Nothing."

"That settles it then." Reaching back over the seat to grab a bag, Clay said, "If he kills us, at least we die together."

Lexi smacked him. "Stop."

Clay rubbed his arm. "All this hitting today. If I didn't know it was pent-up sexual frustration, I'd think you're too rough for me." He rubbed his chin as if putting serious thought into something. "On the other hand, rough can be nice."

"Oh, I'll show you rough."

Clay laughed and opened his door. "Come on, Princess. Your new carriage awaits."

WEDGED INTO THE front seat of the truck between Lexi and their new friend, Kenny, wasn't the way Clay had imagined the night going, but he'd been in worse situations. Kenny on the other hand looked exhausted.

"Long shift?" Clay asked.

"Double, but I'm not complaining. You have to take the work when it's there."

Clay nodded and felt a bit guilty that he'd never put in a full day of work, never mind overtime. "Do you work for the state?"

"I'm an independent contractor. During storms like this there's work for everyone."

"What do you do the rest of the year?"

The man flexed his hands on the wheel as if he didn't want to answer, but eventually did. "I'm new to this area, so I do whatever is available."

Clay's curiosity was piqued, but he didn't ask more.

The man looked over and said, "Sorry. Didn't mean to take it out on you."

"It's all right," Clay said, moved by the genuineness the man exuded. "It happens."

"Yeah, it does."

From beside him, Lexi asked, "Where are you from, Kenny?"

"Not far. Maine. I had a small plow business up there. Nothing big, but good money. Last year my father-in-law passed away, and my wife wanted to be closer to her mother. So here we are." He glanced at Clay. "You English?"

"Guilty as charged," Clay said. "Although I've moved around a lot."

"I did a lot of that when I was younger," Kenny said. "Twenty years in the Marines before I retired. Those were good years, but they don't do much for me now. I didn't think I'd be working this hard this late in life."

Lexi and Clay exchanged a look.

"Enough about me, where are you two headed?" the man asked.

Lexi answered, "Stowe. The event we're going to is actually going to donate furniture to a veteran. You should go and bring your wife."

"Furniture for veterans doesn't do much good if you don't have a house." Although the man's tone was light, there was sadness in his eyes. "Don't go looking at me like that. I'm not referring to me and my wife. We live with her mother for now. It's not ideal, but it's enough. I was thinking about some of my buddies from the corps. Not all of them are doing as well as I am. Furniture wouldn't mean much to some of them."

"The full scope of the fundraiser includes building housing for veterans. At least, I think that's what Sophie said. Am I right, Clay?"

Clay felt like shit that he couldn't remember, but if it didn't, it would from then on. He'd make sure of it. "Yes, it does."

"Fundraisers. I'm sure those people feel good about themselves, but do they make a difference? I know men who are fighting demons that they can't get treatment for because some suit tells them it's not real. I've got a buddy in Maine who has been homeless ever since the first year he came home. He doesn't need furniture; he needs someone to make the government look after those who fought to defend this country. It ain't right for people who give so much to have to wait so long to get treatment. Keep your damn couch and make sure veterans get the benefits they're due. I don't want charity; I just want what was promised. Sorry, I'll come down off my soapbox now. I'm sure the event you're going to will help a lot of people."

Right then Clay knew what he wanted his foundation to focus on. He linked his hand with Lexi's and said, "Kenny, I've been looking for a consultant on a project I'm working on. If you're interested, I'll contact you after the holidays."

Kenny looked away from the road long enough to assess if Clay was serious, then asked, "What kind of project?"

"The Landon Foundation is looking into funding programs to help veterans."

Kenny frowned. "You pulling my leg?"

"Not at all."

"I don't believe in coincidences. You're serious? You work for a foundation that helps veterans?"

Clay didn't believe in coincidences either. It was right up there with a long list of things he'd always dismissed as impossible. The sun had set as the sander pulled off the main road. With no street lights it should have been dark, but the light of the moon glistened on the freshly fallen snow in an almost mystical way. A shiver ran down his spine as he remembered asking for guidance.

Was it a sign of divine intervention or a meaningless chance encounter with a man who just happened to say something that fit what Clay was searching for? Turning, Clay looked into Lexi's eyes and could have sworn he glimpsed forever.

I love this woman.

He brought her hand up to his lips and kissed it. "Lexi and I run it. It's still in the beginning stages, but that's why we could use someone like you. Your experiences would help us help others. It'd be a paid position, of course, and one that could be done via conference calls."

"Hold on, you'd pay me to tell you about my friends?"

"No, we'd pay you to use what you know about your friends to build a network of support for them and anyone in their situation. I'd start you at . . ." He quoted an annual salary that had the older man's jaw dropping open.

Hope came and went from the man's eyes with sad speed. "That would be real nice if it happens. I'll give you my number."

Lexi tightened her hand on Clay's, and her eyes filled with tears. He knew exactly how she felt, but there was no way to prove his sincerity to Kenny right then. All he could do was prove it to him later. "Perfect. We'll contact you first thing after the holiday."

Kenny nodded and kept his eyes forward. He pulled the sander into the parking lot of a motel. "There are hotels farther from the highway, but I've got to get back to sanding. The more time I'm off the road, the more likely it'll be that I'll come across someone else the ice took out."

Clay shook his hand and waited while Kenny wrote his number on a napkin. After pocketing it, Clay helped Lexi out of the truck and retrieved their bags. To his surprise, Lexi leaned back into the truck and said, "Kenny, good things happen to good people every day. Don't be afraid to tell your wife about the job. Go home and Google Clay Landon. He's the real deal."

Kenny smiled. "I'll do that."

Lexi closed the door to the truck and stepped back. Clay put his arm around her and they both stood there, the snow falling down all around them, watching the truck pull away. When she finished waving, Lexi asked, "Should we have asked him to wait to see if there's an open room?"

Clay kissed her briefly. "There'll be a room."

She rolled her eyes. "Oh, sorry, I forgot what a big deal you are."

He chuckled and bent to pick up their luggage. "There you go talking about my size again. All I meant was that most places keep one or two rooms open to accommodate the unexpected, but you can't keep your mind out of the gutter."

They walked toward the office of the motel, their steps quickening as the cold began to nip at them. They were both still smiling until the clerk asked, "One room?"

Clay didn't want to pressure her, but he couldn't imagine not holding her that night. On the other hand, he'd said he would wait for New Year's Eve. Could that ever happen if they shared the same room? The same bed?

"One," Lexi said softly and Clay's blood shot downward.

"I'm sorry?" the clerk said, looking up from the computer.

"One," Clay said more firmly.

One?

Give me strength.

Chapter Nine

AN HOUR LATER, Lexi lay beneath the covers on one side of the bed, staring up at the ceiling. She considered herself relatively experienced when it came to men, but she had no idea what to do. Clay had her completely confused. One minute he was hot and heavy, the next he avoided her touch like he was afraid to catch something from her. "Clay?"

"Yes?" he answered from his side of the bed.

"Is the wall of pillows between us really necessary?"

"Yes."

"Did I say something to offend you?"

"No."

"So you're not upset with me?"

"Not at all."

"Then why do you sound angry?"

"Because I told you that I could wait until New Year's Eve, and I'm damn well going to keep that promise. I'm not going to be the reason you break your celibacy cleanse."

"It was a joke, Clay. A test. We were flirting, and I want-ed to prove to myself that you'd move on if you thought I wouldn't sleep with you that night."

He growled from deep in his throat. "Well, now you know I'm not quite that shallow."

"Yes, I do." She rolled onto her side. In the faint light of the room she could see his profile. He was stretched on top of the blanket on his back with his arms crossed beneath his head. "It really was just a joke."

"Doesn't matter, I said I'd honor it, and I will." Although he'd changed into a T-shirt and lounge pants, he was still covered from head to toe.

"You're serious." She went up on one elbow and looked across at him.

"I am."

"Then thank God you kept your socks on, or I'd be jumping these pillows and ravishing you," she said cheekily and reached out to touch his chest.

He slapped her hand lightly. "No touching until tomorrow."

The light sting on her hand was more exciting than painful. "That wasn't the rule earlier in the Hummer."

"Desperate situations call for desperate measures." He punched the rolled up blanket beneath his head. "Good night."

Lexi flopped onto her back and sighed. Although she liked the idea that he was holding to a promise he'd made her, it didn't make her feel irresistible. In fact, apparently, she was quite resistible. "Good night," she said angrily and turned onto her side. The room was temporarily illuminated by the light from Clay's phone. After hearing him replace it on the beside table, she asked, "Texting someone to bring more pillows?"

"Setting my alarm. Get some sleep. I'll see you at midnight."

"Midnight?"

"That's when my promise expires."

Lexi's body hummed with anticipation at his words. "You're joking, right?"

"Didn't you say you could always tell when I wasn't serious?"

"I was wrong. I have no idea anymore."

"Then I guess you'll have to wait until midnight."

Ridiculous.

Crazy.

So very sexy she almost couldn't breathe.

"I guess I will."

CLAY WAS HANGING onto his control by a thread. He couldn't imagine ever sharing the story of that night with anyone because it would sound crazy in the retelling. Hell, it *was* crazy. He was lying in the same bed with a woman he'd just realized he loved, and he was doing nothing, despite the fact that she seemed more than willing.

He could have carried her into the room, thrown her on the bed and already tasted every inch of her. By now they would be on round two, or three. Her sweet mouth might even be wrapped around him at that very moment. He shuddered.

I'm nuts.

What do I really think this will prove? That I can commit to something? More like confirm that I should be committed.

No, I said I would do this and I will.

He glanced at the clock. Three hours until midnight. Three fucking hours.

"Clay?"

She's not helping. "Yes?"

"We're in a motel. Have you ever stayed in one before?"

"No."

"But you have no problem staying here?"

"Do you?"

"No. I just assumed—"

"That I would be a snob about where we stayed?"

"Yes."

"Just because I haven't done something doesn't mean I think I'm too good for it."

She was quiet for several long moments. "Clay, why did you say that you and I run a foundation together?"

"Because I am in the process of creating one and before you take one of those jobs I lined up for you, I'm hoping you'll consider working with me."

"I don't think working for you would be a good idea, Clay."

"With, Lexi. I'm looking for a partner, not a secretary."

"A partner? What would I do?"

He looked across the darkness at the outline of her. "I don't even know what my role will be exactly, but I want to do this. I need to do this. And it's right up your alley. I've never met anyone as able to jump into a job they knew nothing about and make it look easy."

She flashed a smile at him. "And we could help people like Kenny and his friends."

"Yes, we could."

"We could make a real difference."

"And we could do it together." He reached out to take her hand and jumped when she slapped him back.

"Keep your hands to yourself. It's not midnight yet, buddy."

He rolled onto his back and laughed. "Did I ever tell you how perfect you are?"

"No, but I'm all ears," she said with a light laugh.

"I knew it from the first time I saw you," he said as he went back in time. They spent the next couple of hours talking about everything and nothing, comfortable with each other on a level he struggled to put into words. With her there was no pretense, no game. They simply enjoyed each other.

They were both beginning to doze off when the alarm on his phone sliced through the air.

Chapter Ten

*M*IDNIGHT.

Lexi froze. She didn't know what to expect, but she knew what she wanted. No matter where their time together led, she had a hunger that only one man could ease.

Wordlessly, he picked up one pillow and threw it to the floor. Then another. One by one he removed each of the four pillows that had separated them. Lexi held her breath.

"You're wearing too much clothing, Lexi. Strip for me."

She didn't move. "You first."

He laughed. "Shy?"

"Something like that." Vulnerable was more like it. She wasn't ready to lay herself out for him until she was sure he was willing to do the same for her.

He sat up and pulled his shirt over his head, revealing a perfectly muscled bare chest. With an expert move, he leaned back and slid out of the rest of his clothing in one swift move. Then he smiled and pulled off his socks, dropping them with flair off the side of the bed. Her eyes slid down the expanse of his chest to the throbbing evidence of his arousal.

"Now you," he ordered softly.

She crawled out from beneath the blanket and got to her feet beside the bed. Ever so slowly, she pulled her shirt up and off, then dropped it to the floor. He turned on the light beside the bed and smiled. "So damn beautiful."

She felt beautiful, more than she had in a long time. And daring. She stuck one of her fingers in her mouth, wet it, then drew a circle on one of her nipples before repeating the action with her other. "You're not so bad yourself."

"You still have too much clothing on." His voice was deep and full of promise.

She put her fingers under the waistband on either side of her hips and snapped the elastic. "Oh, no, it seems to be stuck. How disappointing."

He was across the bed in a heartbeat, standing before her. "Let me see what I can do." He kissed her neck hungrily, grabbed her ass from behind and ground her pelvis against his excitement.

Lexi threw her head back as pleasure shot through her. Every place his lips touched came to life for him, adding to the need that was already close to sending her out of control. She gripped his shoulders and lifted one of her legs so he fit more closely against her sex. She moved against him, loving each time her nipples grazed his hot skin.

"I thought that would do it," he said into her ear. "Looks like I'll have to try something else."

He sat down on the edge of the bed and pulled her across his lap face down. There was a roughness to his moves, but Lexi welcomed it. He ran his hand over her upward turned ass as if claiming it as his through her pajama pants. Holding her still with one hand on the middle of her back, he ran his other hand up the inside of her thighs. He cupped her sex through the cloth and moved his hand up and down against it. "I can feel how wet you are already. I'm going to fuck you, Lexi, until you can't remember who you were with before me." He pulled the back of her pajama bottoms down and gripped her cheeks so tight it hurt, but a good hurt.

Lexi remained where she was, draped across his lap. She didn't know what he'd do next, but she trusted him. He slid her bottoms down, inch by inch, until he pulled them off entirely. Then he eased her back onto her feet. "So perfect," he growled, then looked away long enough to grab a condom and sheath himself.

She leaned down and kissed him. As soon as their mouths met all semblance of control left them. He stood and hauled her against him. She dug her hands into his hair and kissed him with all the passion she'd held back. They grasped at one another, frantically sought to bring each other pleasure while greedily taking their own.

He half walked, half carried her the few feet to the wall and slammed her back against it. She yanked him forward, digging her nails into his shoulders as she climbed onto him. Locked in a passionate kiss, he took her against the wall in a wild mating. She arched and met his thrusts. He fisted one hand in her hair and held her up with his other, all while pounding upward into her.

Lost in wave after wave of pleasure, Lexi cried out his name as she came. He groaned and bent her farther back so he could take one of her nipples into his mouth. His tongue and teeth worked her nub in a way that could only be described as sinful magic. She begged for him not to stop when he moved his attention to her other breast and started all over, and she sobbed at the searing pleasure that rocked through her.

All the while he pounded into her, filling her, driving her wildly closer and closer to her second climax. Just before she did, his hand tightened on her hair and forced her face upward toward his. "I'm going to marry you, Lexi Chambers," he growled and thrust into her several times, taking them both over the edge together.

Sweaty, breathless, they stayed as they were, still intimately connected and braced against the wall. "Did you just ask me to marry you?" Lexi asked, trying to gather her thoughts.

He kissed her lips briefly, his breathing ragged and hot against her skin. "I believe it was more of a declaration than a request." He lowered her gently to her feet.

She swayed then steadied herself by placing a hand on the corner of the table beside her. "That's not fucking funny."

He quickly cleaned himself off, dropped the condom in the trash, and swept her up into his arms. "The better response would be yes."

She was still trying to get her bearings when he dropped her on the bed. She scrambled to sit up, but he was beside her, pulling her into his arms. She pushed him away. "How could I say yes when you haven't actually asked me?"

He frowned at her. "You're right." He moved off the bed and dropped down to one knee beside it. "Lexi Chambers, you are the only woman I know who is crazy enough to take on a man like me. I am madly in love with you. If you don't say you'll marry me, I am going to keep you tied to this bed, keep fucking your brains out, until you're so weak from multiple orgasms you'll give in and agree."

Lexi almost burst into happy tears, but instead she burst out laughing. "Now I'm torn. On one hand I could confess that I'm in love with you, too, but you made holding out sound so good I hate to agree too early."

He crawled back into bed and settled himself above her. "Either way you're stuck with me."

She shifted beneath him, widening her legs so his cock came to rest against the lips of her sex. "I sure hope so."

He was instantly rock hard again. "Don't hope—believe."

I do.

I finally do.

MUCH LATER, DRESSED in formal attire, Clay and Lexi walked into the dining room at the hotel in Stowe. It was decorated beautifully in white and gold, but the attendance at the event was a quarter of what had been expected. The storm had grounded most planes and closed the roads until a few hours earlier. Sophie had called and asked if Clay and Lexi would officially represent the Barringtons that evening.

Despite how much he would have preferred to spend that evening in bed with Lexi, Clay agreed to work the party for Sophie. He and Lexi greeted all of the guests and explained the circumstances that led them to being in charge. Well, not all of the circumstances. They were trying to stay on their best behavior, but it was hard. Innocent comments had them exchanging lusty looks and coughing back laughs like children who were under strict orders to be good but couldn't quite hold it together.

"Well, it's good that you were able to come."

"Yes. Yes it was."

More than one person attempted to share concerns about the low turnout or certain subpar meals being served when they first arrived. They quickly realized, though, that they were telling the wrong people. Nothing could wipe the silly smiles off Clay's and Lexi's faces.

The one who almost had Clay feeling guilty was Vincent Moretti, a high-end restauranteur who seemed to want to have a serious conversation. Moretti made the mistake, however, of saying, "I'm surprised you showed up. The snow came down a lot harder and for a lot longer than anyone expected."

Without missing a beat, Lexi said, "Longer and harder is not always a bad thing."

Which sent Clay into a fit of laughter that Lexi joined in on. Shaking his head, Vincent said, "I'll call you after the holidays."

His quick departure only made the whole situation more amusing. *I hope that guy gets laid this weekend. He's all wound up.*

People probably thought he and Lexi had sampled too much champagne, but they hadn't. The high they were both on was solely the result of how good they made each other feel. And the great sex they'd had at midnight, later that morning, and as soon as they checked into the hotel in Stowe.

A courier arrived mid evening with a package Clay had requested. He took Lexi by the hand, pulled her out of the dining room into the hallway, and said, "Lexi, I had this delivered today."

"Stop." He started to go down on one knee when she stopped him. "I can't believe I'm saying this, but I'm in. I'll marry you. You don't have to ask again. The answer is yes."

"I want to do it right this time."

Lexi smiled and cupped his face between both of her hands. "You did. Maybe you didn't do it the traditional way, but you did it your way and that was even better. You and I, we don't fit into the same mold as everyone else, but maybe that's not a bad thing."

"It's not. You're incredible, Lexi."

She went up onto her tiptoes to kiss him. "You are equally wonderful."

He laughed and she joined in.

"Together we're fucking amazing," he joked.

"You got that right."

He opened the ring box. "I still want you to have this, Lexi. It was my mother's engagement ring. It's a red sapphire, not a diamond. My father claimed there was no diamond with enough fire to represent their love." He slid it on her finger.

Lexi looked at it then ran her hand up his chest and pulled him down for a deep kiss. "I love you, Clay. I thought

I knew what love was before I met you, but I didn't."

He chuckled. "I knew I had no fucking clue what it was about, but I get it now. I'm a better person with you at my side. I want to wake up in your arms, fight over something trivial, and have make-up sex every day."

Lexi threw back her head and laughed. "Sounds perfect." Her expression turned serious. "When we go back to Boston, would you be okay with me asking Sophie to help us with the foundation? Not because we couldn't do it without her, but because I want to include her."

"Sure. I'll have Dax clear an office for her in his building."

"Do you think Dax might see the foundation's location as an inconvenience for his business?"

Clay considered her concern for a moment then dismissed it. That was one possibility he refused to believe.

THE END

Love these characters? Keep reading with

Book 4: Let It Burn

Bonus Novella: Just in Thyme

The Barrington Billionaires Series

Book 3.5

A Holiday Novella

by
Jeannette Winters

Author Contact

website: JeannetteWinters.com
email: authorjeannettewinters@gmail.com
Facebook: Author Jeannette Winters
Twitter: JWintersAuthor
Sign up for my newsletter:
jeannettewinters.com/newsletter

Also follow me on:
BookBub
Good Reads

World-renowned chef, Vincent Moretti, could have anyone, anything, anytime. Social events had a single agenda—build his business, which was why he couldn't refuse the last-minute invite to the New Year's charity event. When he learned his investors wouldn't be there, he was angry he'd wasted his valuable time.

Adventurous and loyal Renita Gallo had chosen to stay in Stowe, Vermont for one reason—her father. She wanted to be a teacher. He wanted her to follow in his footsteps and become a chef. When her father became ill and couldn't cater the very important Barrington event at the Vermont resort, she was forced into a role she wasn't prepared for, and into the presence of the most arrogant man she'd ever met.

Renita was confounding, a woman who challenged Vincent, a woman so enchanting he couldn't resist. *Wouldn't resist.* She was also determined to ignore the allure of the devastatingly handsome Chef Moretti.

Vincent *ignited such passion within her that shook her steadfast sense of responsibility.*

Thrown together during a snow storm, more than food will be cooking in the kitchen.

A memory from Jeannette Winters

I love thinking back on my childhood memories, and Christmas was always special to me. It wasn't the gifts because we already knew what they'd be: socks and underwear wrapped in brown paper bags. Things were so simple back then.

My favorite Christmas was one I spent with my father. He'd retired earlier that year and finally could concentrate on things he enjoyed. Christmas music was always his favorite so that year he wanted to make his own Christmas carol booklets for us all. I must have been nineteen and didn't really want to spend each night home typing (there was no computer or printer then), but it was a project we were doing together. After countless hours and all the preparation, we were ready to go.

When we gathered back then, our immediate family consisted of my ten siblings and their families, for a total of forty-five people in the house. My father had me gather everyone together and pass out the sheets. We were all waiting; my mother sat in the middle of us all smiling. She had the voice of an angel. The rest of us not so much (you'd understand if you heard me sing). When my father came downstairs my mother's eyes lit up, but our jaws dropped. He was dressed in a red plaid shirt and was carrying a large black boom box with a microphone around his neck. He made his way around the room and no one escaped their turn at the mic. Christmas was never going to be the same!

And this one, this year, will never be forgotten either. Thank you Mom and Dad for always showing us what is important. Miss you both every day, but your spirit lives on with us. A spirit of love.

One of the greatest lessons our parents instilled in us is to take care of one another. Through this journey of writing, I would like to think that our love and the care we show for each other is because of what we've been shown. Not once have I ever felt as though I was alone. I'm blessed to have family who are on the journey with me. My baby sister Ruth Cardello gave me a nudge to follow in her and my niece

Danielle Stewarts' footsteps. They had already cleared the path for me and welcomed me into the group with open arms.

Writing this holiday novella together is just another example of how this journey has brought us even closer. The three of us cannot get together without talking and laughing about the good ole days. Writing this book brought back all the wonderful and crazy memories of our Christmas parties long ago. Each year another nephew or niece has been added to the mix. Seeing how we've all changed over the years, yet are still so close, is even more special.

Many have told me writing can be very lonely. But when you choose to do it with people you love, it is something you look forward to, filled with times you learn to treasure. We are not just putting words on paper, we are building memories of time we spent together.

So like our parents before us, we hope we are also leaving a legacy for our families to continue. It may not be through writing, but whatever it is, we hope they also remember: *It's always better together!*

Chapter One

RENITA GALLO WAS having difficulty processing what her father told her earlier. *How can the resort be in such dire financial straits? We have the best slopes in Vermont, the staff is always attentive to the guests' needs, and Dad's given his life to this place.*

She had so many questions she wanted desperately to voice her opinion on, but it wasn't the time to do so. Her father, still at home recovering from the flu, made it clear that everything was riding on the success of the Homes for Vets New Year's Eve fundraiser. It was far from the first event that had taken place at the resort, but in the past there had been family reunions and school outings. She couldn't remember anything of this magnitude.

Even before addressing what little staff there was, Renita had gone into her father's office to take one last look at the guest list. There were many names she didn't recognize, but the ones she did meant the resort was about to cater to some very powerful and influential people. It explained why her father was on edge and had spent his vacation last week working. *If you'd have told me Dad, I could've helped, or at least have been prepared for what's about to hit us. Instead, I feel like I'm on a sinking ship without a life preserver.*

She wasn't sure if she was angry about the lack of communication or if it was just good old-fashioned fear creeping in. Either way, she needed to brush it off and do what was asked of her: take full charge of the resort until either her father or the owner, Mr. Prescott, could make it in.

Renita felt anything but prepared to take on such an endeavor. Even though she'd grown up on the resort, she purposely distanced herself from certain areas. The kitchen was number one. Working as the waitstaff supervisor and hostess wasn't what she wanted as her career. But it was a choice she'd made; she was close to her father if he ever needed her. *This isn't what I thought you'd be calling on me to do, though.*

There were many things she was talented at, however cooking wasn't one of them. If it weren't for the fact her father, Ricco Gallo, was the head chef, she'd live on peanut butter and jelly sandwiches or mac & cheese every day.

Sophie Barrington, one of New England's elite socialites, had scheduled this huge fundraiser. Yet one thing after another was going wrong. First there was a massive snow storm, followed by an ice storm taking down trees and blocking roads. Both were common in Stowe, Vermont, but the timing couldn't have been worse. The roads had gone from difficult to drive on to totally impassable. If the resort hadn't been closed for Christmas holiday, it wouldn't be quite as bad, because at least there would be more staff here instead of trapped at home. Now not only was her father not here, but his entire kitchen staff seemed to be out with one excuse or another. They were either snowed in, sick, or their children were sick. That meant she was working with a skeleton crew, but not the ones she'd have chosen to be by her side.

She should be thankful only forty-five of the two hundred guests actually showed up today, but she was in a panic. That didn't mean the others wouldn't arrive once the roads reopened. *Think positive Renita. You don't have options, so suck it up and just do the best you can. The staff will arrive in time, and everything will be perfect.*

After she'd provided what little update she had to the staff, she headed to the kitchen. Each step she took her father's words rang in her head, "You're a Gallo, and we're capable of doing whatever we set our mind to do."

It was great that he had such confidence in her. She, on the other hand, knew and accepted her limitations. If she were being asked to pretend to be a ski instructor, she'd be leaping for joy, as she spent all her free time on the slopes, but this was not her forte, and he knew it.

For years her father had been trying to get her to follow in his footsteps, yet it wasn't something she was passionate about and never would be. Over the years she'd mastered the art of excuses for why something had burnt. *I'm the last person who should be in the kitchen, Dad. It's like you haven't eaten my food before. My burgers could be used as hockey pucks, and my mashed potatoes are like wallpaper glue. I don't think my cooking is going to help save the resort in any way. If it wasn't already struggling, I'd worry I'd be the one to ruin our good reputation.*

Once she'd told the waitstaff what was expected from them for the next several days, she headed to the kitchen so she wouldn't hear the grumbling she knew would follow. Normally she'd give them directions and they'd act upon them, but, like herself, they were all being asked to step it up. She couldn't be in the dining room to coordinate everything while trying to pull off a miracle in the kitchen.

There was one member of her staff she could do without: Tom. He never took anything she said without having to confirm it with someone above her. It was standard procedure for him; each time she'd direct him to the chef, who would always back her. She couldn't have him calling her father now. He was still recovering from the influenza, and she would avoid stressing him at all cost.

Like clockwork she heard Tom shout from behind her. "Renita."

His high-pitched squeaky voice was like fingernails on a chalkboard. She knew she was hypersensitive about it, and it was something she'd need to work on as a supervisor. But if she had her way, he wouldn't be working there. The kid was barely out of high school and as jumpy as they come. His family was one of the regulars at the resort, and Mr. Prescott had given him a job.

"What is it, Tom?" Renita rolled her eyes, not stopping as she responded. There was too much on her plate to play all nice no matter whose son he was. The clock was ticking, and if she didn't get in that kitchen and start cooking something for dinner, the guests were going to start complaining.

"Renita, are you sure you can do this? I mean you're a waitress, not Ricco Gallo."

I'm your supervisor, not a waitress, and no Tom I don't think I can do this. Honestly, I know I can't, but what choice do I have? If we don't shine this week, we'll all be out of a job. When her father came to this country from Italy forty years ago, the Prescotts not only gave him a job but also paid his way through culinary school. She understood his loyalty to them, and for that reason, she'd do whatever it took.

"Why don't you let me worry about the food, and you help the others with setting everything up? The guests should never know we're not fully staffed. So get to work, Tom, and if you do your job right, no one will know any difference." *I may not be Ricco Gallo, but I'm still a Gallo, and we don't accept defeat. Even when it's inevitable.*

"But neither Mr. Prescott nor Chef Gallo are here. I can't afford to get fired; are you sure they've approved you to step in like this? I've never seen you in the kitchen except to grab dinner for yourself."

The truth was ugly and would only cause an uproar. Renita decided it was best to dance around the question. "Mr. Prescott spoke to my father. The directions are to ensure whoever makes it here has an experience they'll never forget." *That won't be hard because once they taste my food, it won't only be unforgettable but possibly not edible.*

Tom was still rattling off something when she went into the kitchen, letting the door swing closed behind her. If she gave him the opportunity, he'd have her standing there for hours debating what wasn't going to change. *I'd appreciate you more, Tom, if you knew how to cook as good as you debate.*

Renita had been in the kitchen a million times over the years but never before had she been so frightened. The huge stainless steel refrigerators she normally snagged a piece of cake or some snack from now seemed like vessels filled with ingredients she had no clue what to do with. *Breathe Renita. You can do this. You have to do this.*

She walked over to the rack of aprons and chef coats. Although her father's coat was too big for her, Renita slipped it off the hook and put it on. *Come on Dad. Let me channel your cooking talents.* Never before had she wished for that, but right now she was going to dig deep. It was time to prove herself, and she wasn't going to let her father down.

Walking over to the large prep station, she reached into the back pocket of her jeans but felt nothing. Then she tried the other one with the same result. Frantically she went to her purse and searched, dumping out the entire contents. *God, no. This cannot be happening. I can't have dropped them.*

When she'd left her house she'd been in such a hurry that she slipped on the ice and fell into a snowbank. At that time, her only concern was if she'd injured herself. She'd never thought to check if the detailed recipes her father had given her were still in her pocket. *Don't panic. I can just ask Dad to give them to me again. No harm done.*

Pulling her cell phone out, she dialed his number. It went directly to voice mail. It wasn't uncommon in the mountains during storms to lose the signal, but the timing couldn't be any worse.

Think Renita. People are expecting food. You have to serve them something. Anything. She walked over and opened the first refrigerator, which she knew had fresh vegetables inside. A garden salad was simple. *No one can screw this up.*

She chopped some romaine lettuce, spinach, cucumbers, and green peppers. Putting everything in a large bowl, Renita added some grape tomatoes. She put the bowl on the table by the door for the waitstaff to carry out. *Not fancy, but it's edible.*

Normally her father had fresh baked rolls to accompany a salad. Even if she had all the time in the world, there was no way could she pull that off. One thing she did have going for her was her ability to think fast on her feet. Walking to the dry goods storage area, she found some sliced bread. She pulled it out and placed it in a basket with packets of butter.

Two things down. Now for the entrée. She stood there with a blank look on her face. It was overwhelming with all the food options staring at her, and yet she had no idea where to start. It dawned on her. She knew exactly what they needed. *It's freezing outside. I need to serve soup.*

Fishing through the pantry she found huge cans of tomato soup. *Yes!* She quickly opened them and put them in a pot to heat. Then she grabbed the bread back out of the basket and buttered one side of each slice. On a large griddle, she laid half of them down and put two slices of cheese on them before covering them with a second slice of bread.

As she turned them over, they were perfectly toasted. Once the other side was done, she cut them into quarters and laid them on a silver platter. She put the hot soup in a matching serving bowl. Proudly she carried them both over to the table. It wasn't much, but she was proud of the presentation.

She pressed the bell for the waiters to come and get the food.

Not bad for my first meal. Not bad at all.

VINCENT MORETTI HAD little patience for waiting for his food, and if he had to, it better be outstanding. He owned several high-end restaurants and was speechless when he saw what was being served. It wasn't an issue of it being buffet style; it was the quality that blew his mind. The salad looked like it came out of a bag, the soup obviously was from a can, and the grilled cheese sandwiches had been drenched in butter.

If the cell service wasn't limited due to the storm, he'd call his friend Brice Henderson and give him a piece of his mind. It wasn't like Brice to pull a prank, but obviously, this was some kind of joke. He'd told Vincent this resort had one of the best chefs, and he'd have to come and try to entice him to join his restaurant that was going to open in Toronto, Canada. *I wouldn't serve this to a kindergarten class. I can't believe Sophie Barrington would hold a fundraiser with food this commonplace.*

If it hadn't been for the fact the roads were closed, and he was for all intents and purposes trapped, he'd have packed his bags and left that instant, as it appeared this trip was a total loss. Upon his arrival, Vincent had inquired on the status of James West and Clay Landon. He had business to discuss with them both, but neither had made it before the state troopers closed the road. *For once, why couldn't I have run late?*

Vincent was hungry and took another bite of his salad before pushing it away in disgust. *If I'm going to be stuck here, I think I better give this so called chef a piece of my mind so he can step it up. Hell, it won't take much to improve on this.*

He made his way toward the door, and as he was about to push it open, one of the waitresses called out.

"Sir, you can't go in there. That's the kitchen."

"I know what it is." *I'm not sure the people inside know what do with it.*

"Only the cooks can enter," she added as he pushed the door open, ignoring her plea to stop.

He had been around restaurants his whole life, so he knew exactly what to expect when entering one, or so he thought. Vincent wasn't prepared to see only one woman waving her hand up in the air in what sounded like Italian. Although she had the sweetest voice he'd ever heard, her tone said she was pissed. She looked like she was barely five feet tall and had lost the battle with a bag of flour. For the little food that was served, the kitchen wasn't in any better shape than the chef. It was so comical to see that it wouldn't have surprised him to have someone jump out with a video camera and tell him he'd been punked. *This has to be a joke. It's the only logical explanation. Because if this was R. Gallo, he wouldn't even hire her as dishwasher, never mind chef.*

She was so riled that he was able to approach without her noticing him. He wanted to laugh as he watched her pounding on what looked like some type of dough. She had a rolling pin in one hand banging on it, and she flipped it with the other. *Definitely not a technique I've ever seen before.* When he was closer, he saw the name on the jacket, Ricco Gallo. *You don't act like a chef, and you sure as hell don't look like a Ricco either. What's going on here?*

"Are you Gallo?"

He must have startled her; she held up the rolling pin as though ready to strike. "You can't be in here. This is restricted to kitchen staff only."

He looked around and only saw her. "So I've been told from your waitress. Are you the cook?" Vincent wasn't about to use the word chef as that would've meant she actually had some skill.

"I am."

The expression on her face had been priceless. Her chin was up in the air, and she actually sounded as though she was proud of it. Why, he wasn't sure. If he'd put anything on a plate that looked that horrible, he'd never cook again.

"Then someone should warn Mrs. Barrington."

"About what?"

Vincent arched a brow and said, "That her guests will have the choice of food poisoning or dying from starvation."

The fire in her eyes amazed him. Once again she went off rattling something in a language he couldn't understand. He may be of Italian decent, but his family had been here for five generations, and he knew only a few words he'd pick up over the years.

When she calmed down he said, "Want to try that in

English this time?"

"I do not know who you think you are, coming into the kitchen and complaining."

"I'm a person with taste buds. Obviously you don't have any or you wouldn't have served that garbage." It was so bad he couldn't even bring himself to call it food.

"Feel free not to eat it."

"Don't worry, I didn't."

"I need you to leave my kitchen. If you haven't noticed, I'm trying to cook here."

He laughed. "Trying, yes. Achieving, no."

Vincent hadn't meant to upset her. He was only calling it as it was, yet he could see she was flustered.

"I'm glad you feel as though you could do better, but unless you're here to help, I repeat, you need to leave my kitchen." Her eyes glistened as she barked at him, yet she held her control.

He had to give her credit, she wasn't backing down. But that was foolish, because once the word got out about how bad the food was, they'd be out of business. None of this was his concern as he turned and walked out of the kitchen. *I have my own business to run. I don't need to worry about some resort that is mismanaged. I don't care how charming the place appears to be; without quality food, it's a ticking time bomb.*

As he made his way back to his table, he couldn't get the picture of her eyes out of his mind. He wasn't one to let tears persuade him, yet there was something about her that was pulling him to return. *Mind your own business, Vincent. Enough has gone wrong already. I'm not here to fix things. Hell,*

I'm not even sure why I'm here anymore. This is a total fucking waste of my time.

Before he sat down, he overheard a couple complaining about the meal. "This is outrageous. When I tell Sophie about this—"

"Excuse my interruption. I understand you are unhappy with the meal. If you wouldn't mind giving the chef another hour, I believe you might have a change of mind." Vincent had no idea what possessed him to interrupt. He was committing to something he knew she couldn't deliver. *At least not without help.*

The woman at the table snorted and said, "One hour. But if it isn't up to my standards, I most definitely will make my call."

Vincent turned and headed back to the kitchen. He knew she needed his help, but how he could convince her of that, was a different story.

The last time he saw her she was standing strong and confident. Now he found her sobbing, holding her face with her hands. Everything told him to stop and turn around, yet he found himself walking up to her and wrapping her in his arms.

He felt her tense, and she tried to pull away. "It's okay. It's just me again."

"What . . . what are you doing . . . here?" Renita asked between sobs.

I wish I knew. "Let me help."

"Why are you being so nice?"

Her beautiful brown eyes searched his face for an answer.

If you find one, please share it with me. "Because I can, and because you need me to help."

That seemed to get her temper going all over again, and she pulled away from him with her hands now on her hips and tapping her toes on the floor.

Vincent almost laughed. No one had ever accused him of being nice when it came to managing a kitchen. He ran a tight ship. Even his sous-chefs were the best in the business. If they couldn't pull their weight, they were cut that same day. Second chances didn't fly with him.

But, as he looked at her, he saw a passion in her eyes. She might not be able to cook, but at least she had spirit. *You, my dear, I might just make an exception for.*

He rolled up his sleeves, went to the sink, and scrubbed up. *Looks like this is a working event after all.*

"What are you doing?"

"Saving your reputation. But if we don't get some edible food out there quickly, even I won't be able to help you."

He opened the refrigerators, amazed at how well-stocked they were. Someone obviously had planned for an elaborate dining experience, but that confused him more. *Why have all this and then open a can? Because if you try telling me that soup was freshly made, I'm calling BS.*

Filling his arms, he grabbed numerous fresh vegetables and laid them in front of Chef Gallo. "You chop, and I'll cook."

He figured letting her attend to the veggies was safe while he searched for ingredients he could pull together quickly and taste as though it was prepared by someone who's seen a kitchen before.

He found salmon and the fixings for a glaze. He went to the prep station but was caught off guard when he was blown away for the second time. She was chopping the carrots as though she'd never used a knife before. *How do you still have fingers?*

Vincent didn't want to shout at her; it was scary enough just watching. Slowly he walked over to her and asked, "Can I show you how?"

She hesitated for a moment then stepped back, nodded, and handed him the knife. It wasn't the right knife for the job. He laid it down and grabbed a different one, holding it up so she could see the difference.

"Watch the way I hold my hands. The knife never leaves the table." Quickly he chopped six carrots all sized equally. He continued until they all were chopped.

"Do you want to try the celery?"

She looked reluctant, but she reached for his knife, and her attempt was better than the first.

"I see you have some skill, but I really shouldn't let you do this. I mean, you're a guest and it's not allowed. The health department would never allow this."

"If they ate what you'd served, you wouldn't need to worry; they'd pull your license." He hadn't meant for the words to be quite so harsh, but he wasn't one who normally held back either.

"Oh, God. I wasn't thinking of that. I only wanted to get something out I knew I could make. Do you think anyone is going to call? I mean, it wasn't that bad, was it? I eat that all the time."

"Then I feel bad for you. Let me answer your first question. I bought you a bit of time to get out some real food, but if we don't, then yes, someone will call. Second, the food was that bad. I have no idea where you were trained, but lady, you're the worse chef I've ever encountered. I can't believe Brice suggested I hire you for one of my restaurants. What did you do, threaten to poison him or something?"

She had a puzzled look on her face and then burst out laughing. "You really believe I'm a chef?"

"You are wearing a chef's jacket and are in the kitchen. What would you like me to believe?" He arched a brow and waited for her to answer.

"Your taste buds." Her smile lit up the entire room.

Damn, you're beautiful, whoever you are. "Then I'd guess dishwasher because your food tastes like you used sink water."

"Ouch. Please don't hold back. It's not like I have any feelings or anything."

She acted hurt, but somehow not surprised by his comment. "I take it you're not Ricco Gallo."

"I might not be able to cook, but at least I have eyes enough to know the difference between a man and a woman."

Oh trust me. I know the difference. And you are definitely a woman. "Very cute. Where is Ricco?"

"He has the flu and the rest of the staff called out for similar reasons or were unable to travel due to the weather. Even the resort owner, Mr. Prescott, wasn't able to get here.

So that left me and the little waitstaff who had come in to work early. They were here to get in some skiing before the big New Year's Eve event. I know you might not believe this, but I was the only option."

He heard her sincerity when she spoke. He expected his staff to step up in a similar situation. However they would've been qualified to do so. "So what experience do you have?"

"Besides my father being a world-renowned chef?"

Ah. Ricco's daughter. Interesting. Vincent nodded.

"Absolutely none. I'm great at taking orders. I'm normally the hostess and supervise the waitstaff. As far as cooking, what you see is what you get."

I definitely like what I see. There was something about her, he couldn't pinpoint it, but he knew he was drawn to her. But right now, he needed to stay focused on the issue at hand.

It had been years since he'd spent any time in a kitchen, usually he was only there for inspections or to review new menu options. He built a successful business but counted on his staff to handle the day to day. He might be a bit rusty, but he knew whatever he put out was sure as hell going to be better than what she had.

"You think you can do better than I can, because why?"

Vincent laughed. "First of all, most people could do better. Second, I am a trained chef, unless you couldn't tell from my cutting skills."

She looked him over from head to toe. He wasn't sure if he was intrigued or insulted, but he found her boldness a turn-on.

"You are dressed a bit too fancy to be any cook that I've seen, but I won't argue. You can handle a knife. What did you say your name was?"

"Vincent Moretti." She didn't seem to recognize his name. He was sure if Ricco was here, there'd be no question about his qualifications. "And you are?"

"Renita Gallo." She extended her tiny hand to his. He found it amazingly soft and delicate as he took it in his.

"So how about I cook, and you watch?"

"No way. I cook, and you help," Renita said firmly.

"Do you want people to eat or make that call?" He waited for her to answer.

"Fine. But I want to help."

He nodded. "Okay, so tonight you learn the first rule in culinary arts."

"Okay, what is that?"

"Don't get in the way of the chef."

Renita grabbed the bottom of the jacket which was almost like a dress on her and curtsied. "Of course, Chef."

Her smile once again beamed. *Maybe this week won't be such a waste after all.*

Chapter Two

RENITA HAD TO admit that having Vincent show up when he did had made things much easier. Although she'd felt that what she'd served yesterday was edible, once she tasted his food she was embarrassed by even the salad.

It was still early morning, but she wanted to check on her father. Picking up her cell phone she dialed his number. The call went through, but there was still so much static on the line.

"How are you feeling, Dad?"

His voice sounded weak. "My fever broke last night, and Maria has been checking. She's almost as bad as you, checking me every hour. With the roads closed, no one can get to the store for medicine to stop this cough."

Renita wished she could be there taking care of him, but her father had insisted she concentrate on the resort first. That didn't prevent her from stopping at Maria's, his neighbor, and asking her to keep an eye on him. And when she asked, Marie seemed very eager to do so. They were both the same age and their spouses had passed away. She didn't normally believe in fate, but she wouldn't mind one bit if her father found someone he could share his life with. Leaving him alone in Vermont with no family around was what held her there.

"I'm glad she's taking good care of you."

"How is the restaurant? Did you follow my recipes?"

No, but don't worry. I have this. Or maybe I should say Vincent has this. "Everything is perfect, Dad. Don't worry about a thing. Just think about getting well."

"How many of my staff showed up?"

"One." She knew that wasn't going to go over well, but she hadn't planned for his response.

"One? That's it, I'm coming in." She heard her father call out, "Maria, get me my clothes. I have to go to the resort."

She knew her father was stubborn enough to do it, even bypass the closed roads and trek through the woods if he had to. But she almost burst out laughing when she heard Maria answer him.

"Ricco, you get back in that bed right this minute, or I'll take all your clothes and throw them in the snow. Do you hear me?"

Her father was swearing up a storm right before the line went dead. She resisted the urge to call back. Maria seemed to have everything under control, so she had to make sure she did the same here. If not, nothing was going to stop her father from coming in, sick or not.

There were many things she didn't enjoy about a chef's life. Getting up way before dawn to prep for breakfast was one of the biggest. Renita was a morning person, but this was too much. Normally, you could find her on a slope as the sun rose, glistening on the fresh powdered snow from the night before. Until her father was well and back in the kitchen, her skis weren't going anywhere, and neither was she.

Even before she opened the door, she could see the lights were on in the kitchen. She was positive she'd turned them off last night. *Please let it be one of the sous-chefs.*

When she opened the door, even with his back to her, she knew exactly who it was. *Vincent. Really?*

He wasn't dressed up this morning. Instead, he was wearing a T-shirt, showing his muscular back, and a pair of jeans, hugging his butt nicely. *Now this is a sight worth getting up for. Might even beat the sunrise on the mountain.*

Renita felt her cheeks warm. *Easy girl. This is not what you're supposed to be doing. Dad has very strict rules about fraternization in the kitchen.* A soft chuckle escaped her as she recalled neither of them were actually kitchen staff.

Vincent heard her but didn't even turn around. "Good morning, Renita. How about you grab the eggs and crack about four dozen for me?"

Here she was having sweet thoughts of how sexy he looked, and he was all business. There were a couple cute remarks she was tempted to make, but she couldn't afford to lose his help. *Or my job.*

She decided not to wear her father's jacket and grabbed one of the plain aprons as Vincent had. Once in place, she prepared the eggs as he instructed.

"Okay, you're going to add some milk and seasoning and

whip them up so they'll be ready for cooking. This will be one of the last things we do, so they won't become rubbery."

She did as he said, but he wasn't clear on how much or what seasoning. Renita put a couple dashes of salt then some pepper. Then she felt him standing behind her, his hand covering hers, which still held the salt.

"Don't be afraid of spices." His voice was husky as he spoke.

Her hand trembled but not from anything except the pure raw desire that filled her as she felt his rock hard body pressed up against her back.

"Relax. You can do this."

Not with you so darn close. I'm not even sure I can breathe, never mind cook. "I think I'd do better if you told me how much, and don't be so vague."

"Recipes are so restrictive."

"No, they mean you make something, and it comes out exactly as you thought it would," she said firmly as she tried not to think of him still behind her. He stepped back slightly but not enough for her nerves to settle.

Vincent placed his hand on her shoulder and urged her to turn to face him. It was bad enough without looking into his honey brown eyes.

"Not the adventurous type?"

Oh, this is what they mean about don't play in the kitchen cause you're going to get burned. "Mr. Moretti, I—"

"Vincent."

"Vincent, is that how they would teach me in culinary arts school?" She swallowed and hoped her answer got him to focus on what the task was. *Feeding the guests.*

"They teach chemistry and how things come alive when you put the right combination together."

Oh, I'm coming alive. And this is not the time nor the place. "I think we should keep the chemistry lesson for another time."

He laughed lightly before heading back to the oven and pulling out homemade biscuits. They were golden brown and smelled heavenly. She wanted to tell him she'd be willing to sample his buns, but that was only going to get her right back where she didn't want to be.

Who am I kidding? It's exactly where I want to be, just not where I should be.

When she turned back to the eggs, she couldn't remember if she'd even put any salt in. When she picked up the shaker, he shouted, "It all about the right amount of spice. And right now those are perfect. Now you'll know how to do them tomorrow."

I would if you let me concentrate on what the heck I am doing instead of what I am feeling. "What else can I do?" *And please don't you dare say check your sausage.*

"I have a fresh fruit salad. If you can plate everything, I'll finish the cooking."

He was back to business, which she liked. There was too much riding on the outcome of this event. Her father didn't say who was coming, but he'd made a point of saying there were going to be some of the most influential people in the country. They didn't know her father wasn't there, and she refused to let his reputation be tarnished. All she could do was trust Vincent knew what he was doing.

Trusting him to cook is easier than trusting myself to behave.

THE NIGHT BEFORE he'd told himself it was a one-time deal, then she was on her own. Yet this morning he found himself back in the kitchen.

Breakfast was usually the easiest to prepare. That wasn't the case today. Renita was sweet and lovely to look at but a distraction that slowed him down. She wanted to talk, and he could listen to her voice forever. At one point he'd been so enchanted by her laugh he couldn't remember if he'd put salt in the hash browns.

Normally he was in full control of what was served, but not so much today. He could've kicked her out, but then again, she was the only reason he was helping in the first place. *Your teary brown eyes got to me. I have no issue with that, but I'd much rather we heat things up in my bed than in here.*

He had two choices: pursue her and say fuck it to helping her, or actually, for once, think beyond his own wants and needs and do something for someone else. *Not just anyone but you, Renita.* Vincent wanted to see her succeed at this. She had heart, and he believed she wanted to learn, but teaching her was going to complicate things. He knew she couldn't afford such liberties right now. Time was of the essence. *Private lessons will have to come later.*

No matter how hard he fought the urge, he found himself watching her out of the corner of his eye. Who could blame him? She was stunning. Whether she realized it or not,

Renita sang softly to herself with each task he gave her to do. *Who would've thought that I could get turned on watching someone plate food? Did she really need to sway those sexy hips to the rhythm? It was pure hell to watch and do nothing.*

When he felt the blade of the knife brush his knuckles he was pissed. Not at Renita, but at himself. It was a foolish mistake that, in all his years, he'd never made before. That didn't mean he didn't snap at her anyway.

"You're done in here. Go help the waitstaff."

"Did I do something wrong?" Her big brown doe eyes were filled with concern.

Problem is what you're doing right. "No. You look preoccupied, and I thought maybe you wanted to keep an eye on your staff." *Instead of me keeping my eyes on your ass.*

"Thank you, but breakfast is complete, and I have to think about the cleanup."

He looked around and wished the dishwasher had shown up at least. Thankfully technology made it so most wasn't done by hand any longer, but still someone had to load and unload the machines.

"It'll only take me five minutes. You can go." She still didn't leave. Something was troubling her, but he couldn't tell what. "Renita, breakfast service went well. We only get a short break before it's time to start the lunch prep." She didn't budge. "Glad to see that doesn't seem to be what's troubling you."

"No. I'm worried about my father. I spoke to him earlier, and his cough is so bad."

"Is he taking anything for it?"

She shook her head. "My father is one of those people who normally refuses to take any medicine. But he needs something to help with this cough. With the roads still impassable, there's no way for me to get him some. Even if I did, I'm not sure he'd take it."

"I can teach you how to make an all-natural one. I'm sure if he was feeling better he'd have thought of this himself."

Renita's eyes widened. "You've tasted my cooking, I should never attempt to make anything medicinal."

He smiled at her. "No cooking needed. I'll show you how to make a tisane by infusing herbs in hot water. Trust me. This will help with coughs and bronchitis. I'll make and you watch and learn."

"Thank you." Renita's eyes softened, and she smiled as she spoke.

Her smile made his heart melt. Somehow she trusted him and that was a mistake on her part. He knew what type of man he was. Yet here he was relishing that she did trust him. *I don't want to break that trust either.*

He gathered chamomile, marshmallow leaf, and thyme because he couldn't find any mullein leaf.

Once again he had her smell each one.

"I thought thyme was for meat."

"It is one of my go to spices that I add to many recipes. But it's not only used for cooking. There are numerous medicinal uses for it as well."

"Wow, thyme. I guess you learn more than just how to prepare a great meal in culinary school."

Putting the herbs in a glass quart jar, he added raw honey and poured in boiling water, filling the jar to the top, and then covered it.

"All we have to do is let this steep for forty-five minutes and then strain the herbs. He'll want to breathe in the vapors while sipping the hot tea."

"I think even I could make something like this."

"You don't give yourself enough credit, Renita. If you wanted to learn how to cook, I know you would and probably kick ass at it."

She laughed. "Maybe I'll cook dinner for you one night and see if you change your mind."

"Deal. But for now, I have a few things I need to attend to before we meet back here." Before he passed her, he gave her a kiss on the top of her head and said, "Good job this morning. Go get some rest."

Walking away, he kicked himself. He had no idea what possessed him to do that. Somehow it had felt natural. *Pull your head out of your ass, Vincent. You're not the sweet, tending, loving guy. Don't pretend to be.*

He went to his room and took a cool shower, trying to clear his mind. Getting dressed again and heading back down wasn't what he wanted to do, but he'd said he'd be there, and it was almost time to go. As he headed toward the door his phone rang. *About time, they get the network back up.*

Vincent shook his head as he saw who it was calling. "Brice. Hope you're calling to say you're on your way, because trust me, this is an event you don't want to miss."

"Why is it that I don't believe you, Vincent?"

Because, we've been friends long enough to know a lie when we hear it. "So I take it you and Lena aren't coming. Even to taste R. Gallo's food again?" *If you do show up, buddy, trust me, you're so going to eat Renita's cooking instead of mine.*

"Tempting as that sounds, we're getting hit with another snow storm here in Boston. Looks like you'll have to enjoy this one without us. Besides, I thought you were making this a purely business trip. You know damn well that if I travel with Lena, she'll have both our heads if we even mention work once."

"Oh yeah, got to love that family life." His voice was full of sarcasm.

"I used to sound a lot like you do now. Trust me; with the right woman by your side, you'll see things differently."

He was surrounded by women throwing themselves at him all the time. They either were looking at him for what he had, or for who he was. He enjoyed their company for what it was, but always knew what it'd never be: anything serious or long term. It wasn't that Vincent was opposed to sharing his life with someone. He'd never met anyone who intrigued him enough to explore anything serious. *Or never let them in long enough to find out.*

"Has he met her yet?" Vincent heard Lena asking in the background.

"Met who?" Vincent asked.

"No one," Brice replied flatly.

"Brice, give the phone to Lena." Vincent knew Lena was the weak link, and it wouldn't take long to find out what really was going on.

"I thought we'd talk business."

"Normally I'd prefer that, but at this moment, I think I'd rather hear what Lena has to say."

"You say that now," Brice said before handing the phone to her.

Her joyful voice echoed through the ear piece, "So, tell me, Vincent. Did you meet her?"

"Somehow I don't believe you're talking about Sophie Barrington because you'd know she hasn't arrived yet."

"Sophie is a wonderful person, but you can meet her anytime. I'm talking about the chef's daughter, Renita."

So, Brice, you let your wife talk you into sending me here in this bitching cold weather under the assumption I was to meet a chef when in fact it was to meet a woman. Nicely played. But it's not going to work. "Yes, we've crossed paths a few times."

"And? What do you think?" Lena asked, and Vincent rolled his eyes just listening to her excitement.

Then he thought about it. How well did Lena know Renita? Was this all a setup? Was Renita only pretending not to know anything about cooking just to lure him to her? *A damsel in distress. Classic move, and I fell right into it.*

"I think she's a fine hostess, but I'm not hiring any at this time. You can have her apply online, and we'll keep her résumé on file if anything opens up."

He heard Lena huff and puff on the phone. "Vincent Moretti. Are you blind? She's beautiful, funny, and so full of life. Renita's amazing."

"And if a position opens up, I'll consider her for the job." He wasn't going to give Lena the satisfaction of knowing he almost fell right into their web.

She huffed again, and he heard her say, "I should've listened to you, Brice. Vincent's hopeless. He can't even see."

The line went dead. He looked at the phone and once again, no service. *Got to love this place. You better be on vacation if you come here. I'm not sure if this is due to weather or location, but either way no one is getting any work done.*

He quickly made his way downstairs and was about to enter the kitchen when he saw Renita approaching him with a young man. *You're going to be sorry the service came back briefly, because you're about to see what an ass I can really be when I run a kitchen.*

"Hi, Vincent. One of the sous-chefs made it in. I guess they are slowly opening up the roads again. That is both good and bad."

"Why is it a bad thing?" *To me, it means I can get the hell out of here anytime. I see no reason to stay for the party. They have my money, and I'm not about to kiss anyone at midnight, so there is no reason for me to stay.*

"Means that more guests are going to be allowed to come, but if we don't have the staff, we're going to be in worse shape than we already are."

He watched Renita closely, analyzing everything she said. *We? I'm just a guest.* Vincent didn't respond to her and spoke to the guy with her. "How long have you been here?"

"Three years."

"Any good?" Vincent asked as he stared him down. He wanted to know how confident this kid was.

"Chef Gallo would be the person to ask."

I like that answer. I can work with that. He hated it when they were so cocky they wouldn't take instructions. Normally those people didn't last long in his restaurant. "Then let's ask him. What's your name?"

"Roberto."

Vincent turned to Renita and said, "I can call or you can."

"Are you really going to check with my father on whether or not his staff is qualified? Who are you to say if Roberto is good or not? I never even checked your credentials. For all I know you're not actually a chef either. I can't believe I let you into my kitchen!"

He thoroughly enjoyed watching her defend her father's honor. She was fiery, and it wasn't just evident in her tone either. Her eyes became so dark they were almost black. *You're either the best actress I've ever seen, or I'm misjudging you all together. Since I can't tell yet, I'll stick around a bit longer but only because you've piqued my interest. And that is not easily achieved.*

"You expect me to believe that you don't know who I am?"

"Of course, I know who you are. You said your name when you introduced yourself. Is that supposed to mean something to me? Because it doesn't." Renita snapped at him, and she was serious as she spoke.

Roberto seemed surprised by the exchange. "Signore, I apologize, for Ms. Gallo. She is under much stress. But she will be better now with me here. I shall take over for her in the kitchen until Chef Gallo returns."

Vincent admired the kid for trying, but he knew there was no way he'd be able to handle everything himself. Hell, he could barely do it, and he was more than a sous-chef. He knew he was going to regret these words, but he said them anyway.

"I'll be happy to have your help, Roberto. I just hope you are more skilled than Ms. Gallo. Otherwise, we're going to have a lot of unhappy people shortly as time is running out, and I need to get in there and start the prep."

"You cannot be serious. Vincent, there is someone qualified to cook here. If you want, I can allow you to assist him, but he'll be the one giving directions, not you," Renita said firmly with her hands on her hips.

"I take direction from no one. Not you, not Roberto, and not your father. Got it?"

"Vincent Moretti, you're impossible!" Renita said and stomped her foot as though it would intimidate him. He would've laughed if Roberto hadn't spoken up.

"Signore Moretti?" Roberto exclaimed.

Renita turned to him. "Yes, Vincent Moretti. He's a guest here."

"Signore. Your reputation . . . I'm honored to meet you." His hand trembled as he reached out to shake Vincent's hand.

Vincent watched as Renita went from perturbed to puzzled. "Do you know him?"

"Si. Un gran chef, a grand master chef. He owns molti grandi ristoranti. If, Chef Gallo only knew you were here he'd—" Roberto exclaimed, full of excitement.

Renita arched a brow then looked back at Vincent. "You're not only a chef, but you own restaurants?"

Vincent laughed and used his best Italian accent, which was pathetic but he did it anyway. "Si, signora."

"Why didn't you tell me?"

"Does it matter to you that much? You questioned my qualifications, and I said I was a chef. If you'd have questioned further, I would've divulged the information."

"Why are you here then?"

"I'm attending the event like everyone else."

"But this is an exclusive group of individuals. They're all—"

"People." He knew exactly what she was about to say. Rich. Powerful. He wasn't going to disagree with her on that, but he didn't like to classify himself that way.

Vincent watched as she changed how she acted toward him. It was as though he was no longer Vincent, but now Chef Moretti. *I don't think I like that one bit. I only want to be Vincent to you.*

"Chef Moretti, would you please be kind enough to assist one more time in the kitchen? With such short notice, I cannot pull this off with only myself and Roberto."

He wanted to pull her into his arms and tell her if she called him Chef one more time, he would kiss her until she couldn't remember her name, never mind his. Instead, he gave her a quick nod and said as he walked toward the kitchen, "Rule two, stay out of the way of the sous-chef as well. Let's go, Roberto. We've got a lot to do."

He left Renita standing there as he walked to the kitchen.

It was going to be much easier with Roberto's help, but he was going to miss his alone time with Renita. *Maybe that's a good thing. I can get through this and get back to my work.*

Chapter Three

FIRST ROBERTO SHOWED up, then within an hour three more of the kitchen staff arrived unannounced. She wasn't sure if Roberto had called them, but somehow their jackets were all pressed, and they each were as quiet as a mouse just awaiting direction from Vincent.

If Dad could only see you now. There wasn't really anything for her to do with the staff all at Vincent's beck and call. She'd only be in the way, but that didn't mean she shouldn't keep an eye on things. Grabbing her cell phone, she stepped out of the kitchen to call her father.

"Hi, Dad. How are you feeling?"

"Almost back to myself since you sent that tisane. How did you know how to make it?"

"Glad it helped." She wasn't ready to tell him exactly how. He was a private man, and he'd never be happy knowing she had been talking about him being sick with the staff, never mind a guest.

"How are things at the resort? Shouldn't you be in the kitchen cooking? Did something happen?" He spoke faster with each word.

"Everything is fine, Dad. Don't worry about a thing." She understood why he was concerned. Mr. Prescott had always been kind to her father, but this was a high-level event that if it went bad, they were all finished.

"What is on the menu?"

I should know this. Sadly I don't. "Dad, I only have a minute and wanted to check on you, that's all. Glad you're no longer coughing, but I've got to get back inside."

"Nita, I'm your father. I know when you're keeping something from me. Unless you want me to get in my car and come there this instant, you will tell me the truth." His tone demanded an answer.

"Dad, you know I'm not a good cook. Actually, I'm horrible. But there's a guest here who's been kind enough to . . . help me."

"A guest is in my kitchen? I can't believe you've let a stranger in there. What's his name? I want to speak to him right now."

She had thought it was crazy when Vincent mentioned how territorial chefs were, but she'd just heard her father confirm it. *Maybe they're all crazy from the heat of the ovens or something.*

"Dad, he's busy right now. Maybe we can call later?" *Like after he leaves.*

"Nonsense. Tell me his name, and I'll call the kitchen so I can speak to him personally."

"Vincent," she said softly, not wanting to say his last name after Roberto's reaction.

"Is that his last name?"

"No. His name is Vincent Moretti he's—" She stopped herself and waited because if Roberto knew the name, she was positive he did as well.

"I know who he is. Are you telling me that Chef Moretti is in my kitchen right now doing the cooking while you're outside talking to me on the phone?"

She wasn't expecting that reaction from him. "Yes." Her voice was soft like a child who knew they were in trouble. But for what she wasn't quite sure.

"He wasn't on the guest list last week."

"No he wasn't. I assume he was a last minute add or filling in for someone else. I never actually asked." *Another poor choice on my part. I'm supposed to be monitoring the entire resort, and I don't even inquire why he's here. I should never be left in charge again.*

"You should be by his side, learning everything you can. It's an opportunity that most are not given. And yet you're talking to me as though it means nothing to you."

Because, it doesn't. I don't like cooking. Just because he's the sexiest man I've ever met and I could listen to him talk about cooking all day, doesn't mean he can teach me to cook. "Dad, he's here to help, not train me. You're the chef, probably better than Vin—Mr. Moretti. Besides, you know how I feel about being in the kitchen, having people try what I make." *I dread it. I know I'll never be as good as you, so why bother?*

It was the same argument they'd had since she was a teenager. He wanted her to learn and take over the kitchen at the resort, and all she wanted was to be out on the slopes.

"You know how you feel about learning how to cook

from me? Trust me, you'll feel different with Chef Moretti. With the right person, it's not learning but connecting, sharing. A man and a woman cooking together can be very enlightening."

Oh, my God. Dad, you've got your fever back because you seem to have forgotten I'm your daughter. "Dad, I don't—"

"Do not Dad me. I'm not getting any younger, and at this rate, I'll never have any grandchildren."

This is worse than I thought. He's trying to get me married off. "Dad, I'm a grown woman who—"

"Would stay on this mountain, trying to take care of me, and never get out and live and find love. If you're not working, you're skiing alone on the slopes or sitting at home reading. And a successful, well-liked, and respected man is there helping you, and you don't want to be with him. Why?"

"Dad, he's not helping because of me. He just doesn't want the other guests to suffer through my cooking." *Can't blame him.*

"Chef Moretti wouldn't care about the other guests. It's not his reputation on the line. It's mine and the resort's. Open your eyes, child, and see; if he is in there doing all the work, he's doing it because of you."

"Me?" *That's ridiculous. He could have any woman he wants.*

"Really, Nita, I don't know what you're looking for in a man, but you'll be thirty before you know it. Your mother and I'd been married eight years by your age."

She was regretting even speaking to her father right now.

As if I don't have enough stress on me already, you're talking like I'm going to be an old spinster if I'm not married by thirty. She wanted to tell him this was a different time; people didn't jump into marriages and live happily ever after. They had careers and lives that also fulfilled them. *Of course that will only open up another can of worms. Because right now I don't have those either.*

"And you think Mr. Moretti will be impressed by my cooking skills and do what, ask me to marry him? Dad, I think you better get back to bed and take something for your fever."

She wasn't trying to sass her father, but what he was saying made no sense at all.

"Maria is not intimidated by my cooking skills. She's in my kitchen making fresh pasta. And she brings me a spoon to taste, and her eyes sparkle when I tell her how good it is."

More information than I need to know, but at least you're eating. "Yeah. Great. I have to get back to work now."

"I hope you understand what I'm telling you."

More than I want to. "Yes, Dad, I do."

"Good. Now do as I say and don't leave his side for a moment. Understood?"

How is it that I'm twenty-six and you've got me wanting to run to my room and hide under my blanket? I thought fathers were supposed to scare the boys away, not push me to them. Do you want me out of the house that much? There are easier ways than this to stop me from living at home.

Renita was no fool. Even though she didn't want to admit it, she'd seen Vincent looking at her, and when he was close to her, she knew there was a mutual attraction. But all that changed the moment she found out he was not one of the skiers here, but he was one of the elite attending the formal New Year's Eve event. He was only flirting with her until the other guests arrived. *He's probably just bored.*

Knowing that made her more determined to keep her distance. She didn't want feelings for someone who'd never reciprocate. And if her father was right, the last thing she needed was spicing it up in the kitchen with Vincent. *I need to keep it professional. Go in, do what he says, and get out. Simple.*

No matter how much she was going to hate that, she'd never disrespected her father before and wouldn't start now.

"Yes, Dad. I understand. Can't wait till you feel better and can come back to work."

She disconnected the call and reluctantly entered the kitchen again. Vincent was barking orders at Karen, one of the other sous-chefs. The man who'd been so kind and gentle with her seemed to be totally different with the staff. He was all business and expected—no demanded—perfection. That was something he wasn't going to see from her. Not in a million years.

Although, there was nothing between them for him to look at her any other way than the way he did the rest of the staff. *Craziness. That's exactly what I am. And I'm not even kitchen staff. I'm supposed to be out in the dining room to make sure everything is perfect. Why did I ever promise to be by Vincent's side? I'm only going to irritate him with my lack of skill.*

As she watched him, she took a step backward. *I don't think Dad meant to literally stand next to him. I think in the same room, actually on the other side of the room, will work just as well. Probably better.*

He must've been watching her while she'd been looking at him because he patted the workstation. "Come by me."

She stood, hoping to be able to get out of doing what he requested. She looked at the others; although still working, they were paying close attention to both she and Vincent. "I thought you wanted me to plate," she said softly.

Never turning to her, he said more firmly, "I want you here with me. They can plate."

When she made eye contact with Roberto, she saw a hint of a grin before he turned away quickly. *I hope the guys don't think that Vincent and I are . . . oh, this is embarrassing.*

Renita held her head up and pretended to be confident as she made her way to Vincent's side. Once there she whispered, "I really think that I'd be better at—"

"If you don't try, you'll never know if you can do it." He reached out and gave her hand a gentle squeeze. "You'll never be the same after a couple of private lessons with me."

Her cheeks flushed as somehow her mind had wandered from the kitchen and into the bedroom. She had no doubt he was not only a master in the kitchen. His confidence was sexy as hell. If he were a spice, he'd be a habanero pepper, super hot. *Remember Renita, he warned you, cooking is all about chemistry. And if you get too close to him, you know you're going to ignite.*

"So what are we making today?" *Please don't say love be-*

cause I'll have to quit my job and move away if you do.

"Why don't you tell me what you know how to cook, and I'll show you how to make it better."

"It's a very short list."

"How about we start with lasagna?"

Oh, God no. That is way too hard. "I can't. Maybe something simpler."

"Grilled cheese?" He arched a brow, but the curl of his lips said he was teasing her.

I think this might be easier if you yelled at me like you do the other staff. That way I won't like you so much. "Maybe something in-between."

"How about we skip cooking and head straight for dessert?"

Renita's tongue betrayed her as she licked her top lip. "Sounds sweet."

She could be as playful and teasing as he could, but somehow she knew she'd just challenged him, and he wasn't going to back down.

Vincent went and grabbed all the ingredients, and she tried to listen and pay attention as he measured flour, sugar, eggs, milk, baking powder, and fresh vanilla. There was more added, but she'd stopped paying attention as the aroma filled her nostrils.

"Did you get all that?"

"Hmm? Oh, yes. I got it." She was lying, but had no plans on ever needing to make a cake from scratch again.

"So tell me what do you smell?"

"Cake batter?" She didn't know what else to say. But it

was a logical answer as far as she was concerned. *Can't be wrong there.*

"Renita, you weren't paying attention. But I refuse to let you fail at this." He turned away and barked, "Everyone out. Now."

She heard the utensils being put down and footsteps hustling out of the kitchen. This was not his kitchen or his staff, yet no one questioned his order. *Can't blame them. He can be pretty damn intimidating.* But it was her job to remind him who was in charge here, and it wasn't him. "You can't—"

"I just did. Now we continue with your lesson. Okay close your eyes and give me your arm."

She looked at him. "Why?"

"You think cooking or baking comes from some paper. It doesn't. You need to use your other senses as well. Now give me your arm and close your eyes."

She gave him her left arm.

He lifted it up and said, "I warn you, if I see you peeking, I'll get a blindfold."

"I bet you have one too." She sucked in her breath not meaning to have said that out loud.

With her eyes still closed, she felt him closer to her. Then his warm breath was by her ear as he said, "I'll be happy to show you when we're alone."

Her cheeks burned hot, but she refused to open her eyes. Not for fear of him, but she didn't want Vincent to see the effect he was having on her just with words. *God help me if he touches me.*

She felt him rub something on her bare arm, a powder of

some kind. Then there was something wet and once again another spot of something dry. This continued all the way down her forearm. She had no idea what he was doing but wasn't going to question him.

"Hold your arm there for one minute. Don't move."

Don't worry. I'm afraid to right now. I think my legs will be shaking if I try walking.

"Without opening your eyes, I want you to smell each spot where I put something."

She lifted her arm and the first thing made her nose tingle, and she almost sneezed. It was spicy and nutty.

"Do you know what that is?"

"No."

"Then taste it. Remember you need to use other senses when cooking."

Her tongue darted out and couldn't identify it.

"Nutmeg. Now do the next one."

"Vanilla."

"Yes, very good. And the next?"

This one smelled sweet but she couldn't get it so she once again licked her arm. "Honey." She actually was surprised how much she was enjoying this game.

"Very good. Now you know what they smell and taste like on you. Now I want you to tell me what they are on my arm."

She stiffened up as there was no way she'd heard him correctly. It was one thing to lick her own arm, but there was no way she was going to do that to him. It was weird, and personal. *And sexy and erotic and a lot of other things I don't want to think of.* "You can't mean that you want me to lick you."

"Yes, I do."

She knew she should resist. Tell him how inappropriate this behavior was, but somehow she was unable to resist. *My body is controlling my brain. Not good, but yet so good.* Before she could move away, Renita felt his arm come up, and instinctively, she reached out and held it. She started by his wrist. Once again it smelled sweet, but she wasn't sure. "I don't know."

"Then use your other sense."

You want me to lick your arm here in the kitchen? You're freaking crazy. No, I'm crazy for even considering doing it.

"Vincent. I can't do th—"

She waited a minute to gather her courage to do as he said. *This is not the cooking lesson I thought I'd get. But damn, he knows how to make me pay attention.*

When she was ready, she brought his wrist up to her mouth, and the tip of her tongue slowly licked it. "Honey? But it smelled different from mine."

"Continue to the next one."

His voice was so serious, as though this actually was a lesson instead of some form of foreplay.

As she did, she found they were all the same ingredients she'd had on her arm. "I don't know why you're having me taste and smell them again."

"Because you needed to learn that even spices smell and taste differently on each person. Now I'm going to lick them all together."

If she thought he meant he was going to lick his own arm she was wrong. Her legs trembled as she felt his tongue start at her wrist and lick up her forearm. She was glad he'd kicked out the staff because right now her heart was beating so fast and she was positive he just made her panties wet. *You make me forget where I am. Who I am. God, you're dangerous.*

"Now I want you to know what they taste like all together."

Before she could ask how that was possible, she felt his lips claim hers. So gently that she melted against him. Her hands reached up and clung to his shoulders for support as his tongue urged her to open to him.

Renita wanted to resist, knew that she should, but instead she eagerly opened and welcomed his tongue into her mouth. Their tongues explored each other, then he sucked hers into his mouth. She ached for more. *This is so wrong but feels so right.*

As she ignored the battle within, calling her to stop, she felt him begin to pull away.

"You can open your eyes now."

I'm not sure I want to, because I'm having the most amazing dream. Taking a deep breath, she blinked them open. He was standing so close and her hands were on his shoulders as though holding him to her. She brought them down by her sides.

"So tell me, what did you taste?" Vincent asked softly.

"What?"

"Think of what you tasted on my tongue."

"Is this still part of the cooking lesson?" She had long

forgotten about the spices as her mind was clouded with desire.

"Unconventional, but yes."

I'd definitely say that was unconventional. "I don't know." *I wasn't thinking about that. Maybe we should try again and this time I'll pay attention. Or not.*

"Do you want to taste again?" He was grinning as he said it.

Had she voiced her request out loud? He seemed to know exactly what she was thinking, wanting. But it didn't matter. *I know what my answer has to be.* "No. I think I've got it."

"And?"

"Cake batter." Even after all his efforts, her answer remained the same.

He smiled at her and shook his head. *You probably expected something much more technical.*

"Not the answer I expected."

"Sorry to disappoint you," she said smugly.

Vincent reached out and brushed the back of his hand on her cheek. "I'm far from disappointed, Renita. But I think this is enough of a lesson for now, otherwise I'm going to need a cold shower before I can finish cooking."

Oh my God. How could I forget that there's going to be hungry people looking for food? And here I am, thinking of what it would be like to be anywhere else with him instead of the resort. She was shaken up, and whether she wanted to face it or not, she was on the clock and had a job to do. This was no vacation or romantic getaway, and she had to remind herself of that. "I think it'd be prudent to have the staff come back in so the guests will have something to eat."

He watched her and finally agreed. "Lunch might be a few minutes late, but it will be served. You can tell them they may enter again. Why don't you make sure the dining room is set up better than yesterday? I think your staff needs your special attention to details because it lacked something this morning."

She was proud that he'd noticed how seriously she took her job. Without another word, she exited the kitchen, rejoicing in the coolness of the dining room. *It was way too hot in the kitchen. But I have a feeling that the North Pole would be hot with him near me.* She feared she couldn't keep her emotions in check and was going to get burned.

Chapter Four

"I 'M TELLING YOU, Renita, I don't ski," Vincent said as he walked down the hall toward his suite.

"I recall telling you I don't cook, and you wouldn't take no for an answer. So if I had to try cooking, you owe me one time on the slopes at least," Renita said with her hands on her hips, challenging him to argue.

"There is nothing I find appealing about being out in subfreezing temperatures."

"Beats the heck out of being in a hot kitchen with no view. The only thing better than skiing at night under the moonlight and stars is skiing at pre-dawn to catch the sunrise. So which do you prefer?"

He stopped and looked at her. Even her bottom lip pouted as though teasing him to say yes. "And doing this gets me what exactly?"

Vincent caved once she batted her long lashes at him and said, "You and me alone on the ski lift all the way up the mountain."

There are so many other places I'd rather spend some alone time with you. Number one would be in my suite where it's toasty warm.

"I promise, you'll love it."

I highly doubt that, but time alone with you does appeal to me. "I'll meet you in the lobby in fifteen minutes. If you're not there, then—"

"I'll be there," Renita shouted as he watched her scurry down the hallway.

I know you will. Vincent went inside and grabbed his ski clothes. At the last minute, he'd decided to pack them in case Landon and West wanted to discuss business on the slopes. Otherwise he'd never ski for pleasure. *But then again, I'm going to now, but the only pleasure is being with you, Renita. If I thought you'd agree, I'd have invited you inside to continue that lesson from earlier because, God knows, we taste good together.*

When he arrived in the lobby, Renita was there in a pink and white snowsuit. He was wondering how much she'd really object to him picking her up and carrying her back to his room. *Probably not as much as she'd pretend. She didn't mind the kiss, and I know if we hadn't been in a public place, who knows where it would've ended?*

Normally, he wouldn't let an opportunity like that slip by, but something told him she wasn't the casual affair type of girl. Maybe it was the innocence that shone in her eyes as she flirted. Although she didn't kiss as though she was inexperienced, he felt she didn't have as much experience as other women her age.

And fuck if that doesn't only make me want you more.

"I thought I was going to have to come and drag you,"

she said joyfully, as she came over and locked elbows with him. "And don't think I wouldn't either. Not much will keep me off the mountain on a night like this."

And only one thing would get me on it. You!

Before long, they had their skis on, and she was trying to encourage him to hop on the lift.

"You do understand that I've never snow skied in my life."

"Really? I thought all you guys skied."

Raising a brow Vincent said, "You mean chefs?"

"No. I mean . . . big businessmen."

"And how many *big businessmen* do you know?" Vincent wasn't sure he wanted to know that answer.

"Besides you?" she asked.

He nodded.

"None. But I watch television, and you see pictures of guys all over the world, relaxing on some beach, or an exotic island, or skiing."

"Don't believe everything you see. Granted, I like to vacation, but when I do, I go where it's quiet, and I can think."

"Then the mountain is just what you want. It is so silent up at the top that you can hear your own heartbeat. That is unless it is a windy day, then you can hear your teeth chatter instead," Renita joked.

"I'm glad you're not in sales, because you're horrible at it," Vincent said as he tried standing on his skis. "Tell me you're not starting me on that mountain." He pointed to the biggest one.

"No way. We're going to start on the kiddie hill over

there. If you can stay up, then we'll take the lift to the top."

Vincent wasn't sure if she was kidding or not. "I'm not uncoordinated in the least. Waterskiing takes skill, and I love it. Both have the same amount of risk." *If I'm going to break my leg, I'd prefer it happen while doing something I enjoy.*

He looked around and there were only a few people crazy enough to be out skiing at this hour. There was no way he would be caught on the kiddie slope looking like an idiot. He considered himself a risk-taker, but starting on the big hill was damn foolish. That didn't mean he wasn't going to do it.

"You have two choices. We either go up on the lift now and see what I've got naturally as I make my way down, or we take off these stupid things and spend the rest of the evening in a Jacuzzi with a glass of wine." He was hoping for the latter of the two.

Vincent knew by the look in her eyes that this was payback for what he'd done in the kitchen earlier. He'd taught many people how to cook, and he'd always kept it to a professional level. The lesson they'd shared did not fall into that category. Not by a long shot. It wasn't that she disapproved of his tactic, but it appeared she was about to give him her version of what a lesson should entail. *I think mine was much more fun.*

"Vincent, you can't be serious. There is no way I'll let you go up that mountain without a private lesson first."

"Great. So let's get out of here."

She grabbed his arm. "That's not what I meant. I don't want you to get hurt."

"We're in agreement on that, but the options remain the same. Which one?"

"Vincent, that's not fair. You're not giving it a chance. Or are *you* not the adventurous type?"

"I am. But I only do things my way."

He loved how she pouted when she didn't get her way. There was nothing about her he didn't find sexy. If she pushed, he'd probably cave and give in to anything she wanted. He wasn't about to reveal that to her. *It's a dangerous power you hold, Renita.*

"Has anyone ever told you that you're stubborn?" Renita asked as they made their way to the ski lift.

"Only when they were trying to be kind." He laughed as he followed her.

She shot back a concerned look, but when she saw his smile, he watched her throw her hands up in defeat. *I'm glad you think I'm joking. You're seeing me at my best. If you saw me in business, you'd come up with a few choice words for me as well. And I'd have earned every one of them.*

Vincent hadn't grown up with money. If people knew he'd been homeless and sleeping in a car right after graduating from culinary art school, they'd never believe it. He'd had the option of going back home to live with his parents and siblings, but he'd wanted to prove to them and everyone else in that small town he could do it. Like most successful people, he'd fought for everything he had, but it came with a price. Distancing people wasn't always pretty. But things moved faster and easier when you only had yourself to think about.

Most days it was the way he preferred it. Yet, meeting someone like Renita made him think about what tomorrow would be like if they were together. That made no sense because they had nothing in common. He loved to cook; she hated it. He hated the cold, and she loved it. So why the hell was he out here about to go down a mountain and risk breaking his damn neck?

It was probably the same thing that was making him want to extend his stay. Leaving on New Year's Day had appealed to him, but not anymore.

Vincent watched Renita's eyes light up as they sat on the lift and began their journey to the top. The moonlight reflected in them, and he could see her excitement the higher up they went. "You're really in your element here."

She turned to him. "You'll understand when you get to the top."

"What's so special up there?"

"It's not what's there, but what's not. When you're coming down the slope at night it's so peaceful and quiet. The only sound is your skis as they cut into the snow. I can do my best thinking and dreaming then."

"What do you dream about, Renita?"

She turned away from him, and he was afraid he'd brought up a painful memory. Being here had nothing to do with him but was all about giving her some stress relief.

"I think about what it'd be like if I weren't here," she said, her voice soft.

Her eyes had sparkled earlier, and he'd have bet she'd never want to leave this place. Right now she looked as though she'd flee if given the opportunity. Had he been misreading her, or was she that complex that she didn't know what she wanted?

"Where would you go if you weren't in Stowe?"

"I'm not sure. That's the problem. I've always been here, but my heart wants to do much more."

"What are you passionate about?"

"Children. I love to be around little ones. When I have free time I volunteer to watch them so parents can enjoy a bit of free time."

"You want to do daycare?"

She shook her head. "No, I was thinking more like a teacher. I haven't told my father yet, but I've taken a lot of classes online and will continue to work toward my degree in education just in case one day I—"

"So, why do you stay?"

The sparkle left her eyes as she spoke. "My father. I'm all he has. I can't go and leave him alone. He's not one who takes care of himself. If I'm not here, all he'll do is work and work some more. That's not the life I want for him."

"Have you ever told Ricco how you feel?"

Renita shook her head. "No. I don't want him thinking I'm unhappy here. Because I'm not. I like it here. It's just not what I've dreamed of doing with my life. Does that make sense?"

"Absolutely. But you can't live your life for him. You don't resent it now, but someday you will."

"You try to make everything seem easy."

"I only look for ways to accomplish what I want without

sacrificing what I need. For you the answer would be to travel back and forth." Listening to her speak of her father made him feel a bit guilty for not spending more time with his parents. It wasn't them he avoided as much as his hometown. It reminded him of everything he didn't have as a child, and he hated it. He always had one excuse after another. Every time he saw his mother, she asked the same damn question. "When are you going to move back here and make me a grandmother?" Vincent was never going to live there again. As far as children, he always protected himself. *I don't have attachments and don't want any.*

"No one wants to come home to an empty house every night."

The way she said it made him realize that's exactly how he lived. He had a fast-paced life, but at the end of the day, he slept and woke alone. It wasn't a bad thing. No one told him what he could or couldn't do. A prime example was his last minute decision to spend a few days here. Brice had said, if he and Lena were there, it would be all vacation, no work. He'd never have done that. *Until now. I'm stuck with no option but a vacation. And down time is not something I do well.*

"If he wasn't alone, where would you go?"

"Texas."

He burst out laughing. "You drag my ass up here in the freezing cold, and you'd rather be someplace warm. I'll tell you what, the roads are open, let's go ring in the New Year in Texas."

They approached the top and had to scoot off the lift. As

soon as Vincent's skis hit the snow he regretted going all the way to the top; his legs went two different ways and he landed right on his ass. *I might not need to worry about where I'm spending the holiday. It might be in the emergency room.*

"Are you okay?" Renita was right by his side trying to help him up. "Are you hurt?"

He raised a hand, not wanting any assistance. "Only my pride." *This time. Next time I can't guarantee I won't need a helping hand. Or worse.*

As he tried to steady himself, he heard her swearing again in Italian. *Spicy little thing when you're mad. I like it. I really wish I understood more Italian, but it's not what you say, it's your emotion when you say it. I like it.*

"Okay. I'm ready." His voice was filled with false confidence. The way Renita looked at him said she wasn't buying it either.

"We can ride the lift back down. You don't need to do this. You *shouldn't* do this."

It'd been a long time since anyone cared if he hurt himself. It was . . . *nice.* But he wasn't one to back down. He'd committed to this slope, and damned if he wasn't going to see it through.

"Not changing my mind. You lead, I'll follow." *Hopefully in the vertical position.*

The first push off went much easier than he thought, but then he dropped to his side. Renita had been watching and was close to being parallel with him, so she cut her skis and stopped to wait. He lifted his hand right away, so she knew better than to offer.

Renita stood there shaking her head. "This is foolishness. I'm not sure which one is worse. You for doing this or me for letting you."

"Letting me?"

"Yes. Technically the lodge would've never let you on the lift without first knowing you could ski. Because I'm with you, the staff didn't question it. So if something happens to you, this is all my fault."

"So you're not really worried about me, just about being blamed for my demise?" Vincent asked, arching a brow and grinning.

"Actually, I'm worried about you ruining a perfectly packed white slope with your blood."

Her tone was so dry that he almost believed she was telling the truth before that sweet smile of hers returned.

"Want to put a little wager on if I make it down?"

"Alive?" Renita teased.

Spunky. I'm glad I don't intimidate you and that you're not trying to kiss my ass to impress me. I hate both things. And you do neither. Very refreshing. "I was actually going to say still standing, but yeah, I like alive too." He laughed.

She smiled. "I'll take that bet. If I win, you cook dinner."

"And if I win, you cook breakfast." He didn't wait for her to respond as he dug his poles into the snow and started his descent. She was not far behind him as he heard her soft laughter getting closer to him.

He was agile and picking it up very quickly. All it took was a bit of coordination, which he had. Vincent looked at each turn logically and was mastering it quite well. What he wasn't expecting was how he'd gone off course and was trying to avoid rocks.

"Vincent. Get back on the trail. You're going to get—"

He heard her scream and turned to watch as she was midair doing flips and landing on her ass. Immediately he cut his skis to stop, pulled them off, and ran up toward her.

Dropping to his knees he asked, "Renita, are you okay? Do you need me to get help?"

"I'm okay. As you said before, only hurt my pride. Here I am telling you to watch out, and I hit one of the rocks myself. Stupid amateur mistake."

He lifted her gently into his arms. "I think this means I should get breakfast brought to me in bed."

She laughed and then rubbed her bottom. "I'm glad you were able to turn this around to be all about you. I thought I was the injured party here."

He became serious. "Tell me, Renita. Are you hurt?"

Shaking her head, she said, "Nothing that won't heal or feel better after a long soak in a steamy tub. So if you don't mind putting me down, I think we can call it a night."

Before he released her, he kissed her lips briefly. "As you wish." *But only this once. Tomorrow night I'll set the plans, and if we end up horizontal, it won't be an accident.*

Chapter Five

RENITA MADE HER way to the kitchen after a very restless sleep. Her mind wouldn't shut off. Vincent was the first person she'd openly shared her dream to be a teacher. Now she was regretting it. *Dreams are meant to be locked away unless you're willing to chase them. And I just can't bring myself to abandon Dad like that.*

Besides being tired, her body felt sore, even after a long soak in the tub the next morning. Vincent had been kind enough to see her to her room, but the way he looked at her, she knew if she asked him in, a lot more than kissing would've happened.

He wouldn't have been her first, but compared to him, she was naïve and inexperienced. He probably was comfortable with a casual love affair, a quick hook-up on vacation and then never see each other again. That wasn't her at all. *Besides, I'm honestly attracted to him, not just physically either. If I don't keep my distance, I'm going to fall further, and it's going to hurt like hell when he leaves tomorrow. Twenty-four more hours, that's all. I can do this. How hard can it be to resist him for just one more day?*

As she opened the door to the kitchen, she heard her father's booming laughter. Although she was thrilled to see him back on his feet and where he belonged, she wasn't used to hearing him so cheery at work. That was usually reserved for guests or at home. He, like Vincent, ran a tight ship. *What has you so chipper this morning, Dad?*

When her father stepped to one side, she was surprised even more. Vincent and her father were laughing and cooking at the same counter. Both had been too absorbed in the conversation to have noticed her. *I wish I had a camera because this is a sight I'll never see again.*

She couldn't take her eyes off them. Vincent was smiling and more relaxed in the kitchen than she'd seen him. *Almost as comfortable as last night when we were alone. Guess he can let go of business for a short time. He should try it more often.*

Thoughts like those were going to get her in trouble. *You'll be gone and will have forgotten my name. I don't think I'm going to be so lucky. You've made me want more.*

It appeared she was no longer needed in the kitchen. She was about to turn and head out to the dining room when Vincent called out to her.

"Renita. Just in time for another lesson."

Oh, no more lessons for me. Especially with my father here, thank you. "I think you gentlemen have the kitchen under control. It's time I get back to my job and make sure the dining room is ready for tonight's main event."

"Nita. You heard Chef Moretti. Come. I shall go and prepare the breakfast while you study." Her father glared at her as only a parent could.

She smiled at him, wishing she could say what was on her mind. Couldn't he see she didn't want to be there? He knew she hated cooking, and now she was being forced to do it with a man who was going to make it impossible for her to concentrate on a damn thing. The entire kitchen could catch on fire, and she wasn't sure she'd notice if he was kissing her or touching her.

She felt her cheeks grow warm. *And this is exactly the reason I need to get out of here.* "Dad, I think you'd be the best person to teach me. Why don't we set a time after this New Year's Eve party is over?"

Ricco laughed and slapped Vincent on the back as though they were old friends. "My daughter has jokes this morning. I've tried to get her into the kitchen since she was a child. Couldn't even drag her in here. You come along, and she walks in all smiles and bright eyes. Chef Moretti, I believe I'm beginning to feel ill again; maybe I should go back home."

"Dad!" She couldn't believe he was so blatantly doing this. What was Vincent going to think? That her father was pushing her to him? Normally her father was nothing but professional in the kitchen. This was a side of him she wasn't used to seeing. It was nice to see him so light-hearted, but Vincent was an off-limits topic. "Vin—I mean Chef Moretti is a guest here, not part of the staff. And you look fine to me." She didn't mean for her voice to sound so sharp, it wasn't meant for her father as much as for Vincent, who was standing by him grinning as though everything was going according to his plan.

"Chef Gallo, I believe your daughter is trying to say she learns best with private lessons." Vincent never took his eyes off her as he spoke, and all she could do was remember that sizzling kiss. *I've learned I want you, but still, have no idea what you put in that cake. And I truly don't care either.*

A mirror wasn't necessary to know her face went from pink to red. Her father should be appalled that Vincent was speaking so flirtatiously, but somehow he seemed fine with it. *Who are you? You've never liked anyone around me. Why now? Why him? Don't you know he's leaving, and if I don't stop this now, it's only going to break my heart later?*

"How about tomorrow morning, Chef Moretti, before you leave? After brunch is served, the kitchen will be all yours."

She gave Vincent a look that said he best not agree, but he didn't heed her warning.

"It's a date." Vincent turned his back to her and continued whatever he'd been doing before she came in and interrupted.

She lowered her voice, hoping the others wouldn't hear. "Dad, I don't need or want any lessons."

Ricco stood there shaking his head. "Oh, my Nita. What am I going to do with you, child?" He waved her away with his hand. "Go to your dining room and make sure it sparkles. More guests have arrived since they opened the roads. Although not all could make it, it must still be spectacular, and with Chef Moretti cooking with me, it shall be."

Renita nodded and left the kitchen quickly before anything else was said. *More guests? How could I have forgotten to check on the latest count? Oh, that's right, because my head hasn't been attached to my body since my little cooking lesson yesterday. I can still feel his tongue licking my arm. God, I wanted to put ingredients all over myself so it'd never end.*

The truth was, it didn't matter if it ended tomorrow or a month from now. It was going to end and the sooner, the better. She wouldn't care if he left right now without even saying goodbye.

Renita stopped in her tracks and looked back toward the kitchen. Part of her wanted to tell him she wanted private lessons today, tomorrow, and always. That was more foolish than taking him skiing. No one ever accused her of acting foolish before. She shouldn't start now. *Vincent, I hate to do it, but there is no way I'm keeping our date tomorrow. It's hard enough now. I'm going home as soon as the event is over. I feel the flu coming on, and I'm calling out of work in the morning.*

She'd never called out of work before and sure as heck never lied about it. But desperate times called for leaving her comfort zone. With how sick her father had been, no one would question if it was true or not. *Yup. Out sick for sure. I just hope I don't really get the flu, because I'm not sure avoiding Vincent is worth influenza.*

"MY DAUGHTER IS . . . difficult at times. She is stubborn," Ricco said as he and Vincent continued cooking.

She's vivacious, stunning, funny, smart, sexy, and tempting as all hell. "I hadn't noticed."

"Chef Moretti, you are too kind."

"Please call me Vincent."

"Vincent, my daughter worries too much about me. Since my wife died many years ago, she had taken it on herself to make sure I'm all right. At times I believe she's forgotten who the parent is."

"I see she loves and respects you very much." It was another thing he liked about her.

"Do you like my daughter?"

He wasn't prepared for that question and had no way to answer. It wasn't something he ever thought he would discuss with Ricco. He was attracted to her, and enjoyed her company more than he'd enjoyed anyone's in a long time. Not since his first love many years before. This man wasn't one of his friends asking out of curiosity. This was Renita's father. How he answered was crucial. Thinking about the right answer wasn't going to happen, so he spoke directly from his heart. And that scared the shit out of him.

"She's a special woman." *Very special.*

"Renita does not belong here, Vincent. I see a look in her eyes that was not there a few days ago. I know she has dreams, although she won't tell me what they are." Ricco stopped working on what he was cutting and was staring into Vincent's eyes. "She's told you, hasn't she?"

"We've spoken." He didn't want to give any information Renita wasn't prepared to share herself.

"Very interesting. Can you tell me what you spoke about?"

Vincent shook his head. "Not my place. But I believe if you asked her, she would tell you."

"You may be right. That wasn't the case before, but

something has changed within her. I think it has to do with you. I saw the look in her eyes when she looked at you. I approve of that. I have a lot of admiration for you. But this is my daughter. If you are serious about her, you'll have my blessing. But I warn you to be very careful and not play with her heart. I don't care who you are, I'll not sit by and let you hurt her."

Wow, Ricco. Way too fast. I'm only here on vacation. I like her, she amazing, but I'm not what she needs. "Mr. Gallo—"

"Ricco."

"Ricco, I'm only here for the event." *Not a lifetime.*

"My point exactly," Ricco stated firmly. "Vincent, you're burning the glaze," he added as he pulled the pan from the fire.

He'd never been so distracted before. "Maybe we need to change the subject for now."

"Yes. No more talk of my daughter in the kitchen. We have hungry people out there, and I don't want them thinking I'm the one sending out burned sauces and unseasoned eggs." Ricco didn't try to hide his laughter one bit.

Vincent couldn't help but join in. No chef had spoken to him like that in years. They all feared if they did, it'd blow any opportunity to ever work for him. If he hadn't just witnessed Ricco's skill, he would've thought Lena and Brice really had sent him here to meet up with Renita. But even Brice couldn't pull off a major snow and ice storm or give Ricco the flu.

So now he was left with a dilemma. Did he approach Ricco with one of the main reasons why he was here in the first place? The fundraiser was a wonderful cause to support, but he could've sent a large donation check without making the trip here. This probably wasn't the right time for telling Ricco he was here to talk him into leaving the resort and working for him. Of course if he pursued things with Renita, that only added to the challenge because he never mixed business with pleasure, and Renita was definitely someone he enjoyed. This entire thing was quickly becoming a quandary.

This is business, Vincent. The one and only thing that matters to you. Don't let your desire for a spicy sweet Italian woman make you forget that.

"Ricco, there is something I would like to discuss with you, if you're free later."

"My daughter?"

That's one subject I don't want to talk about. Not with you or with your daughter, yet. "This proposition is for you." He kept his voice low as not to let other staff overhear. He had no issue with them knowing he'd like to steal Gallo away from this resort, but he wasn't sure how Gallo felt. Normally he didn't care. *Is it this place or this family that has me being less of an asshole than normal?*

"Then I suggest we talk tomorrow after your lesson with my daughter."

Vincent wanted to tell him he already knew Renita was going to blow off that date. It was written all over her face. Although she smiled, her eyes said *goodbye.* And he hated it. Why? He didn't know yet. But by God, he hated it.

Chapter Six

R ENITA WAS GLAD she'd avoided seeing Vincent before the event. Her father was right; she needed to make this glamorous. Mrs. Barrington was expecting elegant, and Renita believed she pulled it off.

As she made her way around the room, she overheard someone say Mrs. Barrington had something special planned that hadn't been announced to the guests. She had to admit it piqued her interest, but she didn't need to worry about such things as she'd be attending this black-tie event, but only as staff. *Good thing, because I have no idea what I'd have worn if I'd been invited.*

It was surprising how many more people were able to make it, even though it had snowed very hard earlier. She thought for sure the roads would be closed again, but they remained open. One thing about Vermont was that weather could change in a blink of an eye.

Now standing away from everyone she took in the entire picture. Everyone was dressed elegantly and appeared to be having a great time.

What was once a rustic look now screamed romantic.

White flowers entwined with branches and crystal teardrop globes with white candles burning inside hung above the long dining tables. The tables had matching flowers in beautiful vases, but each place setting had a long stemmed crystal candle holder, and the lights had been turned low to set the mood. From what she'd been hearing, her efforts hadn't gone unnoticed. She had done her best, and all she could do now was hope it was enough to get the resort noticed in a positive light.

Renita tried to focus on her staff, making sure they were as attentive as possible, and she tried to anticipate each guest's needs. There was one her eyes continued to find, no matter how hard she tried otherwise.

Vincent looked stunning in his tuxedo. Although they never made eye contact, she could tell he knew she was watching him as he was her. She couldn't understand why. There were so many beautiful women, and yet she continued to feel his eyes on her.

At one point Renita saw Clay Landon and Lexi Chamber, the couple who was supposed to be in charge of making sure all was in order, look as if they sipped too much champagne to be in charge of anything. She held her breath, as she watched what looked like a train wreck in the making, as they approached Vincent.

Clay and Lexi didn't seem to take whatever Vincent was saying seriously, which was no shock. She wished she could hear their exchange because all she saw was Vincent shake his head and walk away.

"Nita, you did a lovely job," Ricco said as he stepped

away from the kitchen long enough to check on the guest's reaction to his cooking.

She rested her head on her father's shoulder and said, "I hope Mr. Prescott thinks so when he gets feedback."

"You worry too much about what he'd think. When I am in the kitchen, I don't think about if he'd like the food. My thoughts are only on doing my best, and therefore I put out only something that's pleasing to me. I've no control if they'll enjoy it or not. You need to start looking at life that way."

She'd always done things in the way that others would want. Working at the resort was something she'd done for her father. The fact that she did her job well, didn't mean it was what she was passionate about. *I'm not sure if I will be good at being a teacher. I want it, and I've been working toward it, but who knows; maybe I'll be a horrible teacher just like I'm a terrible cook.*

"Things don't always turn out how we plan."

"Nita, you need to live your life. Not mine. Do you think when I left Italy and came to the United States I didn't miss my family back home? Of course, I did. But I needed to do as my heart desired. I could've stayed and worked in the bakery back home with my papa, but it was not my dream. Just like being here, Nita, is not yours."

"Where do I even begin?" She hadn't meant to say it out loud as it was a question she'd been internalizing for some time.

"Follow your heart. It knows the way."

Well then I'm in trouble, because my heart is torn in several directions right now. "I'll try that."

"You seem to like Vincent."

She looked for him in the crowd. Somehow her eyes always found him easily. "Yes." Denying it was useless, and she knew it.

"You must trust him very much if you shared your dreams with him."

She lifted her head and shot him a puzzled look. "He told you?"

"I asked but he wouldn't betray your trust. He's a good man. They are hard to come by. If you like him, tell him. Sometimes we men are so smart we are stupid, and we need things said clearly."

"He's been kind. Very helpful. That's all, nothing more. We just met a few days ago, and he's leaving tomorrow. After that, we'll never see each other again." It was painful to think it, never mind say it. Whatever her father was seeing wasn't going anywhere. It would pass. *It better because it's going to hurt like hell if it doesn't. Nothing is worse than loving someone who doesn't love you.*

"Oh, my sweet Nita. If your mother was alive, she would be the one to guide you on the ways of the heart instead of this old man. But I love you and want you to be happy and enjoy your life."

"I do, Dad."

"Do you remember me telling you how I met your mother?"

Renita nodded, but she loved hearing any stories about her mother.

"I knew the moment I met your mother. She walked into my father's bakery, and I heard her voice from the back. She sounded like an angel, and I had to stop what I was doing and find out who it was. From that day forward, she came to the bakery at the same time each day until I asked her to marry me."

She saw a look in his eyes that was filled with joy and sorrow at the same time. Renita knew how much he missed her mother. *This is exactly why I can't leave you, Dad. I don't want you all alone.*

"You better make sure the champagne glasses are full, because it's almost midnight."

Ricco gave her a kiss on the forehead. "Happy New Year, Nita."

"Happy New Year, Dad."

She called over two of the waiters, gave them instructions, and did one last walk through. The countdown was about to start.

She walked over to the large window that overlooked part of a mountain that was not used for skiing. However, it was an amazing sight. There was a full moon, and the stars were shining brightly. *Leave here? Why? So both Dad and I can be alone? It makes no sense. I'll go when I have had time to adequately plan.*

A shooting star came over the mountain, and she closed her eyes. It may be a childhood game, but one day she hoped one of her wishes would come true.

"Ten. Nine. Eight." Renita didn't need to turn to see the crowd or watch the ball drop at midnight. The room was reflected in the glass of the window if she watched at an angle. She scanned the images and for the first time she couldn't see Vincent. Her father appeared out of the kitchen again, and this time the rest of the staff was with him. It was a tradition that all staff members rang in the New Year and celebrated, if only for a few minutes.

Dad? Maria? Her father hadn't mentioned Maria was at the resort. *Probably just checking on him like I asked. You're a good woman.*

"Three. Two. One. Happy New Year!" Gold and white balloons dropped from the ceiling, and she could hear all kinds of noisemakers going off.

As she looked again at her father, she was taken totally by surprise. He'd pulled Maria into his arms and was kissing her. Not a quick happy New Year peck either. It was a lip-locking, you're my gal, type of kiss. *Well, what do you know? Guess I don't have to worry about you any longer do I, Dad? It would've been simpler to tell me instead of trying to push me onto Vincent.*

She hadn't heard him approach but only felt his arm come from behind her and turn her toward him. As she looked up into Vincent's brown eyes, he said, "Happy New Year, Renita."

His lips claimed hers. Light and tenderly, but not ending. The noise in the background was drowned out. Nothing at that moment mattered to her except Vincent. She didn't want to admit it, not even to herself, but she was falling in love with him.

At that very moment, Renita had made her choice: to

enjoy what time she could have with him, even if tonight was all she'd ever get. Denying her feelings was causing her just as much pain as embracing them then watching him leave.

Reaching up, she wrapped her arms around his neck and pulled him closer, deepening the kiss. She was going to give him everything she had. Let him feel what she was feeling. *Tomorrow is another day, but at least, I'll always have tonight to remember.*

VINCENT HAD BEEN watching Renita all night. People continued to come up to him to talk business or investment opportunities. He hadn't cared about anything tonight, except for it to come to an end so he could steal her away and have her in his arms.

Once that clock hit midnight, he knew exactly where he wanted to be. *Holding Renita.*

When she pulled him down to her, he thought he'd lose his mind, but they were standing in a room filled with people. Her father being one of them. Although he didn't want to stop kissing her, he needed to before it became something she'd regret later.

"Renita, I—"

"Vincent, please. . ." Her voice was soft and full of need.

The little control he'd had was lost. She needed him, wanted him, and he couldn't hide the fact that he felt the same. "Let's get out of here."

"But the party isn't over."

He didn't care about the party or what anyone was going to think. *Maybe her father.* He looked over to where he'd seen Ricco standing earlier. He was watching them. The look on his face wasn't one Vincent could read, but he'd guess it was one of concern. *I'm not the type of man I'd want for my daughter either. And Renita deserves so much better than me. Someone who'll be with her tomorrow.*

Although he wanted to pick Renita up in his arms and carry her to his room, he needed to think past this. *I don't know what's different about you, Renita, but damn you've got me tied up in knots like I've never been before.* He knew one night with her wasn't going to tell him what he needed to know. *I'm not sure how long I need, but I have to know what this is. Walking away right now is not the answer. Asking her to come with me isn't either.*

"Your staff can handle the rest. No one is going to care at this point; it's only drinking and dancing."

"And the cleanup."

"I'll help you clean in the morning." *Where did that come from? I don't clean tables or do dishes. Hell, up to a few days ago, I didn't cook either, but you seem to have me doing a lot of things I don't do anymore. I'm not sure if I like it or not.*

She was looking up at him as though she doubted him. "You're leaving tomorrow morning, Vincent. Or did you forget?"

No. I didn't. He didn't want to leave her. "I'm extending my stay." He knew it probably sounded as though he was saying it only to get her into his bed. That wasn't the case. Yes, he wanted her, every inch of her, but sex had never driven his actions before. It wasn't going to start now.

"You're staying?"

"Yes."

Her eyes widened, and he could tell she had so much she wanted to ask yet was afraid to ask. "How long?"

Telling her the truth, that he wanted to stay to explore what he was feeling for her, wasn't going to give her an answer. But putting a timetable on it wasn't something he could commit to. "I don't know." *One day at a time.*

"Why are you staying? You don't ski, and I don't think you're enjoying the blustery cold either."

"Maybe I found something that makes the freezing temp more tolerable." He loved how easily he was able to make her blush. The women that normally flocked around him were anything but shy. *Forward, aggressive, shallow, and most likely only interested in either money or a job. You, my dear Renita, don't seem to want me for either. I'm just not sure why you do want me. I think a few more days exploring that more closely will do us both some good.*

"Nita, you have covered for me so much this week while I was sick. It's now time for me to repay that debt," Ricco said as he approached, holding a woman's hand.

"Dad, I can't."

"Consider yourself off duty and enjoy this party. I hear the food is quite good. We make a good team, Vincent. Feel free to join me anytime in the kitchen."

"Thank you, Ricco," Vincent said with a nod of appreciation. "And who's this lovely lady?"

Ricco beamed. "Ah, this is my Maria. She makes the best homemade meatballs. You should come for Sunday dinner."

"Dad, I'm sure Vincent has things to do. Like attend to

his own business, or enjoy his vacation," Renita answered.

"I'd love to join you, but only if Renita and I can bring the dessert. She learned how to make a holiday spice cake." Vincent tried to hold back his grin. He knew damn well that she'd been too distracted to remember a thing about the recipe.

Renita shot him a look that said he was going to pay for that. He gave her one right back. *I look forward to it.*

"Oh, how wonderful. Maybe you and I can do some baking together?" Maria asked Renita.

Vincent put his arm around Renita. "It's our secret recipe."

Maria clapped her hands together. "Oh, my! So romantic. Renita, I'm happy you've found yourself a man like Vincent."

Vincent didn't miss the warning in Ricco's eyes as he spoke. "Yes. It's nice to see her so happy," Ricco said.

"Dad," Renita said as though embarrassed.

Ricco chuckled and shook his head. "Now if you two will excuse us, I'd like to take this lovely young lady for a spin on the dance floor before we head back to work."

Maria winked at him. "Let's leave the dancing to these folks, I much rather a stroll under the moonlight."

Vincent had no issue with the light flirting going on between Ricco and Maria. But he could tell by Renita's eyes that she still wasn't used to seeing her father with a woman. *Maybe you're not staying because of your father. Maybe you're staying because of you.*

They both stood there watching Ricco and Maria walk

away arm in arm. He was finally alone with Renita again, and she no longer had any excuses why she couldn't come with him.

Vincent reached out, grabbing Renita's hand, and led her out of the dining room.

"Vincent, I really can't leave my father here to do my job."

"You can and will. I want you all to myself tonight." He stopped and pulled her into his arms. "Unless you tell me otherwise, I'm taking you to my suite."

Her eyes darkened, and her only response was a slow nod.

Tonight would require self-control to hold back. He'd wanted Renita from the moment he'd laid eyes on her, but he wanted it to be something more than just a physical release. Although his body was aching to be inside of her, he wanted her to want and enjoy it as much as he would.

Vincent took off his jacket, tossed it onto the couch, then loosened his tie. He could see she was nervous so he asked, "Would you like a glass of wine?"

"No, thank you. I don't drink."

Another thing I like about you. He walked back to her and touched her right cheek with the back of his left hand. Then he let his hand glide along her jaw as his thumb stopped to rest on her bottom lip.

"You're a very beautiful woman, Renita. How is it someone hasn't captured your heart yet?"

She swallowed hard, and he felt her heart quicken. "I . . . guess I haven't met anyone I . . . care about enough."

That only concerned him more. Was he about to be the one to break her heart? A serious relationship wasn't something he'd done in a very long time. He was too set in his ways to change now. Or was Brice right, that when the perfect one comes along, it doesn't feel like a change? Instead, it feels like it should've always been.

"I could ask you the same. Why no . . . girlfriend or wife?"

"I'm married to my job."

"That sounds sad and lonely."

"At times, yes. But it was my choice. I wanted to stay focused on building."

"A Moretti empire? What good is it if you don't have anyone to share it with?"

Vincent leaned into her hand and kissed it. Renita challenged him to think differently than he had in a long time. She was so much more than just a beautiful woman. She had heart and brains and one hell of a sense of humor. *Can't cook, but I can live with that.*

"I'm glad you're with me tonight."

"Me too," she said breathlessly.

She was captivating even in her hostess uniform. He couldn't take his eyes off her. He gazed to her slender hips, over her abdomen, and finally, at her voluptuous breasts. *Don't start what you can't finish.* He'd never wanted a woman as badly as he wanted Renita. He wasn't sure he could stop if he simply kissed her. The swell of her breasts was only inches away, begging him to release them from the confines of the thin fabric.

Her tongue darted out, and she licked her top lip. Vincent could hardly restrain himself. But when she said his name so tenderly, there was no longer any holding back. "Vincent."

In one swift move, he pulled her against him, devouring her lips with a hard, feverish kiss. She held him to her, parting her lips to let him inside. He inhaled her sweet scent as he kissed down her jaw to the nape of her neck and back to her lips. *I need you.* A moan of pleasure escaped her and rumbled through him.

He couldn't keep his hands off her and ran them down her back, over her sweet ass, and back up the front to cup her heaving breasts. Without breaking their kiss, he swept her into his arms and carried her to the bed in the other room.

He stood at the foot of the bed and fumbled with the buttons of her blouse. She smiled. "Let me."

Vincent watched each button open as he quickly did the same with his shirt and his pants, letting them both drop to the floor. If he'd thought she was stunning before, she was pure perfection now in her red lace bra and matching panties. "I would've thought you'd be the pink type."

"I have an adventurous side," Renita said playfully to him.

He watched as she reached behind her and unhooked the bra to let it drop. Her perfectly round breasts were begging to be sucked. She slipped her thumbs under both sides of her panties and wiggled out of them as well.

His heart was not the only thing pounding. His cock was aching for attention. He slipped off his boxers then lifted her and laid her down in the center of the bed. Vincent needed to taste her, all of her. He nibbled and kissed her from her jaw to her neck but didn't stop there. He cupped her breasts, plucking at one nipple, and she moaned deeply. Then he sucked the other, teasingly flicking it with his tongue.

"Vincent," she called out as she ran her fingers through his hair. He could touch her forever, but his body was begging for more. As he licked and nipped his way lower, he felt her quiver as his tongue circled her belly button and continued lower.

This was the first time she used her hands and tried to block his path. He lifted his head. "What's wrong?"

She blushed. "I've never . . ."

"Hasn't anyone kissed you here?" Vincent asked as he touched her between her legs.

To know he'd be her first excited him. But he wasn't sure how innocent she was.

"Are you a vir—?"

Shaking her head, she softly said, "No, just not very experienced. I'm sorry. I don't want you to be disappointed. I'm sure you're used to—"

He interrupted her with a powerful kiss. "You're far from disappointing to me, amore mio." Her body trembled as he spread her legs. She quivered as his tongue traced lower, stopping only to nip softly on her inner thigh.

Breathlessly she begged, "Vincent, I can't."

"You can," he said as his tongue licked her center gently. "All you need to do is trust me." He circled her clit then sucked on it. Renita cried out in pleasure, arching her hips off the bed, her moans only encouraging him. "You taste so sweet." He couldn't get enough of her, devouring her feverishly as he felt her tense beneath him.

"Vincent. Oh, please, Vincent. I—"

Her body jerked violently as she lost herself in a powerful release. He continued to suck until her body began to settle. There was no getting enough of her. *Damn, she's perfect.* His hard throbbing cock ached to feel her wrapped around him. He quickly reached down, grabbed his wallet from his pants pocket, pulled out a condom, and sheathed himself.

Her body still trembled when he returned to her as he kissed his way back up her stomach and claimed her breast again. His fingers once again slipped between her folds, which were now wet and ready for him. But he wanted to bring her to the brink again before entering her. His thumb stroked her clit, and she stirred again. This time, she didn't hold back and was moving with him, begging him so she could feel it again. Her hands ran down his back, nails digging in at times as he brought her to the brink and held her there.

"Please, Vincent. Please, no more," she begged softly in shallow breaths.

Sucking her nipple hard, he stroked her clit faster. He needed to feel her release on his cock. Pressing his throbbing cock at her opening, he paused, his mouth taking hers. She was hot and wet, ready for him, and he could wait no longer.

In one thrust, he buried himself deep inside her. She instantly cried out his name again and again. She may not be a virgin, but she was so very tight, and he worried he'd hurt her. He stopped for a moment, still deep within her and raised his head enough to see her face as a tear rolled down her cheek. "Did I hurt you?"

"No, it's . . . I never knew it could be . . . I mean I've never . . ."

She was innocent in her own way. Whoever her lover had been before was selfish, not to please her first. He'd probably done the same in the past, but he could never do such a thing with Renita. *She'll always be first in my life.*

Emotions flooded him with that knowledge. *I love her.*

This was not only their first time together, but he was also giving more of himself than he'd ever thought he could. Vincent slowly began to move inside her, all the while kissing her softly. No thought of his own desire. Only when her hips began to move did he quicken his rhythm. Moving faster and deeper, her cries of pleasure filled the room. As she moaned, her body rocked with a release, causing him to lose control and plunging deep within her; he shuddered with his release.

He collapsed on her as they both caught their breath. He rolled to his side, careful not to crush her. Pulling her close, he kissed her gently and whispered, "Good night, my love."

She responded the same in Italian, "Buona notte, amore mio."

Chapter Seven

RENITA WOKE THE next morning, wondering if it was all a dream. As she stirred in the bed, she felt Vincent's naked body near hers. Never had she felt so good, so alive, as when he'd held her, called her *my love*. But was that just something he did in the heat of the moment?

She knew she was a good and kind person, but he was rich and powerful. This is no Cinderella story. He didn't need to rescue her from anything. Renita might not be living her dream, but she was happy. One thing was missing, and she never realized it until Vincent entered her life. *Love*.

It was a foolish thought. They'd only met earlier this week, yet the connection to him was beyond words. *I don't want this to end. No matter how hard I want otherwise, he'll leave.*

"What's the matter, my love?" Vincent's voice was husky as he was just waking up.

"Nothing's wrong." She wasn't sure how he'd picked up on it, but he seemed very attuned to her emotions. That wasn't good, because it'd make it hard for her to pretend not to care when he said goodbye.

He rolled onto his side and propped himself on his elbow, looking down at her. She knew her eyes told him everything. "Renita, talk to me. Why are you sad?"

She didn't want to discuss it. Instead, she had her own questions for him. *If he wants to talk so much, then I'll be happy to listen.*

"Have you decided how long you'll be staying?" That wasn't the question she'd wanted to ask. If anything that only brought it right back to her, where she didn't want the focus to be.

Vincent brushed a lock of hair away from her face before he answered. "I promised Ricco and Maria we'd attend Sunday dinner. But I can't stay after that. I've already been away too long."

But that's tomorrow. I wanted you to . . . stay . . . oh God. No matter how long, it's not going to be easy. But after a family dinner, it's going to be nearly impossible. "You don't have to go tomorrow. I can make an excuse for you."

"I want to go. Or do you not want me to be there?"

How she wished she could turn away so the truth wouldn't be obvious. But he watched her closely, waiting for her to answer. *He wants to go? I don't know why. I don't want to be there.*

"It's not that I don't want you there, it's just not going to be what you're used to. Maria is going to be doing the cooking, so I don't know what that's going to be like. This is . . ."

"New for both of us."

She smiled up at him. "Yes, it is."

"So my sweet Renita, quit worrying about it. We have today to enjoy ourselves. But don't think for one minute that I've forgotten your private cooking lesson."

Renita rolled her eyes. "Can't we just say we did when we didn't? I'm never going to be able to cook like you or my father."

"You don't have to. All you need to do is cook like Renita, not anyone else. Let it flow from you, all your passion and love, and you'll find what you make is delicious."

"Why is it you make everything sound so easy?"

"No, letting go of things that scare you or intimidate you is never easy."

She laughed softly. "I can't picture anything scaring or intimidating you."

He didn't laugh and his voice became soft and tender, "The thought of never seeing you again scares me."

Her heart skipped several beats. It's what she wanted, but she was almost too afraid to believe it. *Could I be dreaming? He stayed because of me?* Vincent's expression said he was dead serious.

"Me too." She didn't know exactly what that meant for them going forward, but they appeared to be on the same page.

"I was thinking about that lesson."

She shook her head. "Really? Cooking is what you're thinking about right now?"

Vincent laughed, grabbing her and rolling her so she laid on top of him. Before claiming her lips, he said, "I wasn't thinking about food."

She knew there were so many things she should attend to, but none of them seemed to matter to her. Smiling, she gladly melted into his arms. *Let the lesson begin.*

Chapter Eight

VINCENT HAD NEVER been nervous about going to dinner before, but this felt different. He'd told Renita he wanted to go. That wasn't exactly accurate. He had an agenda he wished he'd mentioned to Renita before they arrived at the house.

Better late than never. "Renita, I think we should talk before we go inside."

He could see the concern and panic fill her eyes. "A little late to change your mind. I can see my father looking at us through the living room window."

"No. I'm not backing out. But I haven't told you why I came to Vermont."

"Sophie Barrington's charity event. Or have you forgotten that I saw the guest list for seating purposes? Not saying I may have seated you next to the most boring couple on purpose or anything." Teasingly she batted her eyelashes at him.

He was trying to be serious, but the expression on her face was so darn cute he couldn't help but smile. "What was that payback for?"

"For criticizing my tomato soup."

"You should be thanking me. If I hadn't stepped in everyone would've starved, long before the event started."

"If my cooking was that bad, maybe we shouldn't allow my father to eat my spice cake after all."

Vincent reached out and covered her hand with his. "It's perfection. Trust me; I'd tell you if it wasn't."

She looked at him, trying to judge if he actually would. Then she smiled. "Not sure I like getting the blunt truth all the time, but at least, I'll always know where I stand."

He lifted her hand to his lips, kissing her. "I'm not one who makes a lot of promises, but I promise you, I'll always be forthcoming."

The smile faded. "What is it you want to tell me, Vincent?"

"One of my main purposes for attending the event was to meet your father. Brice Henderson highly recommended him."

"I remember him. He's come to the lodge a few times with his wife, Lena, and their son. I even babysat for them for a few hours one night so they could enjoy a late night ski. What exactly does this have to do with my father?"

"I came to offer your father a position as chef at a new restaurant I'm opening in Toronto, Canada."

Her mouth gaped open, and she pulled her hand from his. "I don't see how seducing the chef's daughter would fall under a normal interview process. Or for all I know, maybe it does."

"Renita, you can't think that I—"

"I don't know what to believe, Vincent. But if you want to offer my father a job, then do it, but I want nothing to do with it. Now if you'll excuse me, I think it's probably best if I go in alone as this is Sunday dinner, and we don't discuss business at the table." Once, again she was rattling off in Italian. He was glad he didn't know what she was saying because it sounded like she wanted to wring his neck. As she reached for the door handle, he grabbed her.

"I didn't need to tell you beforehand. I did it out of respect for you after what we've shared."

She turned to face him again, but the look in her eyes told him his choice of words hadn't helped any. "You're right. You're not obliged to tell me a thing."

"Renita, I didn't mean it to sound so harsh. I was just trying to—"

"I get it, Vincent. It's none of my business."

"My business is separate from my personal life. I've always kept it that way. Sharing with someone, caring what someone else thinks or feels about my decisions . . . this is the first time I've been in this situation. Most likely I didn't present it well. But I wanted to discuss it with you first." Even this was far outside his comfort zone. Normally he wouldn't have shared anything. But he didn't want to do that with Renita.

"I'm sorry I snapped at you. What's happening between us is new to me as well. I've never brought anyone home for dinner with my father before. I know it's crazy, but there wasn't anyone I wanted to before this. So I guess I'm a bit jumpy. Not knowing what to expect."

Her voice had softened, and she seemed to relax. "You're not the only one. Ricco has no problem asking what's on his mind. I'm concerned what that might be today. There are a few things I'd prefer not to talk about." *Like how we spent the last thirty-six hours.*

Renita laughed. "I wish I could say his bark is worse than his bite, but that'd be far from the truth." She tapped her chin with her finger and then added, "Maybe that's why I never brought anyone here before."

"Thanks for the warning. Maybe I should reconsider the job offer. It's bad enough my employees have to answer to me, they don't deserve two of us."

"Just so that you know, neither of you scare me."

He reached over and pulled her into his arms. "Good, because it's not fear I'm looking for from you."

Vincent claimed her lips just as he heard the tapping on the driver's side window. "There is no drive-up service, so if you want to eat, you need to come inside."

Ricco didn't wait for an answer, and Vincent saw him head back into the house.

"We'll pick up where we left off later tonight."

"Looking forward to it," Renita said as she got out of the car.

Vincent got out and reached into the back seat for the cake. As he was standing up, he felt the impact and then cold snow trickled down his neck and into the back of his jacket. Looking up, he saw the twinkle in her eye.

"What was that for?"

"That was for deciding to tell me after we got here. If

we're going to argue, then make it somewhere more private."

"Why is that?"

"Because I didn't even get to finish my make-up kiss."

If he'd been closer, Vincent would've rectified that issue. But she turned and bolted inside, leaving him to shake off the snow before following her. *I might just start another argument on our way back to the resort. Don't want to disappoint you twice.*

RENITA HAD NO idea why she'd been so nervous about Vincent coming to her home. He seemed to fit right in. She and Vincent sat on the couch, and he held her hand gently on his lap. She actually felt like they were a couple, although they'd never brought up the subject. *Maybe we'll broach the topic before you leave.*

The last thing she wanted was to come off like a pushy, insecure woman. Nothing chased a man away faster than that. *Just enjoy what we have. If more comes out of it, be happy, and if it ends after today . . . you'll find a way to be happy again one day.*

She tried to focus on what was being said, but couldn't understand half of it. When Vincent and Ricco spoke it was almost as though they talked a secret language that only chefs would comprehend. If they weren't discussing a recipe, they spoke about the most outrageous thing they'd ever eaten. *I can't believe that these two grown men are competing on who's eaten the most disgusting thing ever. I'm happy my food didn't make it on the list.*

The more they spoke, the happier she was that she decided not to run a kitchen. As she sat watching the fire she couldn't help but think how this house felt so much more like a home than it did a week ago. Maria waited on him hand and foot. And she was here with Vincent. It was a new time, another chapter in her life, and she liked it.

"Would you like to help me with the coffee and dessert?" Maria asked.

"I'd be happy to." It felt a bit odd being asked to help out in her own house. She did live there, at least half the time. But somehow it seemed as though Maria knew her way around the kitchen better than she did.

She got up off the couch but before she got far, Vincent tugged her back to him and gave her a quick kiss. It was sweet and loving, and she glowed as she followed Maria.

Once inside the kitchen Maria poured two cups and set them on the table then plopped herself in one of the chairs. "It looked like the men wanted to talk alone for a bit, so I thought it'd be a good time for us to do the same."

Renita wasn't sure if she wanted to be in either room at the moment. Although Maria had been their neighbor for many years and had practically watched her grow up, she couldn't remember ever having a serious conversation with her. When she couldn't come up with a polite way to decline her request, she took the seat on the other side of the table.

"Vincent seems to be such a nice young man."

"Yes, he is. We're still in the get-to-know-you stage, but I like what I've seen." *Which is every inch of him.* She quickly brushed that thought out of her mind, but it was too late. Maria was very attuned to her reactions.

"Oh, young love. It's a very beautiful thing. But it's nice, even at my age."

Renita saw how Maria's eyes sparkled when she spoke of love. Was it possible that Maria and her father had been speaking on a more personal level before? *And here I thought I played matchmaker. Better not quit my day job because I never saw a thing.*

"It's nice to see my father smiling and laughing again. It's been a long time."

"I understand completely. The heart is something that heals only when it's ready. And also loves when the time is right. I wanted to make sure you're comfortable with your father and me being . . . together."

It wasn't what she'd expected, but seeing them and how they interacted during dinner changed her outlook. Maria was perfect for her father. It was as though they'd been together for years. *Heck, maybe they have, and I've always been clueless.*

"You two didn't have to hide this from me all this time."

Maria looked puzzled. "I don't understand? We never have . . . I mean the only time I've entered your home was when you asked me last week to care for Ricco. Nothing except polite conversation before that."

"But you—"

"Love him. Yes, I do."

Renita wanted to say that it was craziness, to even think after one week someone could truly love a person. But she was not a hypocrite. Although she hadn't actually said the words *I love you* she'd thought them. And they'd called each other *my love* in Italian.

"I'm glad you've finally found each other then."

"And you seem to have found your love as well."

Renita shrugged.

"Why do you doubt it?" Maria asked as she sipped her coffee.

"He's never said it."

"My dear child. Words are so simple to say. How Vincent looks at you, how he treats you, his actions, those things will say something much greater than words ever will. Some men can't say it, but it doesn't mean they don't love you."

"I'll remember that, thank you." Although she was happy to get to know Maria better, she wanted to change the subject. She wasn't ready for any deeper discussion about either of their relationships.

"What do you think they're talking about in there?"

Renita had a good idea but didn't want to mention a thing. That was going to be between Maria and her father to discuss. Just like Vincent had said to her earlier, don't mix business with pleasure.

Before she could answer Maria, the two men joined them in the kitchen, and Ricco teased, "Look at this, Vincent. We're waiting patiently for our coffee and cake, and the ladies seem to have forgotten us."

"Sometimes a woman likes to be sought after. Isn't that right, Renita?" Maria asked.

Thanks for throwing me under the bus. But she wasn't going to back out. "And what better way than through his stomach?" Renita held up a slice of cake for Vincent.

Smiling, he took it from her and bent to give her a kiss on the cheek, before sitting next to her. "You won my heart long before you could cook, amore mio."

Her heart fluttered with joy each time he called her *my love*. Maria was correct. The words may come someday, but if not, she'd have to use her eyes to capture his actions instead. *And yours tell me you care very much for me.*

"I know. You were smitten at the very first taste of my tomato soup."

Everyone in the room laughed as they recalled hearing guests complain about it during the party. If she'd been inspired to be a chef, she might've been insulted.

"Maria, would you join me in the other room, please? I would like to discuss an offer Ricco presented to me, but I wish for us to decide together." Ricco reached out his hand, and Maria smiled at him as she accepted.

Once Renita and Vincent were alone, Vincent's demeanor changed. "The job offer went well I take it?"

Vincent nodded. "I was more than fair."

Oh, I don't doubt that. But don't worry, he's worth whatever you offered. "It's kind of hard to get used to Dad bouncing things off Maria."

"They are happy, so you should be happy for them."

Renita looked over to Vincent. "I am happy." *More than I can tell you.*

"Do I make you happy, Renita?"

She wanted to shout yes, but still was afraid to say the words first. *I don't want to be rejected. My heart will break if he doesn't say it back.*

"I'm happy."

He reached out and tipped her face to meet his eyes. He had the most beautiful light brown eyes she'd ever seen. She could stare into them forever and never get bored. It was like being on top of the mountain and watching the night sky. *Powerful, mysterious, and beautiful.* She could spend a lifetime exploring the levels of him and didn't doubt there were many to be seen.

"I asked if I make you happy."

She nodded. "Yes, Vincent, more than I can express."

"I believe your father is going to take the job."

Nothing like changing the subject. Weren't you supposed to tell me something sweet in return? "You won't regret hiring him."

"I'm not telling you that because I'm concerned about my choice. It's just that he'll no longer be here in Vermont. There is no reason for you to stay here any longer."

Panic filled her. Vincent was right. She wasn't afraid of being alone, but she'd only thought of leaving one day and coming back home to visit him here. This had always been her home. But this house was provided by the resort for the chef and his family. If her father left, she'd need to leave as well.

Maybe that's a good thing. A new year, a new beginning for all of us. "Whether he takes the job or not, I already knew I needed a change. I wasn't expecting so much change all at once, but I guess I should start thinking about what to do next. Because you're right, staying here isn't what I want to do, but going to Toronto with him isn't either."

"I was thinking more along the line of New York with me."

Stunned, she asked to be sure she hadn't misunderstood, "Are you asking me to go with you?"

"What I feel for you Renita is more than I expected. I don't want it to end. I'd like it very much if you came with me and we explored where this is going, our feelings for each other."

"Live with you?" she asked softly. Although she wanted to be with him, she wasn't ready to make that type of leap. He was right; they needed to get to know each other better. Although she was ready to say *I love you* to him, she also needed her own space to adapt to all the changes in her life. "I want this, Vincent. But since meeting you, I've begun to dream again for the first time in years. I've got a lot to figure out and how I'm going to achieve it: where I want to work, what I have to offer, and who I am are all things I need to understand about myself. I can't do that if I'm living with you. Maybe you can help me look for an apartment close by you?"

"I can do that, but let me help you with some of those answers. You're not selfish. You're kind and thoughtful and funny and generous and strong-minded and so much more. And lastly, what you've got young lady is my heart. I love you, Renita. And I'll take you on any terms you want."

Only three words echoed in her mind. *He loves me.* "I love you too, Vincent. And I don't care if we live on the moon, as long as we're together."

He pulled her toward him and kissed her. She was filled

with so much emotion it was almost difficult to hold back the tears. She found herself muttering *I love you* again and again to him as though the floodgates to her heart had opened for the very first time.

"Then it's settled. New York with me?"

She smiled. "With you."

He pulled out a heart shaped silver necklace from his pocket and held it out to her. "My heart is now yours."

When she took it from him, she noticed it was engraved on the back. *Just in thyme. Love, Vincent.*

A single tear of joy rolled down her cheek. She knew she'd been blessed with a man who could show her his feelings and also said the words. He accepted her as she was, a horrible cook and still searching for her career. But what she knew was where her heart was leading her, and that was to Vincent.

"I love you."

"I love you too," Vincent replied.

As he kissed her again, she knew this was the beginning of another chapter in her life. But this story was far from over, and one that would continue to grow over the years. *Yes, Vincent, you arrived just in thyme.*

THE END

Want to read more from Jeannette Winters?

Visit her website: jeannettewinters.com

Bonus Novella:
Midnight on the Slopes

The Barrington Billionaires Series

Book 3.5

A Holiday Novella

by
Danielle Stewart

Author Contact
website: authordaniellestewart.com
email: authordaniellestewart@gmail.com
Facebook: Author Danielle Stewart
Twitter: dstewartauthor
Goodreads
Bookbub

Nolan Saint-Jane is a big enough person to pretend he's happy his sister Libby has married a billionaire oilman. She deserves the best but the sudden change has taken the last piece of family from him. Having spent Christmas alone, brooding Nolan is determined that New Year's Eve will be different.

Holly McNamara travels light. She can't be held down by anything when it's time to run again. New Year's Eve is the perfect time to make a break for it and a chance meeting with a stranger in a coffee shop gives her the opportunity she needs.

When the snow starts to fall, the passion erupts and the truth comes out, Nolan and Holly will have to decide if the new year holds hope for the new life they both need.

A memory from Danielle Stewart

Hanging around mom's house, 1990
Back left:
Nichole (Danielle's eldest sister next to Ruth Cardello with
Danielle on her lap
Jen, Danielle's other older sister holding Luke, Jeannette Winter's son

Dear Readers,
<u>I hope to be like her someday.</u>

My first memory of my aunt Ruthie is actually one of my first memories in general. I'm sitting on my parents' bed with my two sisters. Ruthie's folding up newspapers, making them into hats and boats, telling us funny stories. It's a simple memory, something you'd probably forget if it weren't tied to a tragedy.

When I was young, my baby sister died in her sleep. It was heartbreaking for my family. I don't know why Ruthie was appointed babysitter on that day, maybe she drew the short straw. She would have been in her late teens and she was charged with keeping me and my two older sisters busy while the rest of the family tried to process the grief and sadness that came from our loss.

I learned a lesson that day that I've carried with me for years. On a day full of unimaginable loss and confusion, you can smile. You can listen to a silly story and you can giggle. That day wasn't the last tragedy I've encountered in my life, but it has shaped how I face them. Looking at how she handled it, holding back whatever pain she was feeling in order to keep us smiling, I realize what a gift that was to my sisters and me. My family has a history of facing hardships with humor, and Ruthie is my first memory of that. We were so lucky she was there, and I found myself saying: I hope to be like her someday.

Ruthie has inspired me throughout my life, even when I was sure she didn't realize it. Not many people left the small town we grew up in. But she did. And growing up I heard the stories of her adventures and realized I wanted the same for myself. She may not have felt very inspiring as she hit the bumps in her own road, but I was watching and wanting something more for myself. There I was again, saying: I hope to be like her someday.

When I got older I, too, moved away. I took a job far

from home and met my husband. Three years ago I became a mother and found myself wondering what my future was going to hold. It's hard to remember your worth when you spend your days wiping noses and teaching manners. I wanted to have as much time with my son as I could, and once again I looked to Ruthie for inspiration. She, too, had a toddler and was blazing a path for herself, writing books people loved and still finding time to be a wife and mother. Could I do something I love and still put my family first? Yes. And there I was again saying: I hope to be like her someday.

When I started this journey, wanting to write something worth reading, Ruthie was there for me. At three years old, she had set me on my parents' bed and told me it was all right to laugh. At thirty, she's sitting me down telling me it's okay to put yourself out there. You're good at this, you're worth it, and you can do it. On the days I wanted to quit, she kicked me in the ass. When I questioned my abilities, she reminded me why I was doing this.

I watch her continually pay forward all the success she's had. She surrounds herself with people who spread joy like the common cold, just sneezing happiness all over each other. I started this journey of writing wanting to be like her, hoping to be a successful author. I realize now what I want to emulate is her generous, kindhearted, hysterically funny spirit.

I hope to be like her someday.

Chapter One

NOLAN TAPPED HIS pen repetitively on the text book and stared at the same line he'd been reading for the last twenty minutes. His jet-fuel-like coffee had turned to a cold thick sludge. The café was busy with impatient and distracted patrons hustling to the front of the line and barking out their orders. Clicking the volume up on his headphones, he tried to drown out the chatter.

The halfhearted attempt of the café employees to decorate the dim, overcrowded space fell flat. Old tangled tinsel was taped to the ceiling. Fake sprayed-on frosty snow rimmed each window. If Nolan hadn't spent the holiday alone in a strange place, maybe he could find the magic in the twinkling lights on the fake tree.

The only positive prospect was his sister Libby's trip to visit him for New Year's Day. It had been too long since he'd seen her, and with each passing week the chip on his shoulder got heavier to carry. The mature part of him mustered some happiness for Libby's hotshot, oil-mogul billionaire who'd married her in a quiet ceremony. If anyone deserved it Libby did, having worked every waking minute of her adult life to get Nolan to college and keep them both afloat.

The rest of him was fueled solely by selfishness. Their childhood home was now empty. Everything he'd once depended on to feel connected to his torn-apart family was now even further shredded. Libby and James West were blissful newlyweds, and Nolan was losing the last little bit of family he had.

The music in his ears cut out as his phone began to vibrate. Libby's smiling picture flashed across the screen, one of his favorite shots of her, dressed in overalls with a paintbrush in her hand as she stood on their old front porch. She was trying to make what was old new again. Trying to make what was cracked and ruined whole. That was what Libby had always been to Nolan. The fixer when so many things were broken.

"Hey Lib," Nolan said, trying to sound upbeat. "You guys boarding soon?"

"Nope," Libby said flatly. "All flights are completely grounded. Ice here and a big storm up your way."

"What?" Nolan groaned, giving in completely to his frustrations. "We had plans, Lib. We haven't seen each other in forever."

"I've been inviting you down to tour West Oil for months. You keep telling me you're too busy. Now you're mad because I can't personally de-ice the plane and the runway?"

"You know I don't want to work at West Oil. Touring it is just your way to get me roped in. I'm going to school to be a marine biologist. The oil companies are basically my nemeses."

"I'm sorry, Nolan," Libby said, genuinely. "I miss you so much. I wanted to spend New Year's Day with you like we used to. Chinese food and movie hopping at the theater."

"Isn't there anything your rich husband can do? He has a plane right?" Nolan could hear how whiny he sounded, but he didn't care.

"It's a private plane, not a magic one. It's susceptible to all the same weather related problems as any other plane. There's just no way we can make it all the way to Massachusetts right now."

"What about your charity event in Vermont?" Nolan asked, wondering if his sister was taking that disappointment harder than the idea of not seeing him.

"That's the other reason I'm calling," Libby said in that coy way she always did when there was some bad news to be broken. "I need you to go in our place."

"Me?" Nolan laughed. "You want me to go to some billionaire event?"

"It's not just for billionaires," Libby dismissed. "I'm sure there are a few struggling millionaires there too." Her attempt at humor didn't soften him at all. "It's a great cause, and James is donating a huge sum of money. The giant size check is already there. We just need someone to represent our family and hand it over. Say some nice things about nice people and then enjoy the wonderful party. It'll be good for you. I can hear how down you've been. It's worrying me."

"I'm not a West," Nolan said grumpily. "I'm a Saint-Jane, just like you used to be. He's not my family."

"He's my family," Libby bit back, "and by extension he's yours. I know you're pissed at me. I can tell you don't like how things have been going, but I'm asking you to do me this favor. When have I ever asked you for anything?"

He knew damn well Libby had provided him with all of his basic needs since their mother had moved to a facility for her early-onset Alzheimer's She took care of them all and never complained. To say he'd have nothing without Libby would be an understatement. And she was right, calling in a favor was not something she'd done often. "Aren't you supposed to be there by tonight? Logistically, I'm not sure I could pull it off."

"Yes, and I already did the calculations. You're about a three-hour drive away. I'll give you my credit card to buy clothes, pack a quick bag, and hop in the car. You can time it right to get in between the coming storms and still have most of the day to enjoy the resort."

"You assume I don't have a suit I can wear?" Nolan asked, insult registering in his words. "I know I'm not like all your billionaire friends, but I have clothes."

"Why are you being so snarky?" Libby asked with a huff. "You can't wear that brown suit you wore to Principal Starlin's funeral. You need a tux. Do you have formalwear in your rickety suitcase with the wobbling wheel? I don't know why you won't let me buy you a decent bag."

"Fine," he gave in, not wanting to push his sister any further. He was only able to participate in this internship because of her help. College was only accessible to him because James West had paid for it.

"There's one more thing," Libby said, a hint of apology in her voice. "You need more than a tux for this event."

"Do I have to rent a Lamborghini and pretend to be some stuck-up rich guy? You know as well as I do, I won't pull that off. People will know how poor we were."

"You need a date," Libby replied flatly, unimpressed by the consistency in his bad attitude.

"What?" he chuckled. "I'm up at this internship. I've only been here three weeks. I don't know anyone. You expect me to find some stranger, tell her I'm going to a charity ski event with billionaires, and ask her to go with me in the next hour?"

A kind, soft-featured face appeared in front of him from the café door. Her blue cotton hat was pulled down low, and she was breaking free of her buttoned-up jacket. She stood there expectantly as though waiting for him to address her. As she slipped out of her coat, how could he not notice her with a body like that?

"Sold," the stranger smiled, sliding into the seat across from him. "I love skiing."

"Who's that?" Libby asked and Nolan could hear her smile growing larger by the second. "You do have someone you can take, don't you?"

"No," Nolan argued, refocusing on the phone call, yanking one earbud out so he could hear the woman better. "It's some stranger who just sat down across from me like a lunatic." He wasn't worried about insulting her, considering she'd intruded on his conversation.

"A lunatic who loves to ski," the woman sang, leaning in

toward the phone.

"So it's settled," Libby replied, the overhead speaker at the airport calling out more canceled flights and drowning out Nolan's protest. "I love you, Nolan. I'll text you the details. Drive safely."

The line clicked off, leaving Nolan bemused at this exotic thin-framed woman sitting across from him. She pulled off her hat and placed it neatly in her lap. Her wrists were more bangle bracelets than skin. They jingled as they tapped against each other. Long black hair pulled away from her face and spun into braids woven together like a crown above her ears. Nolan saw a small flower henna tattoo peeking out above the low collar of her tight-fitting red blouse. It was nearly impossible to keep his eyes off that dainty spot where the flower tantalized, begging to be seen.

"When do we leave?" she asked, her eyes open wide with anticipation and excitement.

"We don't," Nolan said, narrowing his eyes appraisingly, trying to measure what level of crazy she registered on the nut-job scale. "I don't even know you."

"Oh gosh," she said as though she'd forgotten the formalities. "You're right. I'm sorry. How rude of me. My name is Holly." She extended her hand for a shake, and he reluctantly obliged, convinced she wouldn't drop her hand until he did. When her cool soft skin touched his, he could almost feel her energy buzzing. "So when do we leave?"

Nolan scanned her face again, waiting for her to break out in laughter, as though the hidden cameras associated with this prank would come out from behind the fake plants any second.

"You're serious?" he asked, lost in that mischievous sparkle in her coal black eyes.

"Dead serious," she said, her shimmering glossed lips rising up in a captivating smile. "It sounds like you don't have a lot of time, and I don't see women lining up to take my spot."

"It's a formal event," he said, his phone chirping with more details from Libby. He flipped the screen for Holly to see the snapshot of the invitation. "Black tie, snooty people, probably nothing recognizably edible for food. Lots of kale and watercress things, whatever that is. Not to mention I'm a complete stranger. Aren't you worried I could be a serial killer?"

Holly laughed heartily, covering her mouth with her hand, the bangle bracelets clanking together. "Sorry," she apologized, her face glowing red. "You are harmless."

"Really?" Nolan challenged, his brow rising at her. With a woman like Holly he could think of a million ways to get in trouble. A mischievous look was now in his eye, but she never flinched.

She went on with her argument. "If you were a serial killer I'd imagine this would be a pretty elaborate scam to get me in your car. You'd have to stage a phone call with someone. Assume I'd volunteer to be your date. Then have a fake invitation drafted up and sent over in a timely fashion. Selecting a victim should be based far more on opportunity, rather than orchestrating something this intricate. Plus, you'd be more personable. Serial killers are notoriously charming when luring people into their trap."

"Hmm," Nolan said thoughtfully, rubbing a hand against the stubble on his chin. "So technically in this scenario you're the serial killer? You found an opportunity, and maybe I'm walking into *your* trap."

Holly opened her mouth to answer, but she couldn't seem to form a proper argument. Nodding her head, she gave him a look as though he'd won.

"I should be worried about you," he teased, the blush in her cheeks exciting him.

"You're right," she agreed, leaning back in her chair and exposing more of the tiny flower tattoo. "By my own logic I am charming the hell out of you. But I'm still coming. If I turn out to be an axe murderer, you can say I told you so."

"I'd be dead," he challenged, tossing his hands up animatedly.

She huffed as though he were being completely exasperating. "Fine," she conceded, rolling her eyes. "I promise to let you say 'I told you so,' BEFORE I kill you."

"Fair enough," he shrugged, convinced she would back out when it came time to actually go through with this. "You're saying you are going to come with me, buy a formal dress, ride in the car for the next three hours, and then hang out at some stuffy event where I have to awkwardly present a giant check to a roomful of strangers? All this on New Year's Eve."

"I'm hearing a new dress, a ski vacation, and the opportunity to meet some billionaires. Is there a better way to spend New Year's Eve?"

"With your boyfriend?" he baited, a wry smile lighting his face.

She nodded and pretended to think on it for a minute. "You could spend it with your boyfriend if you want," Holly shrugged. "Can he find a tux in time?"

He fought the laugh but lost, giving in to her witty humor. Nolan closed his text books and slid them into his bag. Standing, he glared at Holly, still unconvinced.

"I'm leaving," he threatened, completely prepared for her to stay behind, like a sane person would.

"I know a great boutique not far from here where we can get what we need. Judging by that invitation, it looks rustic chic. We'll have to keep that in mind when shopping." Holly hopped to her feet and waited for him to head toward the door.

Was she actually going to come with him?

"Last chance to back out," Nolan offered. She sidled up next to him, a bounce in her step.

"Last chance to uninvite me," she smiled, looking up at him from under her dark lashes.

"I never technically invited you," he corrected. "So how could I uninvite you?"

"You're right," she agreed, pulling her hat back down on her head as they stepped into the cold air. "I guess you can't."

Chapter Two

WHEN HOLLY WOKE up that morning she had a feeling her life was about to change. No. She knew better than that. Feelings and hope didn't get you anywhere. When Holly woke up, she *decided* her life would change.

Now here she was, a brand new designer dress packaged perfectly in the box behind her, as the car drove toward a luxurious ski resort in Vermont. She'd managed to become the passenger in a stranger's car, and that was perfectly fine with her. Maybe it was because he was gorgeous. Or maybe because his eyes were kind and his smile coy in that damaged kind of way. Holly was a sucker for an underdog and Nolan had that look about him.

"I feel like I should have seen your dress before we left," Nolan said, sounding nervous. "You're a bit of a wild card, and I need to not screw this up for my sister."

"The dress is perfect. It matches what I picked out for you, and it's all exactly suited for the event the way it's described on the invitation. I promise." Every girl wanted a bit of a fairy tale. Even Holly wasn't immune to that fantasy. Nolan was the kind of prince you wanted to spin you around the dance floor. Tall. Handsome. A smile punctuated with dimples.

"I'm not sure why your promises are supposed to mean anything since we're strangers." Nolan's grip on the steering wheel was tight, either because of unease about her presence or the black ice the radio kept warning about.

"You just bought me a five-thousand-dollar designer dress. I don't think we can still be considered strangers." The line of trees on the highway was bare, their leaves all blown away by the last blizzard. It had been a winter of record snowfall, and no one knew that better than Holly, since she constantly felt like she was outrunning the cold.

"I feel like I need to tell you something," Nolan said, clearing his throat. "For the sake of full disclosure."

"Okaaay," Holly replied tentatively, drawing the word out. The hair on the back of her neck stood up, unsure of what he might have to say. This whole idea of changing her life by force was suddenly feeling too spontaneous. But in order to make a change, you have to change what you do.

"I'm not sure if you came because you're under the impression I'm rich, but it feels unfair to lead you on. I'm not." His shoulders slumped as he tried to let her down easy.

Holly laughed the same way she had when he warned he could be a serial killer. "I know you aren't rich."

"Well, I . . . uh," he stuttered. "What do you mean by that? I could be wealthy. I'm just letting you know I'm not."

"It's obvious you're not." Holly didn't intend to insult him, but it was clear she had.

"How exactly is it so obvious?" he asked, wounded by

her words.

"It's not you or anything you're doing really. It's also not a bad thing in my opinion," she corrected quickly. "I'm just a really good read of people. My mother was a fortunate teller." Holly raised her hand up to stop herself. "No. My mother worked as fortune-teller. It was all smoke and mirrors. She couldn't see the future. What she could do was read body language and situations. Looking for the clues they were begging her to find."

"What is your body language clue finder telling you about me? This coat's not cheap you know. Maybe you misread me."

"It's not cheap," she agreed, nodding feverishly. "I think it's about what, twenty-five hundred dollars for that blazer?"

"It is?" Nolan asked, running a hand across the fabric and raising his brows in surprise. "It was a gift from my sister."

"Do you know who Dominic Corisi is?" Holly asked, and assuming he didn't she continued. "He's a very wealthy businessman and popular in the circle of billionaires. I saw him with his wife in some magazine not long ago, and he was wearing that blazer. The difference is he was wearing it the right way."

"What's the right way to wear it?" Nolan asked, still sounding insulted.

"It's meant to be worn buttoned up to here," she said gesturing to a point on his muscular chest. "And you wouldn't wear a T-shirt like that under it. You wouldn't leave it wide open, just hanging off of you."

Nolan was at least half smiling now. "Maybe I'm wearing it ironically. People could think I'm so rich that I do what I want."

"No. When rich people do something ironically it still costs them a fortune. At first glance it would look like they weren't trying, but look close and you can see that's not the case," she explained apologetically.

"It's just clothes. You can't judge everyone by their clothes," he said, shaking his head as though her logic was flawed.

"What about that hideous bag back there?" Holly asked, gesturing toward the run-down suitcase Nolan was lugging around.

"Maybe it has sentimental value. It means something to me. Rich people can have sentimental things, can't they?"

"You're right," she conceded, but mostly because she knew how much more ammunition she had for this fight. "Do you have any sentimental ties to your text books?"

"No." He raised a questioning eyebrow.

"They're secondhand, right? Worn-out covers, folded over pages, mismatched notes in all the columns."

"Uh . . . yeah. Whatever, this is dumb."

"Don't misunderstand what I'm saying," Holly said quickly. "There's nothing wrong with not being rich. I wasn't totally sure at first. You were right, the jacket threw me off. At the time I thought it was one of two things."

"I'm afraid to ask," he groaned.

"The first would be," she started, launching right in to her explanation before he could invite her to, "you could have been a male gigolo, and you're so good at your job your clients shower you with expensive gifts."

He laughed, his ears perking up as his cheeks rose in a large smile. "But now you're sure that's not the case?" he asked.

"Only because you told me it was a gift from your sister," she said, letting him off the hook. "So I figure, it's family money, her family not yours."

"Exactly," Nolan answered, suddenly deflating. "My sister married this billionaire oil guy. He has a big empire. Everything's changing."

"Things have a habit of doing that," Holly said, equally as melancholy as she agreed with his point. Change had never seemed to be in her favor either. "Is he not good to her?"

"He is. Libby had plenty of jerk boyfriends before James came along. She's happy now, I can tell." He rolled the stress out of his neck and drew in a deep breath.

"That's good. I'm sure she's well taken care of."

"She is. And no one deserves it more," he grunted, seeming mad at himself. "I'm not unhappy for her. I'm just not sure where I fit into it all. The house we grew up in is empty. She's not there anymore. She was always there. Now she's in this penthouse apartment. Libby wants me to tour West Oil and probably work there. I don't want any of that. There's some history there, and I'm not quite as over it as Libby is."

"What kind of history?" Holly asked, turning in her seat to get a better look at the pained expression on his face.

"My father worked for West Oil, and he died on the job.

They didn't do right by him," Nolan explained.

"I'm so sorry," Holly offered, raising a hand up to his shoulder and squeezing down on the tight muscle. His body responded to her touch in a primal way, a deep drawing in of his breath, a tightening of his jaw. The car was brimming with sexual tension and if she thought it was one sided, she could tell now she was wrong.

"It's history now. Libby's moved past it, so I should be able to. She swears James is nothing like that, and he's running the company completely opposite from how they did when my father died. He wasn't even there at the time."

"That's tough," she said, thinking it all over. "But you're going tonight. You'll go to the party and represent them while giving out a big giant check. That's kind of cool right?"

"Yeah," he shrugged indifferently.

"Hey, I have an idea. Why don't we forget all the drama and just make the next forty-eight hours complete fun? We've got your sister's bottomless credit card, which she clearly wants you to use to have a good time. We've got skiing."

"I'm from Texas, and I'm poor," Nolan replied, seeming unimpressed by her attempts. "I don't know how to ski."

"It's easy," she said, waving off his objections. "You'll pick it right up."

"Really?" he asked, sounding surprised.

"No," she said, pursing her lips thoughtfully. "You'll probably get hurt. But there's a nice lodge and fireplace. Probably a hot tub. What if we just make the next forty-eight hours awesome?"

"You're awfully cheery and optimistic. You know a lot about fashion and money. Should I have been spending my time trying to figure out if you're rich rather than telling you I wasn't?" He glanced at her playfully, only half paying attention to the road.

"There are far better ways a couple of kids like us could spend our time," she said biting down on her lip playfully.

"Yeah," he asked, raising his brows up, challenging her to elaborate.

"I will fit right in tonight," Holly said confidently. She knew she hadn't given him what he wanted, but that was all part of the game. "But not because I'm some rich snob. It'll be because I'm really good at fitting in."

"Well, I'm not," Nolan replied. "They'll spot me from a mile away."

"I can help you with that. Just put your arm around me, and I'll make you look good."

"I don't doubt that," he said, his lips rising in a smile. Her cheeks grew hot with his sudden flattery, and she turned and watched the trees quickly passing by.

Nolan was a good-looking guy. His hair was light, cut short on the side but a little shaggy on top. It was an edgy style, pushed to one side. He had a baby face but was filled out enough to know he was all man. His shoulders were wide under that expensive jacket, and he would be even better looking in his crisp well-fitting tux. Being on his arm tonight would be no chore for her.

"So is it a deal?" she asked, nudging him with her elbow. "Are we going to make this awesome?"

"Awesome? Are we twelve?" he teased.

"Stop stalling and just answer the question. We could have the best time of our lives."

"I don't know anything about your life," he said, sounding too serious suddenly.

"I'm trying to keep an air of mystery. Don't ruin that. It's part of the fun. Just know that when trying to have the best time of my life, the bar isn't set too high."

This weekend could change her life. New people. New place. New opportunity. It would forcibly pull her out of the rut she was living in. It was time.

"Soooo?" she asked, extending the word for effect. "Are you committing to this?"

"I . . . yes. I'm going to forget everything that sucks right now and go to this party. I'm going to chat and eat tiny little gourmet food that doesn't fill me up while I act like I belong there."

"You don't have to belong at the party," she said, returning again to her vigilant watch of the passing trees. "You'll look like you belong with me."

Chapter Three

I T WAS STARTING to become a trend for Holly to have been right. Nolan hadn't been sure leaving his car behind and swapping it for this luxury rental was necessary. But as he pulled up the long, winding, overgrown road toward the ski resort he could tell she knew what she was doing. Besides the fact that the car was amazing and drove like it had the engine of a rocket ship, it blended in far better here than his reliable blue sedan. He probably would have had to park around back with the kitchen staff if she hadn't forced the upgrade.

"Pull in there," Holly instructed, pointing to the covered area in front of the main building.

Nolan reached for his car door after putting it in park but Holly touched his arm gently, leaning in to kiss his cheek. The act shocked him as her sparkled lip gloss left behind a fruity scent as she whispered, "Give him a second, he'll get your door." She gestured to the well-dressed man at Nolan's window. His red hair was gelled over into place and his cheeks were dotted with freckles.

"Good day sir, are you checking in?" he asked in a formal tone. The white gloves and long tails on his black coat made all of this seem over the top to Nolan.

"Yes," he replied as he hopped out of the car.

"And your names?" the man asked, rounding the car to open the door for Holly.

"I'm Nolan Saint-Jane. James and Libby West were unable to make it because of weather. James is my brother-in-law, and he was scheduled to present a donation to the charity tonight. I'll be standing in for him." The long-winded explanation still felt clunky, but Nolan knew he'd probably have to repeat it a thousand times tonight when everyone in the room wanted to know how exactly he'd managed to get an invite.

"Great, I'm Eric. We've had quite a few people unable to arrive due to weather. It's even impacted the staff. You're lucky you made it at all. They cleared the roads a bit but we're expecting even more snow." Eric's voice was fake and cheery but it was clear that was all part of his job.

"If you're going to get snowed in," Holly sang in a chipper tone, "I can't think of a better place."

"On that we can agree," Eric said as he hustled to the back of the car. "I'll bring in your luggage."

Nolan hadn't listened to Holly's suggestion about ditching his old suitcase. It had belonged to his father and before that his grandfather. It was in rough shape but Nolan could still remember the way his father would pack it up and stick it by the door the night before he headed out to a rig on the ocean. Nolan would sneak downstairs when everyone was asleep and tuck some small trinket in the bag for his father. The day he died on the rig someone from West Oil had brought the bag back, and since that day Nolan kept it close to him.

"Oh you didn't," Holly said in an exaggerated way. "I told him to leave that hideous bag at home. I don't care that it's a collectable or cost a small fortune, it belongs in the trash." She rolled her eyes playfully and gave Eric a knowing look as the ugly bag made its appearance. "I question his taste," she added.

"I don't know about that," Eric chuckled. "With a woman like you on his arm I'd have a hard time believing he had bad taste."

"Watch out for this one," Holly joked. "He's a charmer."

Eric escorted them in the main entrance of the lobby just a few steps in front of them.

"Damn," Nolan breathed out, his head on a swivel as he took in every intricate detail of the main lobby. The exposed wood beams looked hand carved and massive, the architecture was shockingly beautiful and well thought out.

"Poker face, kid," Holly whispered. "Wealthy people aren't impressed by anything."

"That sounds awful," Nolan scoffed, snapping his jaw shut and painting his face with intentional indifference to it all. "Who wants to live a life where nothing impresses them?" he whispered, but Holly had no time to answer.

The tall husky man behind the check-in station was greeting them loudly. His smile showed unnaturally white teeth and took up most of his rosy plump face. "Welcome," he boomed in a jolly tone. "You must be Nolan Saint-Jane. James West called earlier and let me know you were joining us for the event in his place."

"He's terribly sorry to be missing it," Holly assured him. "I'm Holly McNamara. Thank you for accommodating us in place of the Wests."

"It's our pleasure. I'm Toby. I'll be right here for the rest of the day and straight through the event tonight."

"That's quite a shift," Nolan cut in, wondering what kind of establishment required that sort of insane grind from their staff.

"The weather has been a mess. You two snuck in during a break in the ice storm, but the roads have been closed more than they've been open. Most of our staff has been detained. I live in a complex at the base of the mountain, so I was able to come in and volunteered to stay."

"I hope you get a chance to get a break and maybe come enjoy the event," Nolan said, still unsatisfied that Toby would be stuck behind this desk for hours to come.

"Thank you, sir." Toby grinned in a way that let Nolan know there was no way in hell he'd be allowed in at the event, but it was a nice offer. "Mr. West has made sure all the special accommodations he had planned for him and his wife have been transferred to you. The room you are in faces the mountain and the view is stunning. The deck has a private hot tub and all the ski equipment you could need has been set aside for you both. I could go through the whole list of upgrades if you like, such as champagne in the room, the chocolate-covered strawberries being delivered."

"No need," Nolan said, clearing his throat.

"We'll just be surprised," Holly chirped, touching Nolan's arm intimately.

"And we just have the one room?" Nolan asked, looking down at Holly, not sure she'd really thought this adventure through.

"Um," Toby said, trying to decipher the question. "We could maybe get you a second room. There have been a lot of cancelations, but I know many people are still trying to get here."

"He's being silly," Holly dismissed with a wave of her hand. "He thinks I need my own room just to get dressed and ready for the event. All the primping and curling, he never gets a moment in the bathroom himself. But we'll make do."

"Are you sure?" Nolan asked, now staring down at Holly seriously. She could push the subject if she didn't want to be stuck in a romantic suite with a stranger for the night. He had no problem thinking of ways to make the room work for both of them, but he didn't want her to feel trapped.

"Positive," she blushed a bit but quickly righted herself. "We'll hardly be in the room at all anyway."

"Oh yes," Toby said as though he'd just remembered something, "Sophie Barrington has been delayed as well. It doesn't look like she'll be able to make it herself. She's asked that I tell all the guests attending the party that for every kiss at midnight one of the homes being built for a returning veteran will be fully furnished."

"Every kiss?" Nolan asked, glaring at Toby to ensure he was telling the truth.

"Yes, apparently she's very creative in her fundraising

efforts."

"She sounds fun," Holly laughed as Toby handed Nolan the room key. "What a wonderful charity. I'm glad we were able to make it out on such short notice."

"And we are so glad to have you. Will you be skiing? Can I have an instructor meet with you on the slopes this afternoon? Or perhaps you'd like to have a bite to eat?"

"We are hungry," Nolan said, the idea of skiing making him want to vomit. Holly had already tried to sell him on how wonderful it was, but he'd decided there was no way he was even trying. The last thing he could afford right now was a broken leg that kept him from returning to his internship.

"Let me call the kitchen and see how things are going. It's been a bit chaotic back there with a lack of staff." Toby picked up the phone and in a hushed tone tried to get a handle on the situation.

A woman next to them with a tall fur hat and matching shoulder shrug leaned in and whispered something that sounded scandalous. "I heard a couple days ago they were serving canned soup and grilled cheese. I'm not sure Sophie picked the right place for her event."

Nolan nodded as though he might agree or at least that he'd heard, and it was enough to appease her. The fur-clad woman shook her head in further disgust and shuffled away.

"I love grilled cheese," Nolan whispered to Holly. "I could go for one right now."

"Shh," she scolded, nudging him with her elbow. "You're making this very hard. I can't keep classing you up if you say stuff like that."

"Great news," Toby proclaimed in excitement. "Our

head chef is back in the kitchen, and he's whipping up some impressive delicacies as we speak."

"Yum. I hope it's something I've never heard of before," he groaned as they walked away.

"That's probably a pretty long list," Holly joked. "Let's get that hideous bag in the room and then grab something to eat. If we're fast we can even ski a bit before we have to start getting dressed for the event."

"I'm not skiing," Nolan said with such finality Holly didn't seem to have an argument to give back to him.

"Really? We're going to be out here in this beautiful place, and you won't even try it?"

"Where did you learn to ski?" he asked accusingly. "I still don't know a damn thing about you. Clearly you come from money the way you're right at home here."

"I learned to ski on the Swiss Alps while away at boarding school. My parents were miserly old monsters who didn't want me."

"Oh," Nolan said as the elevator doors popped open. "I'm sorry."

"I'm kidding," she laughed. "I went to a winter camp a couple years in a row growing up. I'm a quick learner, and I loved it. But I haven't been skiing in a while. You do know this is a ski lodge right? There will be next to nothing to do if we don't ski."

"For the average person maybe," Nolan shrugged coolly. "But do you know who else doesn't ski? James and Libby West. That means he had plenty planned for them to do, and we get to take full advantage of it now."

Chapter Four

"NEVER MIND," NOLAN said as he stood in the doorway of the suite. "Forget what I said about taking full advantage of everything James had planned."

"It looks like a very classy porn is about to be shot in here," Holly said, folding her arms over herself awkwardly.

The blackout curtains were pulled completely shut, the only light in the room coming from the hundred or so flickering candles. Something that was surely against the fire code for a hotel like this, but Nolan assumed money could make those pesky rules go away. A path of rose petals was framed by candles on either side that led to a plush massage table. Near it was a desk full of sensual message lotions, melted wax, and hot stones. The music playing was soft and sexy and seemed to be coming from all directions in the room.

The tub was in the corner of the room on a platform. Steam was billowing up from the cloud of bubbles as though it had just been filled moments before they entered the room. Champagne chilled in a bucket on the table with a tray of exotic fruits laid out around a bowl of dark chocolate, melted by a small tea light below it.

A few logs in the roaring fireplace settled, crackling and sparking. The mantel was adorned with multiple bouquets of red roses. No expense had been spared, no corner of the room had been left untouched by romance.

"So skiing?" Nolan asked, not able to lock eyes with Holly as he dropped his bag down on the bed.

"Are you kidding me?" Holly asked, walking through the room like it was heaven on earth. "I am getting in that bath. Then I'm having a massage. I'm going to devour that fruit. Do you know how expensive that particular bottle of champagne is? This is a once in a lifetime opportunity. I'm not wasting it."

"Where am I supposed to be while you're in the tub? It's right there." He gestured toward the corner of the room where steam still billowed up from the bubbles. He knew where he wanted to be while Holly was soaking deep in the water. Right next to her.

"Oh," she said as though she'd just remembered the logistics of it all. "Okay, forget the bath. I brought a swim suit; I'll just do the hot tub. And the champagne," she said as she swiped it out of the ice bucket. "Oh my gosh, they have their names engraved on the bucket. It actually says *James and Libby West.* How rich is this guy?"

"Apparently very." Nolan grimaced. "The sheets have their initials embroidered on them. This is crazy. We don't belong in this room."

"Is it because of your inferiority complex about your socioeconomic standing or the fact that this is basically a sex den set up for your sister and her husband?" Holly had a wry challenging smirk as she popped the cork on the bottle.

"Both?" Nolan was completely unsure what part of this room was bothering him more.

"I can understand how you're feeling," Holly said seriously, filling her champagne flute and dipping a strawberry in the chocolate. "Maybe you can go back to the front desk and ask Toby for that second room. I'd be happy to struggle through staying in this one."

"Struggle?" Nolan laughed. "Somehow I think you'd manage."

"Or," she said, nibbling seductively on the strawberry, "we could both find a way to make this terrible room bearable." Before he could answer Holly was bending down, her luscious curves aimed directly at him. "Shrimp. The fridge is loaded with shrimp and lobster claws. You said you were hungry, right?"

He was starving, in more ways than one. Nolan had been so caught up in being angry at the world, he'd forgotten what it was like to bask in the glow of a gorgeous woman. A woman like Holly who buzzed with energy and excitement. "I'm hungry," he said, his voice laced with lust he tried to rein in. But it was too late. The shocked expression she shot back made it clear she'd interpreted his meaning.

"Um," she said, swallowing hard and biting at her lip. "Did you bring a bathing suit for the hot tub?"

He shook his head no, moving in closer to her but sidestepping suddenly to grab a piece of fruit. Nolan could see she was holding her breath, anticipating his next move.

"You sure you want to stay in this room?" he asked, as though he were now giving her one more chance to separate herself from this adventure.

"Mhm," she hummed, nodding her reply. "And you do too?"

"Yes," he smiled, pulling the bottle of champagne from her hand and filling his own glass. "What the hell, we only live once right?"

"Right," she agreed, her shoulders finally relaxing some as he clinked his flute against hers. Nolan wouldn't close in on her right now even though he was sure he could. He was positive her body would respond to his touch, and they could spend the next few hours before the party in a haze of pleasure and indulgence. But Holly had still revealed so little about herself and he knew the liability that posed for the evening. He needed to know who she was, why she'd gotten in the car with him, and what her angle was. Then, he'd have every inch of her.

Chapter Five

"DARN," HOLLY MURMURED as she hung up the phone in the room.

"What could possibly be wrong?" Nolan asked as he dipped the plump lobster meat in the melted butter.

"Because of the storm the spa is understaffed and they don't have anyone to come do an in-room massage. What a waste of all this ambiance and product. She lifted a few of the bottles and opened their tops, breathing in their earthy aromas.

The drinking, eating, and relaxing had created a comfortable quiet in the room that Holly was basking in. She rarely got to experience any type of indulgence or serenity these days. But that was not the only thing in the room growing.

It could perhaps be blamed on the ambiance, the flickering candlelight, or crackling fire, but either way it couldn't be ignored. Whatever spell these artfully selected decorations were meant to cast, it was working. Holly could feel herself drawn to Nolan in a primal way.

As he leaned back, stretching and grunting, her eyes fixed

on his biceps that bulged out from his T-shirt.

"Why aren't you sitting down?" Nolan asked, eyeing her curiously. "You've been pacing for the last fifteen minutes. Should we get in the hot tub?"

She rounded the couch and flopped down next to him. "Tell me something real about yourself," she insisted, raking her eyes over his surprised face.

"Why? You haven't told me anything about you."

"I will," she said, "but you go first." She wasn't sure why this felt so urgent. Maybe she needed to hear his flaws or his arrogance so she could tamp down these feelings of desire. Surely he'd say something stupid enough to turn her off. Men could always be counted on for that.

"Fine," he said, tossing his hands up. "This Christmas I was completely alone. I spent the entire twenty-four hours without seeing another living soul. I don't know now if it's the way I wanted it or if that's just how it happened. Is that real enough for you?"

"And you were supposed to see your sister tomorrow for New Year's Day? That fell through. That must have been hard."

"Then you walked in," he grinned, eyeing her intensely. "And a very boring evening of ringing in the new year is turning into . . ." His words trailed off as he leaned in. It was up to Holly now to pull away. She'd have to be the one to tell him the kiss wasn't what she wanted. But that lie felt too hard to speak as he moved in closer.

Laced with champagne and chocolate, their lips collided with hungry passion. She'd been living outside of herself, in such a fake existence for so long, she'd nearly forgotten what it felt like to truly want someone so desperately.

Nolan pulled her onto his lap, never breaking the kiss. Holly worried her thudding heart could be heard over the quiet music still echoing through the room. Her desire for him was almost unbearable as she clutched at his shirt, ran a hand up his back, and finally to his hair.

"Wait," he breathed out, pulling back suddenly. "You were supposed to tell me something real. That was the deal."

"Now?" she asked incredulously, their lips just centimeters from each other. "You can't think of anything better we could do?"

"I can think of a thousand things I'd like to do with you right now," he said, leaning in and nipping at her neck. His lips were smeared with her gloss and his eyes were burning with a lusty flame. "But a deal is a deal. Tell me something, Holly." One hand was brushing her hair back while the other held her tight on top of him. "Why is it so hard for you to answer my questions?"

"Because for some reason, unlike how I feel about most people, I don't want to lie to you."

"So don't," he urged, leaning in for another kiss, this one abbreviated and just a tease.

"My family was very wealthy," she started, dropping her head down to Nolan's shoulder mostly to avoid having to look him in the face as she admitted part of her past. "They imported furniture from Europe and sold it locally. But someone duped my father and tricked him into making a bad investment. Some kind of Ponzi scheme and it ruined him. It ruined all of us."

"Wealth isn't everything," Nolan reminded her, his soft lips breaking into an empathetic smile. "I'm poor."

"And miserable," she countered.

"Not at the moment. Right at this moment I am far from miserable." He laced his fingers to hers and leaned in again. She could feel his hard excitement as she shifted her weight, and her hunger for him built again.

"Take me, Nolan," she whispered, her hand caught up in his hair, pulling him forcefully back into the kiss. "Forget everything else. Just right now, right now this is all that matters."

He lifted her up behind the knees and stood effortlessly. His kisses moved down her neck as he made his way for the bed. "I'm not sure I want to have you in a bed branded with my brother-in-law's name."

Nolan looked around for a better solution. "How private do you think that deck is?"

"I think the better question is how shy are you?" She could feel her body tingling with desire, the anticipation of his hands on her.

"It's cold," he reminded her. "It's freezing out."

"I'm game," she said, cocking an eyebrow up at him. "The hot tub will warm us up."

He moved toward the sliding door of the deck and opened it. A cold blast of air sent her body into a shiver, making their grip on each other more frantic. Painfully tight. Powerful. There was a dusting of wind-blown snow on the deck.

"Ever have sex in a hot tub?" Nolan asked, lowering Holly to her feet as they began frantically pulling at their clothes, fighting off shivers.

They both climbed the steps and sank into the invigorating heated water. At first the warmth against their cold skin stung like needles but it soon melted into an overwhelming complete comfort.

Holly pressed her back against a pulsing jet, the vibration pulsing through her whole body.

"You're too far away," Nolan growled, easily scooping her up and pulling her close. This wasn't something she'd done before, but tonight the light flakes of snow landing in their hair as they gazed into each other's eyes made her feel like trying something new. Nolan was the kind of man you could hand yourself over to; hot tub, back seat of the car, or a rooftop, it wouldn't matter, he'd make sure you got exactly what you needed. Holly could tell that about him.

"I never answered the question before," she said, a little bashful as the bubbling water swirled around her naked body. "I've never had sex in a hot tub before."

"I'm almost afraid to show you how good it can be. You'll be ruined for having it anywhere else. There's just something about the heat, the jets, and being outside that makes it so damn good. I dated a girl who had one. It was a fun summer."

"You'll have to show me," she purred, letting him guide her body. Nolan pulled her arms around his neck and her legs over him. Straddling there above him she had the benefit of perspective. She was able to hold on tight and also look out over the amazing scenery around them.

His mouth devoured her breasts, biting and licking, alternating in a way that had her back arching away then pressing forward, begging for more. When he slid inside her, his firmness filled her so deeply she gasped, clinging instantly to his shoulders.

"Did I hurt you?" Nolan asked, looking concerned. "Do you want to stop?"

"Don't you dare," she said through broken breath as she began riding him, slowly at first then faster, the water making her feel nearly weightless as she moved. Their eyes locked on each other, his face overtaken by the pleasure surging through him.

Nolan's hand clamped down on her hips and moved her at the perfect rhythm as she rocked back and forth, her own burst of pleasure within reach.

Before she could fully climax he laughed, and whispered, "Not yet." In one fluid move he lifted her off him and turned her quickly away. Her back to him, bent over the side of the tub, he introduced her to the magic that was the powerful jet stream.

Aligning her perfectly, her pleasure spot bursting to life, he slid inside her again. This time the gasp was punctuated by a scream of his name. "Nolan, yes! Don't stop."

Whatever pleasure she thought she was about to feel in their last position was a far-off memory compared to the complete overload pummeling her body.

Her chest was above the water, frigid air making her skin tingle and her peaks tightened as Nolan pinched with impeccable pressure. "Harder," she begged, arching her body to give him every bit of herself she could.

"Holly," he breathed her name through her hair, his lips perched over her ear, and she knew he was about to explode just as she was. The jet pulsed, he drove harder within her, and his tantalizing squeezes sent shock waves through her until finally everything burst to life. The snow covered pines, the peaks of the mountains, the sun fading lower in the sky, she was one with it all. She was as big as each of them, and just for a moment as powerful and important. Because from this man she could elicit the most primal pleasure and most intimate connection.

They collapsed on top of each other, nearly going under, before Nolan gathered himself and kept her afloat.

"You were right," she breathed against his lips as she kissed him softly. "That was amazing. You know your stuff."

"No," he said, shaking his head and looking shocked by her. "It's never been like that before. No one has ever been anything like you."

She laid her head against his chest, the water lapping at her chin as she listened to his heart thundering. The flakes of snow grew larger, landing on her lashes and then melting away.

"You make me believe that Nolan. You have a look about you, that you couldn't lie about something like that even if you wanted to."

"Believe it, Holly. Believe every other person is just a way to stay busy until a man like me has the good fortune of meeting you. Believe it because it's true. Not just here in the hot tub either. Life is this thing we do; you make me feel like it's something I can't wait to keep doing."

Chapter Six

THE LAVISH COTTON robes were like wrapping up in a cloud. Nolan put a few more logs on the fire and held Holly tight in his arms as they sat on the plush carpet warming their spent bodies.

"We have to start getting ready for the party," Holly whispered, her body tucked perfectly against his. The reluctance in her voice assured him that she felt the same desire to stay put. She was quickly becoming the small light breaking through the clouds that had been chasing him around.

He pushed her hair off her neck and kissed the silky skin again. "Maybe we should just stay here," Nolan suggested, moving a hand down her body and parting her legs again.

"You promised your sister," she reminded him, though her head kicked back and her legs didn't fight against his motion to part them.

"She promised she'd see me tomorrow. Things don't always work out the way we think. I'd much rather spend the night right here. Finding a hundred new ways to make you shake and scream my name again."

Holly moaned but he could feel her fighting the urge to turn and straddle him. "You have control you know," she said, trying to keep her voice level and unaffected by the heat rising through her body.

"Perfect," he hissed in her ear. "I like being in control."

"That's not what I mean," she purred. "When this is all over you can get in your car and drive to Texas. Maybe it's time for you to meet your sister where she is. Maybe it's time you walk into the life she's living rather than waiting for her to come to you. Put on a Santa hat, load the car with wrapped presents, and go redo Christmas the way it should have been. You have control."

"And would you get in the car for that road trip too?" he asked in a whisper, his lips still pressed to her ear.

"You wouldn't want that," she answered in a breathy nervous laugh. "You're getting the wrong impression of me. I'm the kind of girl you run away with for the weekend. Nothing more."

"So no?" he asked, leaning forward to look at her expression. "If I asked you to get in the car tomorrow and drive to Texas with me you'd say no?"

"I . . . well," she stuttered out. "Why would you want that?"

"You're the first thing in a long time that's made sense to me. You're the first thing that feels good."

"It's a temporary feeling," she argued, her body getting rigid. "You'll figure things out; whatever I'm doing for you right now, you won't need anymore."

"Probably," he agreed. "I won't need you, but I'll still

want you."

"I'm not a good person Nolan," she admitted, pulling her robe tighter as she stood. "We should get ready for the party. You made a commitment to your sister, and I know you're going to keep it."

"How do you know that?"

"Because *you* are a good person. You keep your word. You worry about how people feel. You pay attention. You ask questions to try to figure out who I am."

"You're a good person too, Holly. I wouldn't even be considering going to Texas if it wasn't for you. You're right. It's time for me to meet my sister where she is. A good person knows that."

"No," she laughed. "A smart person knows that. A good person does it. I've missed all the opportunities to do that in my own life."

"Tell me," Nolan pleaded, reaching a hand up and touching Holly's fingertips as she walked away.

"I'm going to take a shower and get ready," she said flatly, unable to look at him. "You're going to do great tonight. Libby is going to be proud she asked you to represent her and James."

When the bathroom door closed Nolan sat staring at the fire, trying to make sense of the disjointed puzzle that was Holly and her explanations. The only thing that did resonate with him was the pain in her eyes that he recognized, having walked around with that heaviness himself.

The ringing room phone startled him and he considered ignoring it, except that he remembered his cell phone was dead, and he hadn't bothered to charge it, too busy indulging in Holly to care.

Nolan rose and grabbed the phone, ready to tell whoever it was to go to hell. He was in no mood for an event update or a dinner reminder.

"What?" he barked.

"You're starting to sound like me," James said coolly. "I'm afraid what I'm calling for isn't going to put you in any better mood."

"James," Nolan said, a bit of apology in his voice. The man had done a lot for him, and he forced himself to remember that.

"I know you're pissed your sister isn't there to spend the day with you tomorrow. I get how much shit has changed and you keep getting the raw end of the deal. I wanted you to know this coming year Libby and I are going to make sure we coordinate better and have more time with you. Plus you know there is a job here at West Oil any time you want it."

"Okay," Nolan said, his head still in a fog from great sex and expensive champagne, mixed with the emotions Holly's words had stirred in him.

"That's not why I was calling," James said, seeming uncomfortable having to extend the niceties required of family. "I got a call from Russell Spicer. He saw you checking in this morning with your date."

"Holly," Nolan said, feeling defensive. "What about her?"

"Russell knows her. Well, he knows of her. She is a con artist. She has a reputation for taking advantage of very wealthy people and then bailing."

"Are you saying she's a criminal?" Nolan asked, looking over at the bathroom and keeping his voice low.

"She has a record," James said. "But no open warrants or anything. Apparently she's found ways now to make sure no one presses charges against her. Probably blackmail and extortion to keep people from turning her in. You can't take her to the party tonight."

"This doesn't make sense," Nolan said, trying to imagine how Holly could be capable of what James was describing. "What exactly has she done?"

"I don't know the details. I just know she's trouble. She can't be downstairs treading on my good reputation to find her next mark. I don't need her associated with our family in any way. Do you understand?"

"I, I . . ." Nolan stuttered out, far from understanding anything James was saying. "I think it's a mistaken identity or something."

"What did she tell you she does for a living? What do you know about her?" James asked arrogantly. "It doesn't matter really. It would have all been a lie. Just tell me you won't take her to the party. If people ask, tell them your date is sick, resting in the room. Then in the morning if the roads are safe to pass, get her the hell out of there."

"But," Nolan said, his eyes still fixed on the bathroom.

"No," James boomed. "This is not negotiable. I get that you're pissed at me or the situation, but this is bigger than any problems between us. This is business. She doesn't go downstairs."

"Okay," Nolan said. "I've got to get ready. Tell Libby I'll call her tomorrow."

"I'm sorry kid," James said, the bite gone from his voice now. "I'm sure you're having a good time. She probably seems like a nice girl. It's part of her game."

"Happy New Year," Nolan said, dropping the phone down and clicking the line dead.

Holly emerged from the bathroom with a towel twisted up in her hair and her robe pulled tightly. "Who was that?" she asked, her cheeks pink from the heat of the steaming shower.

"The front desk," Nolan lied. "Just reminding us we should be downstairs in an hour."

"I better hurry." She smiled. "Sorry I was being weird earlier. Let's just do what we said and make this an amazing night okay?"

"Yeah," he nodded, "it's going to be amazing."

Chapter Seven

THE TUX WAS tight around his muscles when he bent his arms, but Holly had assured him that it was fitted perfectly for him.

"Will you zip me?" Holly asked as she stepped out of the bathroom. His breath caught in his chest as the light over her head glowed down around her like an angel.

Holly's hair was curled into tight ringlets and pulled up and away from her face. Her makeup sparkled and shimmered, matching her vibrant smile. But what he couldn't seem to keep his eyes off of was her body, hugged perfectly in her dress. Strapless and gold, it looked as though it had been designed with her shoulders and long neck in mind. Tight against her chest and flat stomach, it grew full at her waist. Nolan was sure there were names for the type of the dress, the style, but all he could call it was stunning. Her heels matched and were at least three inches high, peeking out from the bottom of the dress.

"I've never seen anything like that before," he said sheepishly. "You were made for tonight."

"You look great too," she complimented, gesturing to his

tuxedo. "We'll make a very convincing couple."

There was still an ache, a hesitation in her voice that tugged at him. James's words were ringing in his ears, but standing in front of Holly, he had to believe there was more to the story. "I need you to tell me something before we go downstairs. I need you to be perfectly honest with me."

"Nolan," she said, furrowing her brows and dropping her eyes down to the ground in what he now read as guilt.

"Please," he said, cutting the distance between them and tipping her chin back up where it belonged, their eyes locked on each other. He'd know now if it were the truth. "Why did you get in the car with me?"

She sucked her lip in and nibbled on it as she seemed to be either mustering the courage or conjuring up a story, he couldn't yet tell. "I needed a break," she whispered, her voice growing some as she spoke. "Haven't you ever just been so tired of yourself, of who you are, that you need a break? I couldn't spend another minute where I was, being who I was. Getting in the car with you, I was running away from that."

His eyes raked over her face, watching every flutter of her eyelids, the way her brows knit together with emotion.

"Okay," he said simply. Leaning down he brushed his lips against hers, his hand resting on her shimmering cheek. "Let's go downstairs."

"Are you sure you want me down there?" she asked, drawing in a deep breath. "You'll do a great job; you don't need me."

"You're right about that," he said, his thumb sweeping across her plump lips. "I don't need you. I want you with me."

Chapter Eight

THE LONG CURVED staircase they walked down was trimmed with pine, holly berries, and twinkling white lights. Just like the thoughtful detail that had been put into preparing their hotel room, the event venue had been equally prepared. The long tables were lined with flickering candles perched in glass pillars of varied heights. White orchids were laced into distressed wood that practically made a canopy over the length of the table. Everywhere Holly turned there was gold, glass, and wood perfectly paired and artfully assembled.

The room was alive with chatter and mingling guests. Sequined dresses caught the candlelight and looked like disco balls gliding around.

"This is amazing," she whispered, squeezing Nolan's arm. She'd been to equally exquisite events with plenty of rich people, but there was something about holding on to Nolan that made this one different. It was the look of awe in his eyes as he continued to carefully map out every inch of her and commit it to memory.

"Poker face," he reminded her, and she couldn't help but

laugh. "We rich people aren't impressed by anything."

"Then I must be poor as dirt," she said, resting her head on his shoulder, "because I'm impressed by you."

"Nolan," someone said as they planted a hearty slap on his back, sending Holly jumping forward. "You're James West's brother-in-law, right? He married your sister, that Lacey girl?" The man's breath was layered with the smell of stale cigar smoke and whiskey.

"My sister's name is Liberty," Nolan corrected, looking annoyed by the man. "And you are?"

"Russell," the man slurred. "A very good friend of James."

"Really?" Nolan asked, perfecting the look of being un-impressed. "He mentioned you earlier and didn't seem to have much to say about you. Didn't sound like a good friend to me."

The sloppy smile dropped from Russell's face as Holly tried to play catch-up and figure out why even-tempered Nolan was being so aggressive.

"This is your date?" Russell asked with a bite in his voice, leering at Holly, his eyes landing on the curve of her breasts as he licked his lips.

"Holly McNamara," she announced with a sweet smile, extending her hand, but Nolan spun her around before she could shake Russell's hand.

"Let's dance," Nolan asserted, beginning to step away from Russell.

"I've got a phone call to make anyway," Russell snarled, and it stopped Nolan in his tracks. He let Holly go and instead grabbed Russell's arm.

"I wouldn't make that call," he threatened, and Holly's heart was thudding nervously in her chest. What had she walked into? "If I were you, and I wanted to walk out of here tonight in one piece, I'd mind my damn business."

When Russell didn't answer Nolan tugged harder on his arm. "Are we clear?"

"You don't know who you're threatening here," Russell finally stuttered out through a look of sheer disbelief.

"Wrong," Nolan corrected. "I don't care. I'm not rich. I have no need for you at all. No power plays, no deals. I have nothing, which means I have nothing to lose. That makes me very dangerous." He released Russell's arm and straightened his bow tie as he looped his arm for Holly to take hold. "That dance?"

Holly tentatively followed him out on the floor. His arms were around her, his mouth hovering over her ear as the music played. "What the hell was that?" she asked, unable to dam the words up any longer.

"A troublemaker," Nolan answered dismissively.

"I didn't think you knew anyone here. What are you not telling me?" She pulled away slightly to get a better look at his face.

"It doesn't matter," he assured her. "Tonight is all that matters, right?"

"Right," she nodded, pained at the idea that tomorrow would be the end for them. Her screwed-up life would be waiting on the other side of the sunrise, and the prospect of a man like Nolan would be nothing but a memory. But that was how it had to be. A man like him, a good honest man who valued family, would never understand her and the things she'd done. "Just tonight."

Resting her head on his shoulder, she tried to fight the warm tears gathering in the corners of her eyes. His cologne was filling her nose, and she clutched at him, never wanting to let go. The hours ticked by too quickly for her liking.

When the music stopped, someone tapped Nolan on the shoulder and Holly held her breath, wondering what this new stranger might want from him. "Mr. Saint-Jane, it's time to present the check on behalf of the West family. Will you come with me?"

"Of course," Nolan said, finally releasing Holly and leaving her feeling completely exposed to the world, away from the shelter of his arms. When he disappeared into the crowd she tried to make her way off the dance floor that was clearing as the charity business began to take center stage.

Russell appeared out of nowhere, clamping down on her elbow. "Sneaky girl," he hissed. "You think you can come here and find a new person to destroy? I know your game."

"Let me go," she said, pulling her arm back.

"I don't know how you got that kid up there to ignore the warning I made sure he got about you, but no one else around here is going to fall for it. I'm going to make sure everyone knows who you are and your association with the West family."

The twinkling lights and flickering candles began to spin as her world was shoved off its axis. The thought of being recognized hadn't occurred to her. The idea that Nolan had been warned about who she was didn't register either. But the idea that her presence would hurt his family, would tarnish their reputation and possibly his relationship with them crushed her.

"Don't," she begged. "I'll go. Just don't say anything to anyone."

"What do I get?" he asked, closing in oppressively on her personal space. Trapped between the wall and his body, she felt a wave of panic set in. The only way out of this might be to make a scene, the one thing she didn't want to do, for Nolan's sake.

"On behalf of James West I'd like to present this check to the Barrington family. We are in awe of Sophie Barrington's selfless efforts to do more than her part in this world. James and Libby apologize for their absence tonight and wanted me to wish everyone a Happy New Year."

Nolan's voice was crisp and confident as it drew the eye of everyone in the room. She wished she could part the crowd and see him on the stage, the spotlight on him. "I'll go," she whispered, trying to move past Russell, but he held her in place.

A thunderous round of clapping began as Nolan finished his speech and Holly used the opportunity to break free. She kicked her knee up into Russell's groin and shoved past him as he bent in half from the pain.

"Don't you dare ruin this for him," she said as she fled out the large mahogany double doors that led to the lobby. She didn't have a plan but that had never stopped Holly before when it was time to run. She'd race to her room.

Change, gather her things, and be on the road before Nolan could realize she wasn't floating around the party looking for him.

Chapter Nine

NOLAN CIRCLED THE room twice, wondering where Holly had disappeared to. The room buzzed as plates began being served and people settled into their seats. Holly wasn't at their assigned table either. A prickly heat rose up his back as his eyes fixed on Russell.

The pudgy faced man was leaning in, grumbling some kind of drunken message to the man next to him. A hearty laugh boomed from the two of them, and Nolan heard him call out his words. "I tossed her the hell out of here."

Never in his life had Nolan wished to be two people more than right this minute. If he were capable of it, he'd split in half and leave a part of himself here to demolish Russell while the rest of him ran off to find Holly. He eyed Russell one more time before realizing the man wouldn't be that hard to find in the future if he wanted to hand out a beating. But Holly could be gone for good if he didn't catch her now.

Darting out the door of the event and back toward their room he fished out the key. If she was there, standing in their room, he wasn't sure he'd bother trying to talk to her.

He wasn't sure he'd be able to do much besides kiss her. Pushing his way in, it only took a moment to realize she wasn't. The beautiful dress hung in the doorway of the bathroom. Holly's bag was gone. The room was silent.

Remembering the car keys he'd tossed on the dresser he was certain he'd find they were gone. Of course she'd take the car. How else would she get down the mountain, especially in this weather?

His cash, the watch Libby had sent him for his birthday, and his expensive blazer were exactly where he'd left them. Anything of value a con artist would probably take was right where he'd left it. But the most important thing she hadn't taken were his car keys. Holly's only conceivable exit strategy.

Dialing her number he balled his hands into fists as it went straight to voice mail. The sensation of being choked started to overtake his body forcing him to start yanking at the tuxedo frantically, ripping seams and popping buttons, not caring how much it had cost. Slipping into his jeans, a T-shirt, and his winter coat, he headed toward the lobby.

Just as he'd said, Toby was still manning the front desk, busy on a call when Nolan rushed toward him.

"Toby," he asked breathlessly, "have you seen Holly?" Maybe it was the urgency in Nolan's face or the worry in his voice, but Toby quickly turned the call over to the person next to him.

"Is everything all right?" Toby asked in a hushed voice, looking nervous about upsetting other guests passing by.

"Have you seen Holly?" Nolan asked again, banging the

solid shining wood desk that separated him from Toby.

"She was just here a few minutes ago," Toby explained. "Is she all right?"

"What did you talk about? Tell me specifically what she said."

"Nothing really, we were just chatting. She asked if the roads were clear and if I was worried about getting back to my apartment tonight. Holly seemed concerned about me traveling the roads."

"What did you tell her?"

"That my roommate has a truck and we only have about two miles to drive. If the main road most guests take up here is too icy, we take the service truck road behind the hotel because it's shorter and not as steep."

"Can you walk it?" he asked, looking out the window at the huge white flakes coming down and coating every surface. "Where would it take her if she did?"

"You wouldn't want to," he said, twisting his face up in confusion. "It's dark now and the only things down there are a few apartment complexes, a really cruddy bar, and a little supermarket."

"A cab wouldn't come up here right now, right?"

"No, we've heard from the local transportation companies that they won't be coming up the mountain."

"But they'd make it to that area right? Where the apartments are?"

Toby shook his head, clearly trying to get what point Nolan was driving at. "A cab would be more likely to go to the apartment complexes than try to get up here."

"Did you see Holly leave?" he pressed.

"No, we were talking, and then she walked off that way," he said, pointing to the elevators.

"Are you talking about that woman a few minutes ago?" the girl next to Toby asked as she hung up the phone. Her hair was slicked back into a tight bun, accentuating her harsh and sharp features. "I saw her go out the side door."

"Did she have anything with her?" Nolan asked frantically.

"Just her bag on her shoulder. I thought it was strange but figured maybe she was just getting some air."

"Show me where the access road is," Nolan demanded, feeling ready to drag Toby out from behind the desk if he had to. Luckily Toby was obedient by nature and ready to help.

He rounded the desk and his feet skid for a moment like a rushed cartoon character as he tried to get his footing. "You can go out these doors and through the trees there. You'll come to the parking lot where all the staff parks. The road opens up just about a hundred feet past that."

"Thanks," Nolan said, setting out in a run.

"Wait," Toby called. "You can't walk down there. You aren't dressed for it, and there is more snow coming. It would be irresponsible of me to allow you to."

"It would be straight up dangerous for you to try to stop me," Nolan called out his warning over his shoulder as he continued to trudge through heavy wet snow. He dialed Holly's phone again and it instantly went to voice mail. But as he passed the parking lot he had something even better.

Footprints.

The quick falling snow was threatening to cover the trail Holly had left behind, but that only fueled Nolan to move faster. The wind whipped at his face and his sneakers slipped comically out from under him every few steps, but he didn't slow down. "Holly," he called out, wondering how she'd managed to make this trek alone in the dark. He'd flipped on the flashlight on his phone but that hardly gave him enough light to ensure he wasn't about to walk straight off a cliff.

The thought was crossing his mind as his feet slid in opposite directions, sending him rolling down the next ten or so feet of the road. His head thumped against a log and he knew instantly the skin above his eye had been cut. A warm drip of blood trailed down his face as he got back to his feet and started brushing off the wet snow. If he'd taken a fall and gotten that banged up the same could have happened to Holly. Or worse. He struggled to shine his light down on the footprints that were quickly vanishing under the new snow. "Holly!" he called again. But the night was so still and quiet that only his echoing voice could be heard coming back to him.

Unsure if the marks in front of him were still footprints, or if they were Holly's at all, Nolan considered tracking back the half mile to the ski resort and asking for help in the search. If she'd fallen, rolled off the road, or was unconscious every second would count.

He looked up the hill then back down. Holly was tough and determined. If her plan had been to reach the small bar by the apartments and hope for a cab to be willing to pick her up, then almost nothing would have stopped her from that.

Nolan ignored the throbbing cut on his head, the icy wind striking his face, and the water soaking through his sneakers. The only thing that mattered right now was finding Holly.

Chapter Ten

HOLLY SHOOK THE snow off her hat and pulled off her gloves. The bar was a dirty windowless box with ripped bar stools and plumes of cigarette smoke. There were only about five or six people scattered around, all looking up at the television coverage of Times Square. A singer performed to the large crowd in the streets and the clock counting down to midnight showed less than five minutes.

She'd like to say this was the worst place she'd ever rung in a new year but at least it had booze. She took a stool and ordered a drink from the languid woman behind the bar. Forgetting her makeup was still dialed up to formal-event level, she smiled when the woman gave her a curious look. It wasn't until she caught her reflection in the mirror behind the bartender that she remembered what a paradigm her life really was. Just a pretty face with too much makeup and soaked boots. Alone as the ball dropped. Alone like usual.

"You coming from a party or something?" the bartender asked, sliding her the beer she'd ordered.

"Yes," Holly replied, not offering anything else.

"You going to kiss someone at midnight?" a burly man

two stools down asked, leaning uncomfortably close to her, practically lying across the stools between them.

"No," she said flatly, taking a long drag off the bottle of beer.

"A pretty girl like you can't spend the holiday like this," he protested, getting to his feet. He wore a plaid shirt that he'd outgrown, his large round stomach peeking through the gaps between the buttons.

"I really don't want to break this bottle over your head before I have a chance to drink it all. Can you just sit down?" She turned her attention back to anxiously peeling the label off her beer. Nolan was all she could think about. By now he may have realized she was not at the party. He could have even gone back to the room and figured out her stuff was gone. With any luck he assumed she caught a ride out and was gone for good. She was clueless why he hadn't confronted her when he'd heard about her past. The best she could assume was that he was being the gentleman she knew him to be. And that was even more reason to leave before she exploited that too.

"I'm not saying we have to make out," the man said, attempting a bit of class as he pulled a comb from his back pocket and tried to tame his snarly hair.

"Sir," Holly said, finally turning her full attention back to the man, "you are a representative of the United States Marine Corp." She gestured at his tattooed arm. "You ride with a motorcycle club dedicated to protecting children." Holly pointed at the patches on his snug leather vest. "A good man, right?"

"Damn good," he boomed, pounding one hand over his heart like a caveman trying to communicate.

"I'm going to turn back around, drink my drink, and stare off into space while I wait for the cab I called. And I'm not going to worry about anyone bothering me because a good strong man like you is here. I'm going to be perfectly safe and free to wallow in my own misery just like everyone else here."

The large man puffed up his chest and tossed back his shoulders. "Damn right," he said, scowling at all the other patrons in the bar who couldn't care less about Holly and her speech. "No one's going to bother you while I'm around."

"Thanks." She smiled. "My name is Holly. I really appreciate you saying that."

"Name's Killer," he said, flashing his yellow crooked teeth. "Um, my name's actually Stuart."

"Happy New Year, Stuart," she offered, tipping her head and then turning back around to glance at the dwindling minutes on the Times Square clock. It was amazing what making something someone else's idea would achieve. Reminding Stuart what a good man he was, reminding him he had a responsibility to help keep Holly safe, defused the situation. That was her super power. That was what she'd learned over the years to harness and wield when needed.

"Holly," she heard Nolan call as he burst through the heavy wooden door of the bar. Looking like a wild animal, a trail of blood trickled down his face. He squinted and waved off the smoke someone had just puffed by his face.

"Damn," she whispered, shaking her head solemnly. "He

actually found me."

She knew instantly her words were a mistake when Stuart the Killer snapped his head around to see Nolan. *This is what it looks like when a plan backfires.*

Chapter Eleven

"HOLLY," NOLAN SAID, closing in on her though she didn't bother to turn around and face him.

"Is there a problem here?" a giant man made up of hair and tattoos asked, slamming a hand to Nolan's chest before he could reach Holly.

"Stuart," she scolded, touching the stranger's arm gently, finally acknowledging Nolan's existence. "It's all right."

"Doesn't look all right to me," Stuart asserted, shoving Nolan backward, sending his body tumbling into a nearby table and his mind into a blind rage.

"Who the hell is this?" he asked, wondering how Holly had managed to make allies in the time it took to leave him standing alone at the party.

"Stuart, really," Holly said, putting her body between Nolan and the beast. "He's not the problem. I'm the problem. Just let him go. Nolan, just go."

"I'm not leaving here without you," Nolan asserted, his eyes fixed now on Stuart, his center of gravity stable and ready for the giant to come at him again. "We need to talk."

"You need to go get your head checked," Holly said, gesturing up at the cut that was still bleeding. "It looks like you need stitches."

"I'm fine. But I'm not leaving you here. We need to talk. I don't care what that asshole Russell had to say. I want to hear it from you. I know there is more to the story." Nolan glared at Stuart, watching for the slightest flinch.

"What if there's not?" Holly asked, her voice cracking with emotion. "What if I am exactly what he says I am? What if it's worse?"

"I don't care," Nolan lied, shrugging off the idea that anything could keep him from the feelings he had for Holly. "I just want to talk to you. I'm not ready for you to leave and not look back. Maybe you'll be okay, but I won't be. So if that matters to you, talk to me."

"Damn," Stuart gaped, his giant paw-like hand coming up and covering his heart. "Don't do this to him Holly. The guy's hurting."

"He's hurting because of me," Holly said as though Stuart deserved some kind of explanation. "I'm not a good person."

People in the room began a loud countdown that signaled midnight was approaching quickly. Just twenty seconds away.

"That was this year," Stuart chuckled. "In fifteen seconds you get to start all over." Like he was moving two tiny chess pieces on a board, he moved Holly by the shoulder and then did the same to Nolan until they were an inch or two apart.

"Five, four, three," Stuart boomed out loudly just as the ball was about to drop.

Nolan looked deep into Holly's eyes, searching for the piece of her he believed to be completely authentic. A low pathetic cheer rang out as the clock struck midnight and Nolan pulled Holly in the rest of the way for a kiss he never planned to stop.

It suddenly all felt brand new. The year, Holly, his outlook. Holding her, their lips on fire, crashing together.

"Nolan," she said, pulling away.

"Yes?" he asked, full of hope.

"That cut is disgusting," she said, arching her head back and pointing up at his injury. "We need to clean it up and put a bandage on it if you won't get stitches. Plus you need dry clothes; you're soaked, and you're going to get sick."

"How did you get down that two miles without ending up exactly like this?" he asked, gesturing at the mess that was him.

"Running away," she said apologetically, "is kind of my thing. I'm good at it."

"Then I better hold on tight," he said, grabbing her hand in his and lacing their fingers together. "Because I don't want to look around again and not see you there."

"Man," Stuart said, choked up with emotion and a hiccup. "What a guy. Don't let go of this one, Holly. He's one of the good ones. I can tell."

"Me too," Holly agreed but her words were laced with worry, rather than optimism. "Let's go get you cleaned up," she said, tugging him toward the door. "Happy New Year, Stuart."

"You too, Holly," he called far too loudly for the small

room. "You can do this. It's a new year."

They stepped out into the cold, and Nolan looked down at Holly curiously. "Do you make friends like that everywhere you go?"

"I know how to handle people. That's all it is, manipulation. Don't look so impressed." Her cheeks pinked either from the cold wind or guilt.

"Tell me, Holly. Tell my why Russell thought you were such a big problem. It's not going to scare me away. I just want to know."

"Later," she said quietly. "We've got a long walk back to the hotel. We should just focus on that."

As they made their silent trek back up the snowy hill toward the glowing light of the lodge, Nolan watched Holly's face carefully in the low light cast by the moon, now that the clouds had blown away in the cold wind. There was a heaviness in her expression that made Nolan positive the ringing in of the new year hadn't freed her of the pain she was carrying.

"Holly," Nolan said, breaking open the stillness of the night with his words. "No matter what, everything is going to be all right. I promise. You're going to be all right."

She laughed, a breathy defeated laugh. "Thanks, Nolan. When you say it, I get as close to believing it as I ever have before."

Chapter Twelve

HOLLY SPUN THE knobs on the bath and poured in nearly the whole bottle of fragrant bath bubbles. The smell of ginger and spices filled the room as Nolan looked in the mirror to inspect the cut over his eye.

"You need to warm up in the bath," she said, coming up behind him and guiding him gently to the tub. She stood in front of him and helped lift his shirt over his head. Tugging at his belt buckle, she dropped his pants down and he stepped out of them.

"Come in with me," he said, leaning down and kissing her neck gently. "There's room for both of us." Before she could answer he was working the buttons on her shirt.

When the water was steaming and their clothes had all dropped away, Nolan and Holly sank into the tub, facing each other, a mountain of bubbles between them.

"I haven't taken a bath since I was ten years old," Nolan laughed, lifting a handful of the bubbles and blowing them over at her.

"I started out by just targeting the man who ruined my father," Holly said, launching unexpectedly into the explanation Nolan had been waiting for. "I just wanted to hurt him the way he'd hurt us. My mother really was a fortune-teller. That part was true. I learned very early how to manage people. I used that to take down Bruce Mulldon. I thought that would be the end of it."

"What did you do?" Nolan asked, trying not to spook her but wanting to know more.

"I pretended to be a call girl," Holly said, clearly not proud of what she'd done. "I basically had my own sting operation. I recorded him trying to solicit me and then I blackmailed him with it."

"Is that what you do to other people too?" Nolan asked, thinking about the men Russell surely associated with.

"No," she said indignantly. "That was crude and very simplistic. The things I do now, they are enough to crush these men and their whole empires. But I don't do it for my own gain. I live very modestly. I travel, I don't stay anywhere too long, and whatever I make from these men goes to the people they've hurt. My targets aren't random."

"Oh," Nolan said, an unexpected wave of relief flooding over him. "Why didn't you just tell me? I can be down with a good Robin Hood scheme. Nothing wrong with robbing the rich and giving back to the poor people they stole it from in the first place."

"It's not quite that simple. Nothing I've done is. It's muddy and messy and not something that lends itself well to having relationships. I've made the choice to live this life alone. I'm in too deep to stop now."

"Do you want to stop?" Nolan asked, reading the pain

on her face.

"I think so," she shrugged. "I'm tired and even though what I'm doing is supposed to be a victimless crime or a justified one at least, it's not without its stress. I don't sleep. I don't rest or relax. Getting in the car with you to come here, I meant what I said. I just wanted a break from myself, from who I've become. For the first time I wasn't running toward the next target; I was running from myself."

"What you're doing is not the same as who you are," Nolan corrected. "Who you are is the woman who put her arm in mine and promised to make me look good here. The woman who saw how unprepared I was, how bad I hurt, and knew she could help."

"I'm so torn," she sighed. "If I stop what I'm doing then these assholes keep winning. But if I keep doing it, I may not recognize myself soon. Lately, there have been times where I've lost perspective. Where the opportunity for a big windfall of money has almost tempted me from doing what I know is right. Once I cross that line, I won't come back from it."

"I don't know what you should do," Nolan admitted. "I don't have that answer. But I stand by my promise. No matter what, you're going to be all right."

"How can you know that?" she asked, a bite of anger in her shaking voice. "I have no marketable skills outside of being a manipulating con artist. I have nothing."

"I know you'll be all right because you won't be alone. You can run from your past, you can run from your mistakes, but I'm not letting you run from me."

"Since when do you have things all figured out? You were the one spending Christmas alone, trying to decide what level of miserable you wanted to be for the rest of your life."

"You're right," Nolan admitted. "But then I met you, and I started to look beyond the next five minutes. I started to believe I could feel things again that I'd been ignoring."

"I'm so tired Nolan." Holly sighed, and he knew she wasn't just talking about the late hour and the long day they'd had.

"I'm going to wrap you in a towel," he began, rising up from the tub. "I'm going to pick you up and put you in bed. I'm going to close those blackout curtains and pretend the sun doesn't exist tomorrow. I'm going to hold you and tell you as often as you need to hear it, that everything is going to be just fine. Your life is going to be amazing."

Tears rolled down her cheeks as she choked back her emotions. "Nolan, I'm so glad you brought me along. I'm not sure I'd have made it much farther without this."

He gave her his hand as she stepped out of the tub and, just like he promised, wrapped her in the plush oversized towel. "Trust me Holly," he whispered as he scooped her up and moved toward the bed. "If you hadn't gotten in my car, I'm the one who wouldn't have made it."

Chapter Thirteen

THE PHONE BY the bed rang and Nolan stirred from the soundest sleep he could remember experiencing in a long time. The hotel room was still completely dark thanks to the blackout curtains pulled tightly closed. He groaned at the incessant ringing of the phone and slapped at the nightstand to try to make it stop.

When the ringing continued, he fumbled for the phone and answered in a groggy voice.

"You're still sleeping?" Libby asked, sounding concerned. "It's almost one in the afternoon. You must have had a great time last night."

"I did," he said, ready to roll to his side and kiss Holly awake. But the bed was empty and cold. "I . . . uh," he stuttered as he clicked on the lamp near the bed. "I can't talk though; I have to go."

"You know James got some phone calls last night about you," she said.

"It's not a great time," Nolan protested again. "I will call you back."

"People said you spoke very highly of him and his charity

work. That means a lot to me. I really am sorry we couldn't be together."

"Libby," Nolan said directly as he saw no sign of Holly anywhere, "I love you. But I have to go." He clicked the phone that was mercilessly tethering him to one spot.

"Holly," he called out, knowing she wouldn't answer. Last night when her body, warm and silky from the tub, curled against him, he naïvely believed she would give him the chance to help her. The thought that she might run again never crossed his mind. And that was the problem. *Idiot.*

He grabbed his cell phone and wondered if calling her was even worth the effort. If she didn't want to be found, she wouldn't bother picking up. The nightstand no longer held his keys. She'd taken them this time.

Punching his hand into the wall, he growled at his own stupidity. He'd let her slip right out of his arms. The sinking feeling in his gut was taking over as he looked around the room. There was nothing else he could do but pack his stuff, take a shower, and call a cab back to his own car at the rental lot. With any luck Holly would be kind enough to return the rental and not cost his sister the replacement fee of a sports car.

The water in the shower was so hot it reddened his skin and steamed the bathroom to the point he couldn't see a couple inches in front of him. This was how he'd been living before he met Holly. In pain, unseeing, alone. And now he'd have to return to it.

Lost in thought, he hadn't noticed the shower door pull

open until the rush of steam flowing out gave way to her silhouette.

"Holly?" he asked, reading the sexy curves of her naked body. "You came back?" He was already fully hard, as she silently stepped into the shower, throwing her long hair off her shoulders and closing in on him. Her arms were wrapped around his neck, her cool body pressed against him and pulling the overload of heat off him as she kissed him deeply.

Tipping her head back, she braced against the wall and parted her legs as he wordlessly began to touch every pleasure spot he could get his hands and mouth on. Nolan could sense how his movements screamed the urgency he was feeling to have her, but he didn't care. Nothing tasted better than her skin, when he'd thought it was out of his reach forever.

Dropping to his knees, the hot water beating against his back, he tasted her core and devoured the shiver that rolled through her body. She responded instantly, sending his tongue into an excited flurry. In only a few moments she was calling his name, begging him not to stop.

With a final shriek of pleasure escaping her sweet lips, she collapsed into his waiting arms. They sat in the steam and pulsing water and stared in disbelief at each other. He knew what had formed his expression, the thought that she'd be gone for good and then returned so suddenly. But he wanted to understand the look of bemused wonder on her face.

"What is it?" he asked, running his thumb along her chin.

"You thought I left?" she asked, her face crumbling some with sadness. "You thought I'd taken off again for good?"

"I woke up and you were gone. So were my keys."

"I'm so sorry," she said earnestly as she cupped his face in her hands. "I'm not leaving. Well, I am," she corrected and his heart sank, "but you're coming with me."

"Where?" he asked, having hoped they'd stay barricaded in this hotel room, living on champagne and chocolate dipped fruit for the foreseeable future.

"It's a surprise. You'll have to get dressed."

"Oh," he groaned, kissing her neck. "I was hoping we'd quit wearing clothes for the rest of our lives."

"It might make the road trip more fun," she teased, standing up and stepping out into the cool bathroom. "Hurry up. We need to get on the road soon."

Nolan rose, braced his hands to the slick tile, and shook his head. Having Holly around had made his life chaotic, unpredictable, but mostly—worth living.

Chapter Fourteen

HOLLY TOSSED NOLAN the keys and prayed she hadn't missed the mark this morning with this surprise.

"Where are we going?" he asked, sliding into the driver's seat and looking at the interior of the car that was loaded with beautifully wrapped presents and festive decorations. It smelled of pastries and hot coffee as Holly handed a cup over to him.

"I thought we should drive to Texas," she said, placing a red Santa hat on his head. "We should surprise your sister and her husband and celebrate Christmas together."

"We missed Christmas by a week," Nolan countered, looking unconvinced.

"I've missed Christmas for the last five years. I want to remember what it was like to actually enjoy it with people. I went out this morning and got absolutely every ridiculously cliché thing you can imagine, and we're going all in."

She clicked on the radio and pushed a CD in. As a holiday song began to jingle, she danced along in her seat. Pulling on her own hat, a green elf with built in ears, she began to sing.

"Have you lost your mind?" he asked, looking her over and losing the fight he was waging against his smile. The dimple in his cheek grew deep as he laughed at her off-key rendition.

"Yes," she said loudly over the music. "It's been lost for a long time. But I feel like I'm finally finding it. I feel like myself again. Thanks to you." She slid her hand into his and squeezed tightly.

"Do you know how long of a drive it is from Vermont to Texas? And, I hear there is some bad weather up and down the coast. It'll take us forever to get down there. I've got my internship."

"Life is short, Nolan. School, the internship, all your plans. They will be there when you get back. But making memories with people you love isn't something you can play catch-up with. It's finite and fleeting. Let's have a do-over."

"And what about you?" he asked, concern on his brow. "Are you still taking a break from who you are?"

"I haven't done one unethical thing all year," she said, beaming. "That's pretty impressive. I think I'll keep it up."

"This year is exactly fourteen hours old," he said, checking his watch and raising a brow at her.

"A new record for me." She laughed then let her face fall serious. "I don't know who I'm going to be or what I'm going to do next. It's pretty scary not to have that answer. But at least there is one thing I know."

"And what's that?" he asked, brushing her hair back.

"At least I know who I'm going to be with as I figure it out."

"And once you do?" Nolan asked, looking worried as he anticipated her answer.

"I won't need you anymore," she said flatly, her serious look breaking quickly into a smile. "But I'll still want you."

THE END

Want to read more by this author?

Visit authordaniellestewart.com

Family Holiday Recipes

Ruth's Dynamites

Ingredients:

5 large green peppers

3 large onions

6 stalks celery

1 tbls crushed red pepper

1 tsp black pepper

3 lbs lean hamburger

1 10 oz. can tomato paste

¼ tsp salt

Instructions:

Brown hamburger. Add chopped peppers, onions into medium and small pieces to meat and simmer for 2-3 hours stirring often.

Add tomato paste salt, pepper, and crushed pepper. Simmer another ½ hour.

Serve on torpedo rolls

Enjoy a little piece of Rhode Island history.

Jeannette French Meat Pie

Ingredients:

2 lbs. ground steak hamburger

1-lb. ground pork

1-small onion

½ tsp salt

1 tbls. Bells turkey seasoning

1 sleeve of crushed saltine crackers

2 ready-made pie crusts

Instructions:

Cook finely chopped onions and hamburger and ground pork until fully cooked. Drain any excess fat. Add salt and Bells turkey seasoning. Add one sleeve of finely crushed and mix well.

In a ten-inch pie pan, place one crust on the bottom. Fill with the meat mixture and cover with the second crust.

Bake in 350 degree oven for 50 minutes or until golden brown.

Let cool for 15 minutes before serving.

Many French people enjoy putting ketchup on top. You decide.

Danielle's Christmas Pie

Ingredients:

1 10 inch graham cracker pie shell in pie pan

Marshmallows-regular size

Walnuts-chopped

1 cup flaked coconut

2 eggs

1 pint milk

½ cup sugar

1 tsp vanilla

Instructions:

Fill the bottom of the pie shell with the marshmallows. Cover with walnuts. Cover with coconut.

Mix the eggs, milk, sugar and vanilla. Pour the mixture over the walnuts and marshmallows.

Bake about one hour in the pre-heated 300 degree oven.

Family Photos

Ruth Cardello, 1971

Ruth Cardello, 1974

Jeannette Winters and Ruth Cardello, 1970

Danielle Stewart

CPSIA information can be obtained
at www.ICGtesting.com
Printed in the USA
BVHW040215131118
532999BV00017B/244/P